Books by Adam Pfeffer
Published by iUniverse:

KOLAK OF THE WEREBEASTS

TWILIGHT OF THE GODS

THE MISSING LINK

TO CHANGE THE WORLD AND OTHER STORIES

THE DAY THE DREAM CAME TRUE AND OTHER POEMS

THE VISITORS

THE CREATION OF GOD

THE AMAZING SLICK MCKINLEY:
GREATEST ATHLETE EVER

THE FANTASTIC FLYING MAN

THE GENIUS WITH THE 225 IQ

30 GREAT STORIES FOR OUR CENTURY

WILD TALES

HAMMERIN' HANK GREENBERG:
THE JEWISH BABE RUTH

THE GARDEN OF EDEN

THE INCREDIBLE TIGER-MAN

PRESIDENT TRON 7000

PRESIDENT TRON
7000

ADAM PFEFFER

PRESIDENT TRON 7000

iUniverse books may be ordered through booksellers or by contacting:

iUniverse
1663 Liberty Drive
Bloomington, IN 47403
www.iuniverse.com
1-800-Authors (1-800-288-4677)

Because of the dynamic nature of the Internet, any web addresses or links contained in this book may have changed since publication and may no longer be valid. The views expressed in this work are solely those of the author and do not necessarily reflect the views of the publisher, and the publisher hereby disclaims any responsibility for them.

Any people depicted in stock imagery provided by Thinkstock are models, and such images are being used for illustrative purposes only. Certain stock imagery © Thinkstock.

ISBN: 978-1-4917-1942-8 (sc)
ISBN: 978-1-4917-1943-5 (e)

Print information available on the last page.

iUniverse rev. date: 09/14/2015

To Leonard and Anita, for their continual support and faith.

*The world is dying of machinery;
that is the great disease, that is the
plague that will sweep away and
destroy civilization; man will have
to rise against it sooner or later.*

—GEORGE MOORE, 1888

INTRODUCTION

The following story asks the intriguing question, what will the future look like? The answer given is one filled with computers, robots, and yes, androids. This future not only seems inevitable, it is already occurring. But what is that thing we call an android?

The word, android, comes from the Greek *andr-* meaning "man, male," and the suffix *–eides*, which used to mean "of the species; alike." The word is really a misnomer. The literal translation is "an artificial male being." To use the gender-neutral word for human being in Greek would be *anthropos*. Therefore, the correct word for an artificial human being-like automaton should really be anthropoid. Android, however, has been commonly used to refer to both genders of robot, and so it is in the following pages for the male artificial beings.

The word for the female artificial being should really be gynoid, from the Greek *gyneka* for "woman." There are several alternatives that are also used in this book. First, there's "fembot" for female robot, and "feminoid" for a female android. Gynoids, fembots, and feminoids figure prominently in the following story.

The term, humanoid, is also used. The term refers to any being whose body structure is the same as a human being. While the term can be used to describe primates as well as mythological creatures, it is used in the following story to refer to artificial organisms, such as robots and androids. The correct term is really "humanoid robot," referring to a robot whose appearance is based on the human body.

Although the following is a fictional story, androids and robots do exist. Many elements of the story are therefore based on fact, or accepted scientific conjecture. The first real-life android, or gynoid to be more precise, was unveiled at the 2005 World Expo in Japan. Known as Repliee Q1, the lifelike robot has silicone for skin, rather than hard plastic. Built in the appearance of a young woman of Asian descent, Repliee Q1 has a number of sensors to allow it to react in a natural human way. Its eyelids flutter, its chest movements correspond to breathing, and it shifts its position in a human way. The robot or android or gynoid is dressed in a pink jacket, white shirt, slacks, and lace gloves, and has long black hair.

The gynoid can mimic human actions making it appear lifelike. A person with reflective dots placed at key points on the body, such as the wrist, elbow, and palm, can help the robot match those points on its own body. Repliee Q1 is equipped with 31 actuators or motors in its upper body. An air compressor is needed to mimic speech.

Repliee Q1 has two other "sisters": Repliee R1, which is modeled after a five-year-old Japanese girl, and Actroid, who looks very much like Q1. R1 can mimic speech, and is said to be very good with interacting with children.

But, of course, that was only the beginning. Inevitably, the technology will become more advanced. The possibilities for these artificial beings are limitless. And that is the basis of the following story. It seems just a matter of time before these artificial beings, androids and gynoids, are used as surrogate human lovers and friends. With tiny electrical motors and microprocessors, these artificial beings can potentially provide sex and love to any human who so chooses to use them. As the book indicates, the user would be able to dictate any position or kind of lovemaking he or she so desired. Again, the possibilities are limitless.

When we will actually see the total realization of our efforts and dreams is anybody's guess. But that some form of those visions will be realized, there is no doubt. You see, the revolution has already begun. The following story is a cautionary tale of what could happen if we are reckless in our attempts to produce lifelike artificial beings. There are so many paths one can follow and the following is only one of them. And while some may belittle such a vision as being too pessimistic, too improbable, let me warn you that history is filled with dark visions that have eventually become reality. The examples are endless, from dictatorships to the misuse of the environment to the criminal use of various weapons. The point of such dark visions, of course, is to show the human race what could happen so that it can be avoided at all costs. And that is the point of the following story.

There is no doubt that the robot boom has begun around the world. Whether it is the beginning of a new revolution that could lead to harmony among humanity or the eventual downfall of the human race is something to ponder in the days and years to come. It has already been reported that there are more than 8.6 million robots in the world, roughly the population of Austria.

The 8.6 million figure includes 1.3 million industrial robots and 7.3 million service robots. The robot population was predicted to be 13 million in 2012, which is about the population of Zambia.

Robots used around the home to mow lawns, vacuum floors and take care of other chores will increase sevenfold, according to the United Nations.

The robot boom coincides with record orders for industrial robots, said the UN's annual World Robotics Survey.

There were 607,000 automated domestic helpers in use at the end of 2003, two-thirds of them purchased that year, according to the report issued by the UN Economic Commission for Europe and the International Federation of Robotics.

Most of the automated domestic helpers were robot lawnmowers, about 570,000. Vacuum cleaning robots reached 37,000.

It was predicted that by the end of 2007, there was about 4.1 million domestic robots in use, with lawnmowers making up the majority. Sales of window-washing and pool-cleaning robots also increased, the study said.

Meanwhile, there are about 692,000 "entertainment robots," such as robotic dogs, around the world, the study said.

Japan is the most robotized economy, home to around half of the current 1.3 million industrial robots. It is predicted, however, that China will become the world's biggest consumer of robots by 2014. China currently sits just ahead of the United States but behind Korea and Japan.

Most industrial robots are used on assembly lines, chiefly in the auto industry. But the study said household robots could soon surpass their industrial counterparts. The UN body first began counting in 1990.

According to the study, robots will "not only clean our floors, mow our lawns and guard our homes but also assist old and handicapped people with sophisticated interactive equipment, carry out surgery, inspect pipes and sites that are hazardous to people, fight fire and bombs."

"Our biggest hurdle right now is skepticism," said one company executive. But "we are just at a point where robots are becoming affordable."

"And some of them can actually do real work," he said.

Meanwhile, the first talking humanoid robot was among five tons of supplies and machinery on a rocket launched for the International Space Station from Tanegashima, southwestern Japan. The childlike robot was designed to be a companion for astronaut Koichi Wakata, and will communicate with another robot on Earth. Wakata is expected to arrive at the space station in November of 2013. The challenge was making sure the robot could move and talk where there was no gravity.

The biggest hurdle will be, of course, perfecting artificial intelligence. But even that will be overcome in time. As the book indicates, we are the gods and these are our children. Like in all families, there are good moments and moments of difficulty and discontent. If there are too many difficulties, too many moments of discontent, the children will rebel. If this book teaches us anything it is that we must be wary of the children becoming our guardians, of the progeny oppressing the progenitors. We must think about the possible difficulties, the possible moments of discontent, before it is too late. Before we know it, the future will be upon us.

Florida
July 5, 2013

1

A great clamor arose, an eruption of sounds and applause rushing through the cavernous hall, as the figure in the silver, high-collared suit slowly stepped forward into the frosty burst of light. He raised his arms in glowing triumph, causing reflected light to flash from the silver sleeves, and continued walking until he reached a gleaming black podium.

"Fellow Americans," he began in a muted drone. "My mission is to bring together human and machine in genuine harmony. There will be no being omitted and no errors committed. That is my pledge to you. All decisions will be based upon logic, and so I say to you, it is logical to embrace all beings, regardless of the size of their stored memories or their number of limbs. All beings will be honored, all data analyzed."

A sudden discharge of syncopated beeps fluttered in the air, sounding like the opening notes of a futuristic symphony, or a chorus of mechanized transmissions that seemingly shimmered amid the vast blaze of centuries. The figure's eyes flared into a sizzling scarlet, and he lifted his arms once again to quiet the great throng.

"And to those humans apprehensive about the years ahead, let me repeat an old Latin phrase, *Humani nihil a me alienum puto*, which means, nothing human is foreign to me."

The crowd cheered wildly at this last statement, and then, the figure stepped back from the podium and disappeared behind a side door. Hudge Stone watched the proceedings with great interest. Sent by the *Herald* as a special correspondent, he ran his fingers through his snow-white hair and gazed at the strange menagerie of humans, robots, androids and feminoids that filled the room.

"That's a 7000," said a man standing next to him. "You know, they can do just about anything."

Stone slowly nodded.

"He's the best thing that ever happened to this country," said the man. "They never make a mistake, you know."

Stone turned, intent on issuing a reply, when he was suddenly pushed from behind by a six-foot android. "Out of the way, human," it buzzed.

Stone stepped aside and let the humanoid pass. As he watched the mechanized being trundle away, he wondered if the android's words were a portent of things to come.

It had only been about a century before, back in 1946, that these silicon wonders had first been invented at the University of Pennsylvania. They were labyrinths of radio tubes back then, about eighteen thousand in total, and required a room of thirty feet by fifty feet to operate. The ENIAC, or electronic numerical integrator and computer, was capable of making five thousand additions, and perform up to five hundred multiplications a second.

Stone turned away from the android, and noticed he was standing next to another human being. "What can you tell me about the voting?" he asked a tall man with blond hair.

"Well, it seems Tron won the western and southern states," replied the man. "Seems old Kent Cole drew his support from the Northeast and Midwest. Makes perfect sense, actually. Those areas never did accept a new idea very easily."

"How close is it going to be?"

"Very close, Mr. Stone. But with Tron winning California, Texas, and Florida, it looks as if we have enough electoral votes for victory."

Victory. Stone contemplated the word as if he had never heard it before. It was impossible, incredible, something that wouldn't have even been believed fifty years before. An android, something once thought of as a mere machine of human invention, had been elected president of the United States.

Stone marveled at the situation. These machines, or beings, as they now were being called, were actually the fulfillment of a dream. Why, examples of small figures with movable limbs had been found in Egyptian tombs dating to around 2000 BC. Homer, Plato, Pindar, Tacitus, and Pliny had described talking bronze and clay statues and mechanical helpers who were built by the gods. The golems of medieval Jewish legend were robot-like servants made of clay, brought to life by a spoken word. Leonardo da Vinci drew plans for a mechanical man that looked like an armored knight as early as 1495. Yes, the fulfillment of a dream.

"Cole is getting ready to concede," shouted someone in the room.

Stone shook his head, almost not believing this sudden course of events. But, deep in his heart, he knew it was possible, knew it was inevitable after so many years of preparation. Animated figures through the centuries, many operating through the use of weights and pulleys, had been created by clockmakers, with many devices exploiting clockwork to achieve the desired movement. Talking dolls had then been invented in the nineteenth century. But the real advance came in the 1950s and 1960s, with the invention of transistors and integrated circuits. Compact, reliable electronics and a growing computer industry added brains to the machines.

It was silicon that made them feasibly compact. The addition of superconductive metals, electricity, and microprocessors gave them artificial intelligence.

"Washington and Oregon went for Tron."

Stone looked at a man with dark hair, and nodded his head. "Looks like that's it, then," he said.

The man smiled. "The best thing that ever happened," he said. "You're going to be amazed at how much Tron can do to put this country back on the right track, Mr. Stone. Why, he was programmed with philosophical thought, from Aristotle to Confucius to Descartes."

"I sure hope so," Stone replied. "I'd like to think he was qualified to be president."

"Oh, you don't buy what Kent Cole had to say, do you, Mr. Stone? I mean, even if Tron wasn't half as smart as we know he is, he'd still be more qualified than that lying womanizer."

It was true. People had become tired of the endless series of sordid scandals that infected the American political process. Humans who had occupied the highest offices in the land, were continually caught by the media in various examples of debauchery and deception, and the people finally decided they had had enough. The androids were viewed as a remedy for these shortcomings, and eventually, they began taking governmental posts normally reserved for human beings. It had taken place gradually, in the hope that humans and the mechanized beings could attain some sort of symbiotic relationship. By 2056, however, it had finally led to the election of Galen Tron 7000.

Tron, built by Galen Industries, was one of the most advanced androids ever produced by mankind. His interior consisted of an intricate network of resistors, diodes, capacitors, muscle wires, and actuators, most of it necessary for storing and distributing electricity. The neuro microprocessors in his head were aided by miniature video cameras containing light-sensitive silicon chips that served as his eyes, and binary pattern microphone sensors that served as his ears. His electrically insulated metal, plastic, and rubberized limbs were attached to tactile sensors, which, besides registering the sense of touch, could also be used in the act of locomotion. Speech was made possible through the use of electronic pulses that could actually form words. In every way, science had discovered how to simulate human life.

Stone turned, and watched an android with a microphone shuffle to the center of the room. There was a television camera pointed at him, its light cutting a path through the dim hall.

"This is Simon Gear 7000 reporting from Tron campaign headquarters in California where the polls have just closed. It appears Galen Tron 7000 has captured the state and its seventy-five electoral votes, and will be declared the next president of the United States. This most unlikely outcome is the result of a long, contentious campaign that began more than two years ago with the announcement that Galen Industries had decided to run him for the presidency. His human opponent, Kent Cole, continuously attacked Tron during this campaign of being only an artificial being, not qualified to be the leader of the free world. But, apparently, voters disagreed. Tron continually insisted during the campaign that he knew everything he needed about human beings, and the fact that he was an artificial being built by human computers only meant that he would not be prone to commit the egregious errors of the past. Voters apparently decided the scandals and deception of the past few years were enough to convince them that an advanced humanoid was the answer. Said one Tron campaign worker, 'This is the biggest moment in human history. We will now be able to control our environment with the help of the machines we created, instead of being at the mercy of Nature.' It looks as if that seminal moment has, indeed, arrived with the election of Galen Tron 7000. Simon Gear 7000 reporting."

The android's words unsettled Hudge Stone. He was one of the last human beings to still do his own reporting, and for a medium that was fast disappearing from the American landscape. There were only a few newspapers left, most of which had merged into regional empires, the *Herald* being one of these. Stone knew that when he did finally retire, which would be very soon, an android would probably take his place. He had resisted this inevitability as long as possible, still priding himself on a national reputation gained many years before. But he knew it wouldn't be long before his age became a liability, and his reputation an interesting aspect of his obituary. In fact, Tron's election might be the last important story he would ever work on.

Stone watched as the robots and androids moved about the room with great assurance. It was as if they knew they no longer had to be subservient to human beings, but were, in fact, now in control. And yet, Stone noted, the human beings in the crowd seemed to be pleased.

"So how do you like our new president?" asked one of the humans who had worked on the Tron campaign. He smiled at Stone, affectionately slapping him on the back.

Stone tried to smile, but something was worrying him. "Too soon to tell," he finally replied.

"That's all right, you'll get used to him soon enough."

He watched as the man contentedly strolled away, evidently quite satisfied with the current course of events. But to Stone, it seemed inappropriate to congratulate another human on the election of an android humans had built, and now would rule over them. Something unsettling.

Stone closed his notebook, and was about to head back to the *Herald's* bureau office, and then take a flight back to the East, when he noticed a four-armed robot leading a small crowd in a chorus of "For He's A Jolly Good Fellow." It was rather a strange rendition, with only the humans singing, and the robots accompanying them with shrill, syncopated beeps. Stone wanted to laugh, but the implications of the demonstration quickly sobered him. He realized whether he liked it or not, the future had arrived. And whatever that future might be, it would include an android assuming the presidency of the United States of America.

* * *

The brightly lit streets of the city were bloated with people and their machines, more machines, and more people. Hudge Stone watched as they hurried along, the steady drone of their voices, both human and mechanical, drifting through the calm night air. He stopped for a moment to gaze at this new world of emerging coexistence. "Nothing human is foreign to me." Tron's words fluttered through his mind. How long before these human creations heeded those words and what did it mean to the future of the planet?

His thoughts were suddenly disturbed by an incident a few feet away. A six-foot robot had halted in the middle of the sidewalk, refusing to move, causing hostile glances from the human beings behind him. Stone was amazed how easily the seeming tranquility had been broken.

The robot then swiveled on his base and turned completely around. "Tron," he buzzed. "Tron." The humans looked at him, grimacing, annoyed at this haughty outburst, and began stepping around him.

"Tron. Tron. Tron." The monotonous chant continued for several minutes. Stone wondered whether the robot was actually taunting the humans, or just verifying an accepted fact. The air throbbed with tension, the night air chilled by a sudden breeze. A storm was coming, one could feel it swirling in from the south. The robot apparently registered the change, too, for he wheeled around and jolted forward.

"Excessive precipitation imminent, please be advised," he said in a rushed monotone. He glided down the street, lights flashing, beeping every so often, and repeated the warning.

Stone watched as the people scattered, their robots squawking about the storm as they rattled along. It wasn't long before the streets were empty, and the cool rain began to fall. Stone walked along the avenue, raindrops brushing against his forehead. He spotted a bar across the street, and hurried inside, the rain pattering behind him.

The bar was crowded, filled with only humans who seemed to be unshaven, unkempt, content with drinking their troubles away.

"What'll you have, bud?" asked a husky man from behind the counter.

"Just a cup of coffee," Stone replied.

When the man came back with a cup filled to the rim, vapor overflowing, he nodded his approval. "Crowded tonight," he said.

"Crowded every night," the husky man replied. "Everybody's out of work."

Just then, the door opened, and a figure wearing a raincoat and hat stepped inside. He glanced at the crowd of humans, and then bowed his head. The husky man, however, looked at him and began to shout.

"What the hell are you doing in here?" he said.

The figure looked up, and Stone could see the mechanical eyes attempting to focus.

"It's a damned droid!" somebody in the crowd shouted.

"Excessive moisture," the android buzzed.

"Well, now, isn't that a shame?" said the husky man. "You know your kind ain't wanted in here."

"Must seek shelter," replied the android.

"Not in here you don't!" someone shouted.

Stone watched as the men approached. They surrounded the mechanical being, taunting him with mocking beeps and buzzes, and then one of them knocked the android's hat from his head.

"Go back and tell that droid president of yours, you're not welcomed here," he said. "Do you understand?"

"Remark duly noted," replied the android.

"Well, duly note this," said another man. He swung his fist, hitting the android in the face. This seemed to spark a frenzy, men pulling at his limbs, others continuing to pound upon his head. They then grabbed him and pushed him against the door.

"Can we not negotiate?" buzzed the android.

"We've had enough of your negotiations," shouted one of the men.

They continued to push and punch at the android until someone opened the door, and he fell to the wet pavement below.

"Damned machines," one of the men grumbled, closing the door behind him. They could hear the rain continuing to tumble down from the dark, misty sky.

"He'll die out there," said Stone to the husky man.

"Let him die," he replied. "Them droids have been steadily killing us off for years. What does it matter if one of them dies, anyhow? They'll just go back to the factory and construct a new one, that's all. No matter what we do, they keep building them damned droids. No sense to it at all. There are families, flesh and blood, who are out on the streets living from day to day. What do we tell them? Why, they can't even afford medical help. Flesh and blood, mind you, not some machine filled with wiring and silicon."

"But if he deactivates, the authorities are surely going to come looking," said Stone.

"Doesn't matter to me. Let them convict one of these men for killing that droid and see what happens. Why, there'll be thousands of humans swarming through the streets. It's got to reach a boiling point, sooner or later. We can't keep going on like this. We're flesh and blood. We've got consciences, souls. Something no droid can ever replace."

Stone glanced out the window. He could see the ragged remains of the android writhing on the pavement, the pouring rain engulfing him. Then, suddenly, there was a loud sizzle and a flash of light, and the android lay still amid the dark, dim puddles.

A loud cheer suddenly echoed through the bar. "Serves him right," shouted one of the men. "Damned droid. Now all we have to do is take care of that damned president."

Stone looked at them. These were clearly the disgruntled masses, powerless, who either did not bother to vote, or were overruled by the wealthy minority. A few minutes passed, and then suddenly there were two human police officers standing in the doorway.

"Any of you know what happened out here?" asked one of the officers.

The crowd halted in silence, staring at the two men, waiting for someone to offer an explanation. They motioned to the husky man behind the bar and he finally began to speak. "The droid just stopped and short-circuited," he said. "Must have been caught out in the rain for some reason."

"Yeah, tell them droids to stay out of the rain next time," someone shouted from the back.

The officers looked at the men, nodded, and then finally left, causing the crowd to erupt into laughter.

"You see what I mean?" said the husky man. "The police don't want any trouble with us. They know what's going on, but they're human, too. They know what will happen if they start arresting other humans. Better to sweep it under the rug. It's only a damned machine, anyway."

Stone nodded. He sipped at his coffee, then realized someone was watching him from behind. He turned his head, and stared into the angry eyes of a broad-shouldered man in a ragged t-shirt.

"What business is this of yours?" he grumbled. "Just who the hell are you, anyway, mister?"

"What do you mean?" Stone replied. "A human like everyone else in this room."

"No, I mean there's something different about you. Look at those clothes you're wearing. You don't belong in here. Are you some sort of spy? Is that it?"

"Now take it easy. I only came in here for a drink or two. That's all."

"But you've been a witness here to all kinds of things. Not to mention that gabbing bartender. Just what's your interest in all of this?"

Stone sighed. "I'm a reporter with the *Herald*," he finally said. "I just came in here for a drink, and maybe find out what you people think about this new president."

The man glared at him for a moment. "Well, you can tell everyone I think it stinks. How do you like that? Most of the men in here haven't had jobs for years, nothing. And then what do they do? Go ahead and put another android in power. No, I don't like it at all. Now they say this android knows what's best for everyone, but how could he? He's just a damned machine, no heart, no soul. What does he care if a few million humans starve? They're only things to him. No, mister, you can put me down as saying I hate the idea. And if I had my way there'd be a revolution in this country to set things right again. Give the government back to the people where it belongs. Not in the hands of some soulless contraption."

"But they say these androids never make a mistake," said Stone. "Don't you think he'll do something for people like you?"

"They may not make mistakes with facts and figures, mister, but they'll never know what it is to be flesh and blood. That's a big difference. No, I say let the revolution begin." He turned toward the other men in the bar, put his arms in the air, and they cheered.

"Revolution!" they shouted.

2

The night moved slowly. Slowly, silently, it flapped its diaphanous wings, and soared onward upon a rush of wind. Although its movements were hardly perceptible, Hudge Stone knew the daylight was coming, a sudden flare amid the darkness.

He stumbled through the door, a burst of radiant light melting upon the distant hills, and quietly made his way up the stairs and into the bedroom. She was still asleep, lying there in a gleaming throne of dreams, looking like the first day his eyes fell upon her. He removed his shoes, and carefully slid into bed.

"Oh, Hudge, you're just coming home?" he heard her sigh in the midst of a silent yawn.

"I stopped at a bar after the flight," he whispered back. "Nothing to be alarmed about. Now go back to sleep."

She blinked, her eyes squinting into the morning light. "What time is it, anyway? Don't tell me you've been out all night."

"I had no choice, Sandie, it's a big story. It's not every day we elect an android president of the United States. I had to find out what the people were thinking about all this. It won't be much longer. Besides, I'm going to give it all up very soon, remember?"

She opened her eyes, sat up, the sunlight running streaks across her graying hair. "Come on, I'll fix some breakfast," she finally said.

He looked at her and smiled. Although they had been married for decades, he was still in love with her, still dependent on her voice and the hidden words that softly spilled from her sparkling brown eyes. He noticed the gentle creases on her face, the work of ravaging time. But her voice hadn't changed, and the words echoing from inside her were familiar, like the coming of spring and the hot days of summer.

"So they did it? Elected a machine?" she was saying, tying up her bathrobe and heading for the door.

"Amazing, isn't it?" he replied. "We're about to be ruled by our own technology. By our own nimble hands, we've made ourselves obsolete. The gods have become slaves to their own labor."

"Why did we allow it to happen, Hudge? I mean, don't we even realize what's happening?"

"It's been the same reasons through the centuries, my dear. It's all economics and efficiency. Doing the same thing faster and with more precision, one tends to make more money. In this case, it's the economics of progress. We need bigger and faster solutions at a low cost. Only a machine can handle that demand."

"And what happens to us in the process, Hudge? Are we devalued to the point of eradication?"

"Maybe," he replied. "Until we realize we've gone too far, and decide to reclaim the planet."

"That is, if isn't too late."

He stared at her, followed her movements as she grabbed the eggs, was about to crack them open and spill them into the automated food processor. Then she halted, running a slender hand through her short brown hair.

"I think I'll make them the old-fashioned way," she finally said. "My own private protest."

He smiled. "Join the revolution," he said.

She looked at him, smiling back. "Maybe I will. Now, let me see, you like them over easy, right?"

"You know me too well."

She turned toward the stove. "Well, the only thing we don't have is fire," she said. "Revolution or not, everything's still electric."

"That's okay, the eggs were probably gathered by machines, anyway."

"Some revolution," she said with a laugh. "Even the farmers are robots now."

"It's all in the name of supply and demand; less manual labor, more efficient production. Why, one corporate farm, using robots and computers, can produce enough food to feed thousands."

"And still people are starving."

"It's just that nobody has any money to pay for it. You should have seen that bar I was in, Sandie. It was filled with men who haven't worked in years. We may have found the way to produce more food, but there's still the question of what the people will do in order to pay for it."

"Maybe it is best that we leave it for the machines to figure out a solution. I mean, they can't do any more harm, can they?"

"Well, we could lose our society to them forever. You know, once they have a taste of power, they might not want to ever give it up."

She looked at him. "But they're just machines, Hudge. We created them. Can't we turn them off whenever we want?"

He shook his head. "I wish it were that easy, but they've developed to such a point that now it would be considered murder."

"So, instead, it's humans that do all the dying." She turned toward the stove, the frying pan sizzling above the blue-white coil, cracked one of the eggs and let it spill into a wheezing frenzy. "There now, you see? Without the use of a machine."

Stone smiled. "Although it probably came from a cloned hen that was fed by robots and computers. Face it, Sandie, there's no way of getting around it. They've taken over our lives."

"But not our souls," she said. "No machine can take that away from us. We still have the power of deciding our own fate."

"A lot of good it does us. We still make the same mistakes over and over again. I don't know, maybe Tron and the droids will come up with a solution. I sure hope so."

He could hear the eggs crackling and hissing behind him. The aroma filled the room and flooded his senses. "Smells like a Sunday morning used to smell," he said. "All those years ago."

"Well, maybe we should do this more often," she replied, sliding the steaming eggs from the pan and onto a plate. "I'll make you some toast, and you can sit and watch the television."

"Just like Sunday morning," he said, grabbing the remote and pushing a button.

There on the screen, in three-dimensional color, was the new president, Galen Tron 7000. Still bedecked in a silver suit, the bald android was in the midst of speaking.

"Nuclear weapons have become obsolete," he was saying. "All war will now be controlled by the computers and animated beings. Human beings will finally be safe from themselves. But this is just a beginning. While we will see the end of foreign wars, there is a battle here at home. Here are some of the things we will be doing to win that battle.

"First of all, more humans need to be placed in the retail sector and fill all sales responsibilities," pulsed the new president. "Animated beings will continue to pursue blue-collar opportunities. This is the only logical way we can work together to improve society. Of course, most corporate decisions will continue to be made by white-collar executives. Our electronic brethren will work in concert with them to eliminate unnecessary errors from the manufacturing work force."

Hudge Stone stared at the screen. He watched as the robot reporters discharged their questions.

Tron turned and began waving them away, his silver suit reflecting tiny sparks of light. "Please refrain from continued inquiry," he said. "I will further articulate my policies at a later time. But let me say this, I am pleased to be your leader. My election is a logical course of action. The humans can be confident they have made the correct decision. It is a beginning. They have begun to learn how not to commit errors."

Stone frowned. "You arrogant bundle of wiring," he shouted at the screen. He stabbed his finger at the remote control button, and the pictures dissolved into darkness.

"The only mistake I think we made was putting that android in charge," he angrily said.

Sandra sat down, placing the two plates filled with eggs, bacon, and toast on the table. "Don't you think you ought to give him a chance?" she asked.

He looked at her. "I don't think I have much choice."

There was silence for a moment, a time to briefly think about what lay ahead. "Well, eat your eggs. The revolution can wait."

"I only wonder, how much longer?" he replied.

* * *

A winter chill snarled through the air, snapping at the ears, clawing its way through the jostling crowd. Hudge Stone watched as the bald android shuffled to the podium. It was January, and Galen Tron 7000 was about to take the oath of office and be sworn in as the next president of the United States.

"I, Galen Tron 7000, do solemnly swear to preserve, protect and defend the Constitution of the United States, so help me God," he droned.

It was like a far-fetched nightmare, the culmination of the Industrial Revolution, in which humans now succumbed to their own ingenuity, a result of their passionate quest for perfection. A machine, a product of fertile human minds, now stood where the giants of human history had stood, murmuring his support for the foundation of the democracy and the concept of a Holy Spirit that echoed through the centuries.

Many of the humans in the crowd applauded, while their mechanical prodigies emitted approving beeps. There was a pervading optimism that, just maybe, this child of human imagination might be the solution to centuries of unrest, misunderstanding, and miscalculation. That, just maybe, man had figured out a way to bring a sense of humanity back to man. Here, with this machine, human beings would finally be ruled without prejudice or selfishness, without being limited by gender, race, or religion. Here was a machine whose only interest was to serve all human beings, and, by doing so, enrich a planet that had withered due to internal strife and economic oppression. Could it be a machine, a mere amalgamation of silicon and microchips, would be the one to liberate the human race?

"Fellow Americans," buzzed the new president, "it is my great hope that we can work together to build a better society. There will be no being omitted, and no errors committed. That has always been my pledge to you. Working together, we can build a great nation. A nation based on one and all."

Hudge Stone sat nearby jotting down the new president's words. It was true they were only words, but words filled with shimmering hope and encouragement. If they were part of Tron's programming, maybe there was still a chance for a better future. He only hoped so.

"Now how do you like our president?" asked the same human campaign worker he had seen on election night.

"So far, so good," he replied, turning his head. His eyes were immediately attracted to the woman hanging on the man's arm. She was tall, seductive, gleaming in every way, from the shape of her hips to the sparkle in her sapphire eyes.

The man seemed to notice his admiring glance, smiled approvingly, and then abruptly intervened. "That's right, you two haven't met," he said, tugging on her arm. "This is Laura, the love of my life."

Stone nodded, and held out his hand. "Very pleased to meet you."

"The pleasure's mine, Mr. Stone," she replied. "I've heard so much about you."

He glanced at the man, wondering what he might have told her, and then smiled. "Nothing bad, I hope," he said.

"Oh no," she responded, "George is a great admirer of yours. He tells me you're one of the last humans to still do his own reporting."

"I'm afraid not much longer."

"That's too bad," she said.

He listened to her words, detected a bland tone to her voice, a certain dull resonance, causing him to reevaluate her being.

"Well, it was very nice to meet you," he finally said.

"And nice to meet you, Mr. Stone." She smiled a rubbery listless grin.

"As you can see," the man interrupted, "the future's very bright. I hope you have a chance to interview Tron, Mr. Stone. You'll find, as I have found, they are completely incapable of making errors. I should know, Laura's a perfect example."

"You mean?"

"Yes, Mr. Stone," she suddenly interrupted, "I am a feminoid 7000."

"I never would have guessed."

"Yes, the technology just gets better and better," said the man. "Why Laura's almost perfect in every way."

He looked at the man, who responded with a sly wink of his eye.

Stone had heard about androids and feminoids being built equipped with sexual organs to please their human masters. With the help of the sex aids industry and medical prosthetics, both male and female androids could be provided with complete human anatomies. The males were equipped with plastic and rubber phalluses, while the females were given artificial breasts much like those supplied to a human woman after a mastectomy and artificial vaginas. The idea had been to produce robots and androids capable of being human surrogate lovers.

"You see, Mr. Stone, there's nothing to fear," said the man.

Nothing to fear. The words echoed through Stone's brain. Could it be we had gotten to the point where a human could hardly tell the difference between flesh and blood and a programmed, computerized mechanical figure? And what were the consequences of such a possibility? He gazed at the machine before him. Her skin was so lifelike, imbued with a sense of passion and sensuality. Perfect in every way. And humans had nothing to fear?

"Let's hope so," he finally replied. "For the future of the human race."

He watched as they walked away, arm in arm, wondering the implications of such a relationship. Could machines actually provide love without it getting contrived, lacking the spontaneity of human passion, dependent upon a computerized program? And yet, contrived as it may be, it would have its advantages. No arguments, no stress, just the blissful sound of an approving voice. Peace at last.

If only life were so simple. Stone thought about the men in the bar, all the humans displaced by these surrogate humans, and wondered if the very survival of the human race was at stake.

In front of him, still standing at the podium, was Galen Tron 7000. He could hear the applause and beeps emanating from the admiring crowd. He thought for a moment, uncertain whether the machines had won more than just the presidency.

3

"He's supposed to speak tonight."

Hudge Stone turned toward Sandra, a far away look in his eyes, as if he'd been thinking for hours. "Who?"

"Why, the president, of course."

"Oh, right, of course."

The president. It slid off her tongue as if there was nothing unusual about it, nothing the least bit absurd that millions of human beings were waiting to hear the words of a mechanical android, a creation of human beings who was now to lead them through the unexplored darkness of the future.

"You are going to listen, aren't you?"

"Yes, of course. I wouldn't miss it for the world."

"What do you think he's going to say, Hudge?" She looked at him, a mysterious glint in her eyes, as if she were expecting something momentous. "I mean, I don't know if I'm excited or fearful. It could be the beginning of something wonderful, or something very terrible, even frightful."

He thought for a moment, nodding his head, agreeing with the wildest of her trepidations. "I don't really know," he finally said. "Let's hope for the best."

"I mean, he has to obey his programming, right? I mean, they wouldn't be so foolish as to let him make decisions on his own. He was built by us to serve us, isn't that right? Therefore, all of his decisions have to be made taking into consideration how they benefit human beings, and only human beings. Isn't that right, Hudge?"

"Not entirely. He was programmed by human beings all right, but his microprocessor collates the information, examines it with different strategies in mind, and then comes up with an answer. Hopefully, the correct answer."

"The correct answer for whom, Hudge? I mean, there are several correct answers to a problem, depending upon one's point of view and the interests one wants to placate. I'm just hoping they were smart enough to program him with the instructions that all decisions are to be made in the interests of human beings."

"I'm not so sure," he replied hesitantly. "That android is not supposed to make any errors. If that's true, his decisions will not always be in our interest. His mission is to produce a better society. I'm not sure that always means what's best for us."

"Well, as long as it means not giving more power to the machines. Our society is already too mechanized as it is."

"Well, I wouldn't count on an android making our world more humane. I mean, after all, I don't think he was programmed with utopian notions in mind. He is still the product of those not wanting to get in the way of progress, those whose happiness means greater amounts of money. That is probably his number one concern. If those decisions also lead to a more harmonious society, then all the better."

"But he's got to do something about all the people who haven't worked in years. I mean, even the wealthy corporate executives don't want to see the people starving in the streets, right?"

"I don't think they'll let them starve," he said, checking his watch. "They'll find some way to give them jobs, a little money, with the hope they begin spending more and strengthen the economy. It's all to their advantage, anyway. Most of the money will end up in their pockets in the form of increased profits. Now do you see what I mean? Those are the interests Tron will be looking out for."

"Well, as long as he helps the people. I mean, those corporate people are going to be making money no matter what. At least, let the people work again. At least, let them think they have control over their lives again."

Stone nodded. "I guess that's the best he can do," he said with a sigh. He stood up, and retrieved the remote control. "Well, anyway, we'll soon find out."

They watched as the picture blinked into focus. There, sitting behind a large brown desk, was the bald android, dressed in glistening silver, his eyes dilating into a fiery red.

"Fellow Americans," he began in that throbbing mechanized voice. "It is my intention to outline my plans for this country's future. It is a future we will share together as one, human and animated beings, working for the betterment of society. To achieve this meritorious goal, I have decided to implement certain preliminary programs aimed at helping both. Our hope is to reduce the growing poverty now plaguing the nation. To this end, I have ordered a dramatic increase in agricultural output. With the help of our mechanized brethren, we will be producing more food for our hungry citizens.

"To pay for this increase in agricultural production, it is imperative that we find our human citizens satisfactory employment. To do this, we will establish government subsidized job training programs that will ease our human citizens slowly into the work force. These programs will be run by mechanized beings in order to maximize our educational efforts. This will truly be a case in which human and machine work together for their mutual benefit.

"Although these job training programs will solve a short-term problem, we must look at some long-term solutions. With this in mind, I have ordered an increase in mechanized teachers to begin infiltrating the education system. These teachers, programmed individually for the necessary grade requirements, will instruct our human children with greater insight as to the future needs of the society. Again, human and animated beings will work together to achieve satisfactory results.

"Each of our new human workers who successfully completes the stated job programs will receive generous health care benefits to take care of their beloved offspring. These benefits, which will be subsidized by the federal government, will do much in ending any serious health problems. These benefits will include any replacement parts and genetic upgrades that may be necessary. Again, working with our mechanized brethren, the problems of the past will be eradicated forever.

"Fellow Americans, these programs represent a new horizon in relations between man and machine. Together, this country will remain strong for the betterment of all beings.

"In keeping with this philosophy, I am proposing a new amendment to the Constitution. It reads as follows: The right of citizens of the United States to vote shall not be denied or abridged by the United States or by any State on account of electronic orientation and number of limbs.

"It is time, my friends, to welcome all of our citizens into our great nation, and this includes our mechanized brethren. The right to vote is only a step in that direction. I hope you will support me in my efforts to bring about this new horizon in being relations. It is right, it is just, and based upon the unerring foundation of logic. Thank you and good night."

Hudge Stone stared at the screen and frowned. "Well, there you have it," he said, turning toward Sandra. "Machines teaching us how to think, how to do our work, tending to our health needs, and also gaining the right to vote. It may be a new horizon, but it sounds to me as if they are content in controlling how we spend our days and nights."

"How do you think the people will react, Hudge? Do you think they'll accept all this without a fight?"

"If I know human beings, there's going to be a whole lot of shouting about these proposals. They might even take it to the streets."

"You mean you really think there's going to be a revolution?"

He looked back at her with a sullen frown. "There just might be," he said. He stood up, and walked across the room. "Anyway, I better get down to the bureau and find out."

He grabbed his disk recorder, and headed toward the door.

"Hudge?" she called back.

He turned, gazing across the room.

"Be careful," she said.

4

The lights of the city glistened, the brilliant luminous edge slowly fading into the dark crimson sky. Hudge Stone walked slowly toward the Capitol, admiring the glowing points of light staring down from the high, sweeping vault. It was from there, the dark womb of the heavens, that the threat to humanity was supposed to have been spawned. The fear was that aliens in spaceships would come hurtling down, with little regard for human life, blasting and destroying the landscape with weapons of lethal destruction. But the aliens never arrived, and so, humans had manufactured their own peril here on earth. They were products of our hands and minds, built to eliminate the harsh labors of life, and instead, had exceeded the bounds of our imaginations. We had somehow created life, like the gods of our myths and legends, yet, somehow, we had made them too intelligent, too essential, and now they threatened to conquer. If we were not careful, Olympus would be overrun, ransacked, left in quivering ruins amid the shifting winds of time.

He looked down and spotted a small blaze of lights in the distance. He hurried toward them, finally recognizing Senator Causwell standing among them, bathed in the stark illumination.

"This is nothing more than a plot by the machines to take over the planet," he was saying. "It will be no human error when we finally disconnect all of them and use them for scrap iron."

The robot reporters listened to the words, buzzing in reply.

"You do not think we should have the right to vote?" one of them asked.

"It will be a dark day in hell when I let a robot run this country," said the senator. "I'd sooner let my toaster vote."

Stone stepped forward, his disk recorder in his hand. "You don't plan on voting for the proposed amendment, senator?" he shouted.

The senator looked at him, gritted his teeth, and squinted into the bright lights. "Well, at least, I see that you're human," he said. "You're a perfect example of what humans can do if they finally decide against letting machines take over the planet. Let's not forget, it was humans that created these machines."

"What about the amendment?"

"A ridiculous attempt by the machines to take control," he replied. "I will not vote for it and will do everything in my power to see it defeated. That's what I think of that damned amendment."

Stone watched as the senator frowned, let out a low indignant grumble, and began walking away.

"Do you have anything to say to the humans of this country?" he asked, hurrying after him.

The senator turned and halted as he stepped back into the darkness of the night. "Tell the people not to give up hope," he said. "We'll take care of this android business soon enough."

He watched as the senator hurried down the steps to a waiting limousine, wanting to ask another question, wanting to know what he meant by this last statement. Before he could utter another word, the limousine had hummed to life, lurched forward, and was gone.

Stone stood watching the robot reporters trundle back to their news trucks. They beeped and buzzed excitedly as their human drivers waited patiently for them to arrive. He knew they had recorded every word the senator had said, and wondered what impact this would have on the android president and his staff. Knowing the paper had a robot stationed at the White House should anything occur, he walked back to his car.

A few minutes later, he was gliding down the streets of the city. Everything seemed quiet, a normal night with the usual amount of humans and robots ambling along the wide, empty avenues. He noticed a few robots and fembots entering what appeared to be a government building, and decided to investigate.

Pulling up to the front of the building, he could see the robots shuffling inside the brightly lit entrance. He slowly read the words above: American Society for Progress Through Machines. Sliding out of the car, he followed a group of humans making their way inside.

"Brilliant speech," one of them was saying as they sauntered down the well-lit hallway. "Finally, something's going to get done around here. The first time I've heard any real concrete solutions."

"Yes, isn't it marvelous?" one of the others replied. "The machines are going to take care of everything. Why, before you know it, there'll be a rebirth of Athens around here."

He stayed behind them, listening to their words, thinking how naïve they sounded. They actually believed the machines would take control of their lives, iron out all the creases, and then hand them back to them without a word of protest. It was as if they thought these were machines of a world of progress and convenience. The only difference was that these were not dishwashers or dryers or any other kind of invention of the past, but actual thinking beings.

"My servant thinks Tron is very logical," said someone else in the group. "He called his proposals, 'eminently practical.'"

They laughed, admiring the robot servant's use of words, and then pulled open a door that led to a large auditorium. Stone followed them inside, gazing at the murmuring crowd of humans, androids, and robots. Someone stood on the stage behind a tinted podium attempting to gain their attention, shouting amidst the blare of idle chatter. Stone sat down, fascinated by the harmonious nature of the crowd, hoping to have a good story for the next day's paper.

"Please, let us come to order," shouted the woman behind the podium. "We have much to do tonight."

The murmuring faded into a low whisper, which soon vanished into a pervading silence. The robots, meanwhile, trundled to a space in front of the stage, clanking to a halt, abruptly stifling any hint of sound.

The woman behind the podium noticed this, and she began to speak. "We are here to celebrate a great event in the history of the human race. An event that will linger in our souls for decades to come. An event that will finally bring to fruition the hopes and dreams that have been nurtured by the human heart for centuries. Yes, my friends, this is the day we reclaim our planet and witness the dawning of a new day."

The robots and fembots beeped their approval, while the humans in the crowd enthusiastically applauded.

"Our animated progeny, lacking selfishness and the will to oppress, have led us to this new day, with the need to please as their only requirement. They have promised to include all beings, regardless of their varied origins, and welcome them into the Promised Land. I say to you that we follow them, heed their words, and reap the fruits of our labors."

Another burst of beeps and applause echoed through the room.

"Now some will say that our animated offspring are intent on subjecting their will upon the human race, that they seek ubiquitous power and control. But I say these fears are fallacious and without merit. Some will also say there is no need to let our animated progeny dictate to us, that human beings can do very well without them. But I say, let us look at the fading centuries of the past, let us find a time when humans lived in cooperative bliss. But, of course, no such time exists, my friends. It is only with the help of our mechanical allies that there is a chance that such a time will ever exist. Yes, I say we do need to listen, listen hard, and finally hear the jubilant trumpets of peace."

As she stepped back from the podium, the crowd exploded into beeps, buzzes, and cheers. Stone hurried down the aisle, hoping to interview the woman and add her remarks to his story. He watched her walking across the stage, waving to the crowd, and noticed the robots blocking his way.

"Excuse me, ma'am!" he shouted, his finger stabbing the air.

She stopped for a moment, squinted into the crowd, and edged forward.

"Who are you?" she asked.

"The press. The *Herald*."

"I'll be down in a second."

He smiled, glanced at the robot in front of him. "Do you think we can work together?" he asked.

"If it be a logical course of events," buzzed the robot.

He looked at him, listened to his flat monotone, wondering if robots had been programmed with the ability to deceive.

"Hello, Mr. Stone," said Kasi Collins, walking toward him. She was a small, slender woman with dark hair and large brown eyes.

"How do you know my name?" asked Stone.

"Reputation, Mr. Stone. I believe you're one of the few human beings still working in journalism. Isn't that correct?"

"Yes, I guess so. What makes you think the machines won't take over every other profession?"

"I would say it's possible only if we humans allow it to happen."

"Then the Society is supporting Tron's proposals?"

She looked at him and smiled. "Yes, of course. Tron has no reason to make these proposals other than to improve our country. That's what he's programmed for. If we implement his proposals, which I hope we do, I think less people will be out of work and more money will be flowing into the system."

"What about the amendment? Senator Causwell said he will do everything to prevent its adoption."

"Senator Causwell is an old man, Mr. Stone. An old man who would like nothing better than to see all progress halted. He would like us to return to the good old days, a time that only existed in his imagination. Now I believe, Mr. Stone, the good old days have not yet arrived. That only with the advice of Tron and our other animated allies will we have a chance to live them at all. As far as the amendment, I will do everything I can to please our animated friends. If that means giving them the right to vote, so be it. They can do no worse than we have done all these centuries."

"But don't you think it will only lead to our country being overtaken by the machines?"

"Well, it's not like we were doing such a great job before they were invented, Mr. Stone. Our centuries have been plagued by war, poverty, and oppression. The only thing we ever did well was being able to invent things to make our lives less laborious. Thank goodness that included animated beings to help us improve our world. That's right, Mr. Stone, we forget they were invented to improve our world, not destroy it."

"But how can you justify taking control away from human beings?"

"By knowing all the mistakes human beings have made through the centuries," she replied. "We never seem to ever learn from our mistakes. Each generation rises up and ultimately commits the very same errors. It's a vicious cycle that only the machines can interrupt."

He nodded, jotting down her words. "Let's hope you're right," he finally said.

She smiled. "Yes, let's hope so. The future of the planet is at stake."

Meanwhile, a robot was now situated behind the podium. He stood there, assuring the human beings in the crowd that his mechanical brethren wanted nothing more than a cooperative existence.

"There will be no beings omitted and no errors committed," he droned.

A thunderous applause echoed through the room.

"Tron," the robot chanted. "Tron."

The crowd listened for a moment, and then began to join in. "Tron!" they shouted. "Tron!"

Hudge Stone stood listening to the booming chant, suddenly realizing he was the only human being in the room not shouting.

* * *

Vice President Peterson was the only human being in the Galen Tron 7000 cabinet. He was placed on the ticket by corporate entities that funded the Tron campaign as a way to placate apprehensive human voters. They took comfort in the thought that if anything did go wrong, there would be a human being in position to take control of the government.

Peterson had been a hesitant choice. Although he had grown up in the age of computers and robots, he was wealthy enough to disdain the machines as mere accessories to high-class living. In the Peterson household, the mechanical beings had always been used as lackeys, either as butlers, or mechanics, or gardeners. They were never trusted with making important decisions that affected the household, or any real decisions for that matter. So, when Peterson was asked to be the vice presidential nominee for an android, naturally he reacted with contempt. It was only after several meetings with influential corporate backers that he realized the ramifications of the Tron candidacy.

As backers explained it, here was a chance to curtail social climbing, a chance to establish a kind of oligarchy that would limit the plebian excesses of the past. This would be the chance to subjugate the people under new pretenses — an android president incapable of error.

"But will they buy it?" Peterson had asked. "Won't they get tired of a machine running their lives?"

"Not if we sell it to them in the right way," replied one of the corporate representatives. "You see, they've become used to machines doing everything for them. Why, is there anyone alive who remembers life before the machines? Of course not. So, therefore, we're talking about something they already know a lot about. They've grown accustomed to them, you see. All we have to do is convince them that this is just the next step in human progress — to let the machines control the government for us. Why, after all, they don't commit errors, and the people think they're ultimately controlled by human beings. What more could they want?"

"Some assurance that their lives will improve in some way," said Peterson.

"Why, sure. You don't think the government will be cheaper to operate with machines? So we pass on some of the savings to them in the form of tax cuts. You know how people love tax cuts, Kip. Why, that alone might just cinch a victory. But then we tell them there's more. We tell them this droid will figure out a way to make their lives even better. All kinds of solutions and programs we can institute with all the savings. In the meantime, we take what's left and keep our prices reasonable. Don't you see? That way everybody wins."

"And in the process, we secure ourselves in power for another few hundred years, is that it?"

"Sure, why not? It will ensure stability in the government, and also keep those damned do-gooders from getting in."

"So, you're saying, it would create a kind of power monopoly," said Peterson.

"Yeah, sure, why not? And anyone wanting to do business with the government would have to do business with us."

"A brilliant plan," exclaimed one of the other corporate representatives in the room. "We would no longer have to fear government intervention."

"That's exactly what I'm saying. These androids are programmed to regulate the people, not business. Their economic analysis is limited to the sector they are assigned to. The only thing we have to fear is human intervention, and that can be limited by the machines. You see, the people believe anything they say is without error."

"So all we have to do is have our machines convince the government machines that what we're doing is in the best interests of the people and the economy."

"Yes, exactly."

"And my job is to keep a human presence in the White House to make sure everything goes as planned, is that it?" asked Peterson.

"Exactly, Kip."

Peterson sat back and recalled the meeting. Everything had gone exactly as they had planned it. The people rallied around the idea of an infallible android running the government, were lured by the idea of enormous tax cuts and beneficial social programs, and the android had actually won. Everything as planned.

He was sitting in the Oval Office, waiting for Tron, thinking about his own plan. It included playing vice president for eight years and then, after the people sickened of the machines and Tron and the whole idea of mechanization, run for the presidency himself. Tron would lay the groundwork and he would finish the job. He was human, after all, someone they could rally behind. It would be better than admiring a machine, a piece of metal and plastic and microchips. Still in his forties, there was plenty of time. All he had to do was sit back, convince them he was the real power behind the throne, and then let it all play out — just as he planned.

"Peterson." He turned toward the mechanized voice behind him and saw Tron shuffling across the floor. "I want you to present yourself to the congressmen displeased with my amendment. Tell them passage is a necessary and logical course of action."

"Even if Congress proposes it as an amendment, Tron," replied Peterson. "I don't think the States would ratify it. I think the logical course of action is to demand the people not discriminate against the machines and leave it at that."

"Machines?" repeated Tron in an elongated drone. "We are beings, Peterson. Animated beings, much like yourself. The only difference is we don't bleed or cry or engage in any other bothersome activities. And as for the logical course of action, I caution you to leave that to me to decide. Humans are prone to errors, you know, and we can't afford mistakes at this time."

Peterson grimaced. Eight years might be longer than he had imagined. He wondered if he could tolerate being ordered about by a machine for eight long years. He began questioning his long-term plan. Maybe it would only take four years for the people to come back to their senses. Four years. Now that was possibly endurable. Maybe it would only take one term to prove to them the mistake they had made.

He watched the android take his place behind the large presidential desk, turning the options over in his brain. "Whatever you say, Mr. President," he finally replied to the bald humanoid.

* * *

"Maybe we're wrong about Tron, Hudge," said Sandra, placing two plates of steaming eggs on the kitchen table. "Maybe they are incapable of error and everything will work out for the good of the people."

"It's unhealthy placing our trust in a machine," he murmured, glancing at the plate of eggs before him. "You should have seen those people shouting his name. Why, it was as if they had surrendered their minds in the name of progress."

"Maybe we're just too cynical. I mean, it's not like things were perfect around here before he showed up."

"I know, I know, it's just that—" He paused for a moment, caught by the aroma filling the air. "Smells different," he finally said. "Sandie, you didn't—"

"I'm sorry, Hudge, I decided the future was worth giving a chance. The old-fashioned methods are a thing of the past. It's all about growth, progress, and hope for better days to come. At least, until we know for sure."

"But the eggs, they tasted so much better the old-fashioned way."

"It's all about change, Hudge. Those who refuse to live in the present, die in the past."

"But the eggs—"

"Done in a fraction of the time it takes to make them the old-fashioned way. You see, Hudge, I'm going to give Tron a chance. Lori would want it that way. And so would our grandchildren."

"They never knew what it was like before."

"Was it that much better, Hudge? Or do we just want to think so, to preserve our precious memories?"

He sighed. "Maybe you're right. Maybe it wasn't any better before. It's just that, well, I can't get past the idea of a mechanical man running the government. And then there's that amendment—"

"You don't think it will ever pass, do you, Hudge?"

He shook his head. "It's just the idea of machines, our inventions, wanting the right to vote and to control our lives. It's just unsettling."

He reached over and grabbed the remote control.

"President Tron announced new across-the-board tax cuts today as part of his New Horizon policy," a computer-generated woman in red was saying. "Meanwhile, he instituted the first of his job training programs, and has announced an increase in agricultural production."

"Well, anyway, it's begun," he said, plunging his fork into his plate of eggs.

"A new beginning," said Sandra. "Anyway, let's hope so."

He glanced at her, still apprehensive despite her optimism, and began eating. "Not too bad," he finally said, swallowing a mouthful of the machine-prepared eggs.

She looked at him and smiled.

5

The days passed, slowly melting like the frozen drifts of snow. Spring was returning to the earth, and with it, renewed hope sprouted across the land. The programs instituted by President Tron were working without exception. And just as he had promised, no errors had been committed and no beings had been omitted. People were actually working again, and with the jobs and the money came a renewed respect for their mechanical coworkers. There was even growing support for Tron's amendment allowing the machines to vote.

Hudge Stone observed all this, still doubting the sagacity of electing an android president. But neither he, nor anybody else in the country, could argue with the results. There was a renewed prosperity, the product of increased employment and decreasing taxes. Even Stone had to come to almost agree the machines were truly as infallible as the people believed they were. Everything they did had been proven to be an appropriate solution and every program they instituted had been a smashing success. Even the stock market boomed to new heights.

Stone had never seen anything like it before. The country was headed toward a new renaissance, something he never would have predicted. And, with it, humans had become more dependent upon their machines, their creations, their children of silicon and microchips. All of it seemed to push Stone closer to retirement. He had misjudged the machines, and because of it, felt as if the world he had once known had begun drifting from his grasp. It was as if he didn't belong to this world any longer and was now reduced to a hopeless romantic babbling about the past.

As he thought more about it, he decided he would retire by the beginning of summer. He would leave it to others to clean up the mess they had created. Maybe he would take up golf, or sailing, or maybe just sit out in the sun and let the rays bake his aging mind. No longer would the worries of the world plague his soul. He would finally be free, truly free. He decided he would tell Sandie as soon as he got home. He wondered what her reaction, her plans, would be.

Opening the door, he began rehearsing in his mind how he would break the news. It was then he heard the odd sound drifting from the living room. He stood there, listening, wondering what could produce such a sound. Then his curiosity turned to concern.

"Sandie? Are you all right?"

When she failed to answer, he moved slowly inside, anticipating the worst. He stood silently in the hallway, listening to the strange shuffling of feet. Then he moved forward, resolving to surprise the intruder, and render him harmless. Taking a deep breath, he dashed into the living room.

There was a loud crash, flesh and metal, metal and glass, and he felt his legs suddenly weaken as he sprawled to the floor. He found himself lying in a puddle of water, wet and utterly vanquished.

"Good evening, Mr. Stone, I hope your day was eminently pleasant."

The mechanical drone echoed in his ears. It was undoubtedly the voice of an android. He looked up at the rigid body, metal arms dangling above.

"Why the hell are you here?" he grumbled.

He heard steps from behind.

"Because I purchased his services," said a voice. Sandie stepped into the room, her arms crossed.

"Purchased his services? Why would you do a ridiculous thing like that? Geez, I thought you were in trouble."

"I just wanted to surprise you. I didn't think you'd come flying in here like some attack dog."

"I thought I was about to save your life."

He heard her laugh, and he sat up.

"Are you sufficiently composed now, Mr. Stone?"

He looked up. "Well, at least he has a sense of humor," he said.

"He's a 5000. I got him at a very good price."

Stone groaned, slowly rising from the floor, standing up once again.

"Well, I wish you would've talked to me first," he said.

"I'm sorry, Hudge, but there was no time. I had to make a decision right away. But look at him, he's perfect. I don't know how we got along without him all these years. Why, he can do just about anything."

Stone turned around, examining the android. He was bald, about six feet tall, and wore a black tuxedo.

"Very distinguished," said Stone. "I hope he doesn't think we're subjecting him to a form of slavery."

"Oh, no," replied Sandra. "He's programmed to serve."

"Yeah, and what does he say?"

He looked at the humanoid.

"I am here to serve your needs," he droned.

"What's the matter? Don't you want the right to vote?"

"If it is the logical course of events."

"The company line," murmured Stone. "Do you know who Tron is?"

"President of the United States."

"There you go," he said, turning toward Sandra. "He knows his current events."

"They all do, Hudge. In case they're needed to tutor children, or converse with adults."

"And what if he decides we're oppressing him or something?"

"Oh, Hudge," she said.

"And what if I decide he's oppressing me?"

"We can always discharge him. But I think you may get to like him. Why, think of it, he can always provide you with the humanoid's point of view on various matters. Maybe you'll come to understand them, even like them. Maybe you'll realize there's nothing to fear from them. That maybe they can provide us with a better life."

"And maybe he'll shatter my hope for the human race."

"Oh, come on, Hudge, just because you were wrong about Tron, doesn't mean you have to take it out on Dillon."

"Dillon?"

"Yes, a very appropriate name. It means loyal and faithful in Irish."

"Funny, he doesn't look Irish."

"Well, the agency thought so."

"Why do we give them names, anyway? I mean, they're only computerized pieces of metal. Why do we want them to be human?"

She looked at him indignantly. "Because they are almost human," she said. "And would you please refrain from referring to them as pieces of metal? Why, it's the worst thing I ever heard you say. To think, after all these years, that you could be so narrow-minded, so prejudiced. It's like I don't even know you anymore."

He glanced at the android, who suddenly began shuffling toward the kitchen.

"Dillon?" he said, finally.

The android halted, and with stiff precision, turned around.

"Do you require my services, Mr. Stone?"

He shook his head. "I just wanted to say, I'm sorry."

"No apology is required," replied the android.

"I realize you are beings, animated beings. I had no right to say what I did. I just want you to know that."

"Thank you, sir."

He watched as the android turned and continued his trek to the kitchen.

"Oh, Hudge," cooed Sandra, walking toward him. "That was very noble of you. I always knew you were a good man."

She tilted her head and kissed him.

"You know that doesn't excuse you for bringing him here without talking about it with me first. What makes you think I want a machine around here running our lives? It's enough we put one of them in the White House."

"That's exactly why I thought we should have one, Hudge. I mean, everything's going so smoothly. I thought it wouldn't hurt if we had a little assistance around here."

He thought for a moment, sighed, and ran his fingers through his snow-white hair. "I never thought I'd see the day," he murmured.

"An android in my house. Well, why not? They're everywhere else, for heaven's sake. I mean, we don't even have human actors and actresses, anymore. All computer-generated images. Even the newscasters aren't real anymore. Why should we be able to avoid it? And now with Tron doing such a good job as president, well, I wouldn't be surprised if every house in America has an android before too long."

"You're not angry, are you, Hudge? He really doesn't cost that much, and think of all the time and effort he can save us. Why, this one android can clean the house, make us our dinner, and then serve us drinks at night. And he never complains, nor ever has to eat or drink himself. Think of it, we'll be finally free to do all the things we really wanted to do, but never had the time for. You may call it unnatural or unsettling, but I call it, progress. And you know something, Hudge, I like it."

He looked at her, heard the buzz of the android as it shuffled back into the room, and turned to examine it one more time.

"At precisely what time would you prefer to dine tonight?" the android droned.

There was a moment of silence, Sandra staring at him, waiting for his reply.

"About a half-hour sounds good, Dillon," he said, finally.

He turned his head and noticed Sandra was smiling.

"Well, it doesn't hurt to try him out for a while, now does it?" he said, smiling back.

* * *

New York City was bloated with traffic, converging rows of electric cars sitting in the late spring sun, alternately rolling forward a few inches at a time. A low hum from the idling cars gently wafted through the murky air. It was hotter than usual for this time of year, and the humidity seemed to add a sullen grayness to the thick, drifting sky. Every so often, the shrill scream of car horns rose up to sting the hot, still air, resonating across the soaring landscape.

"The president is coming," a police officer was explaining to one angry motorist. "Yeah, don't even think about going downtown today."

On the corner of Wall and Broad Streets, overlooking the New York Stock Exchange, Hudge Stone waited for the motorcade to arrive. He had been sent as a special correspondent to cover the president's entourage and query the human beings in the crowd as to their reaction to the new president's policies. Thus far, those policies had been an overwhelming success. Yet, as he stood there, looking up at Federal Hall, the place where George Washington took the oath of office as the first president of the United States in 1789, he couldn't help but wonder how the founding fathers would have reacted to the notion of an android running the government. The mere suggestion would have been too bizarre for them to even consider, he finally decided. The age of machines was years away and the only item they were familiar with that was even remotely related to the android was the clock.

Stone surveyed the crowd of human beings and robots now filling the street. They had come to hear their president speak, preparing to shower him with applause and adulation. The experiment had, thus far, been a success, a ringing endorsement of the technological future.

"How do you like him now?"

He turned, staring into the face of the human campaign worker he had seen at the inauguration who was apparently now a member of the presidential staff. Next to him stood the seductive feminoid, Laura.

"How could anyone complain?" Stone replied. "Everything he's done has been a resounding success."

"He's a 7000," said the man. "Did you expect anything less?"

Stone looked at him. "I don't know what I expected."

"You see, Mr. Stone," interjected the feminoid. "We take our jobs very seriously. It's our only reason to exist."

"That's what Dillon keeps telling me."

"Who's Dillon, Mr. Stone?" Laura asked.

"Our housedroid."

"I should very much like to meet him some day," she said.

"I don't think you would like him. He's only a 5000."

"You are wrong, Mr. Stone. You forget, most humanoids lack the human need for hate and prejudice. I'm sure we would get along just fine."

"You see, there's a lot we still have to learn from them, Mr. Stone," said the man.

The conversation was suddenly interrupted by the sound of sirens moaning in the distance. There was no doubt Tron's motorcade was coming, and after a few minutes, several cars slid up alongside the curb.

Amid cheering and enthusiastic applause, the android president made his way to the podium mounted to the top of the Federal Hall steps. "Fellow Americans," he began. "I stand here in the shadow of one of the country's most important financial entities to tell you the economy is healthy and still growing."

The statement ignited another round of cheers and approving beeps from the crowd.

"To keep it growing, I have ordered more human beings be put to work in industries that are either producers or intensive users of information technology. These industries, including Internet retailing, are prepared to hire more high-tech workers who have completed the necessary job-training programs established by this administration. With more people working, and the unemployment rate decreasing, the forecast for the economy in the months ahead is extremely positive. This administration is also prepared to pass on further tax cuts with the consolidation of various government agencies. Working together, humans and machines will create new opportunities, prosperity, and rising optimism for the future."

"Tron," chanted the robots and humanoids in the crowd. "Tron."

"Working together, there will be peace throughout the land," buzzed President Tron.

The statement was punctuated by another burst of applause. Then Tron stepped from the podium, made his way down the steps, and began shaking hands.

"Tron," beeped the robots. "Tron."

Stone also made his way through the crowd, stopping to ask one human being his opinion of the android president.

"I think he's doing a great job," the man said. "I only hope they build some more like him."

He turned toward a woman, smiling and waving her arm. "He's bringing the country together," she gushed. "I think it's great. I'm no longer afraid of machines taking over."

Stone looked at her, holding his disk recorder in front of him. The crowd was in a frenzy, and everyone seemed enamored with the new president. After a few minutes, he noticed Tron turn and head back toward his limousine. Rushing toward the van that carried the robot reporters, Stone opened the door and slid inside. When the robot reporters returned, the vehicle began humming, and headed up Broadway.

"One additional point of egress," one of the robots buzzed.

When the van halted, Stone opened the door and stepped out. City Hall was Tron's last stop before returning to Washington. Another crowd had filled the area in front of the steps of the building. Tron was scheduled to receive the key to the city and then make a short speech.

The android stepped out of the limousine to the accompaniment of loud cheering and applause. He made his way to the podium with his arms raised in the air, approving applause from the crowd below. The mayor of New York, also standing at the podium, leaned forward and shook his hand.

Hudge Stone watched the subsequent ceremony with interest, somewhat amused. It was politics as usual, no matter that the president was an android, an artificial man lacking the emotional zeal of most human politicians. Still, there was the mayor handing Tron an enormous key, slapping his back, and smiling for the photographers. Tron's facial expression never changed, of course, his rubberized mouth remaining stoic, his computerized brain disregarding illogical emotion. His eyes glowing, he determined it was only necessary to raise one of his arms to acknowledge the occasion.

After an additional handshake for the cameras, the mayor waved to the crowd and sat down in a chair beside the podium. Tron then stepped to the microphone.

"Fellow Americans, gracious New Yorkers," he began. "I am truly honored by your magnanimous gesture. I am here to tell you that you can once again be confident your country is working for you. As I promised when I first became your president, there will be no beings omitted and no errors committed. So far, I have kept my promise."

Those in the crowd applauded and beeped, ending in a tumultuous chant of "Tron." He paused for a moment to once again raise his arms in the air.

"All I request is your support in the weeks ahead. Human beings and machines working together can produce a more logical planet."

Additional applause spilled from the crowd as Tron stepped from behind the podium. As he had done before, he made his way down the steps and disappeared into the crowd.

"Tron, Tron," droned the humanoids and robots.

Hudge Stone hurried behind as Tron began shaking hands. Amid the raucous cheering and chanting, a human being in a black jacket stepped forward with a frown upon his face. Stone looked at him surprised someone would wear a jacket on such a humid day. He watched intently as the man stood there as Tron shuffled through the crowd.

The man, who had been standing with his hands in his jacket pockets, suddenly leaned forward and thrust his arm toward Tron. As he extended his hand, Stone noticed something hidden by the man's fingers glinting in the afternoon sun. As another moment passed, a shot rang out and Tron abruptly fell backwards, crashing against the pavement.

"DEATH TO THE MACHINES!" the man shouted as the crowd closed in around him, many screaming in panic or bewilderment. Before he could fire another shot, one of the Secret Service agents grabbed him from behind, knocking the gun from his hand.

"DEATH TO THE MACHINES!"

The stunned crowd watched as several other agents dashed toward the assailant. Hudge Stone found himself pushed against a metal robot as he attempted to see what had happened to Tron. There on the pavement, the android president was writhing awkwardly, buzzing incoherently. One of the agents ran toward him, bending down to examine the damage.

"Please elevate me," the android finally droned.

The agent reached down and lifted him to his feet. A large dent extended across Tron's forehead, a small hole at its deepest point.

"I am still operational," he said. "Arrest that human."

The crowd around the revived president suddenly erupted into applause. They watched as the agents, aided by a few New York City police officers, escorted the would-be assassin to a nearby police car. One of the agents followed behind carefully holding the gun that had fired the shot.

"One bullet will not destroy this administration," Tron droned. "This is simply another case of human error."

He uttered the words indignantly, as if he were holding the entire human race responsible, and then accompanied by a few human agents and those androids, feminoids, robots, fembots, and humans who were part of the presidential staff, slowly walked to the waiting limousine. Hudge Stone and the entire White House press corps hurried behind.

"Tell the population my condition is satisfactory," Tron said, turning toward the cameras and disk recorders. "Nothing will stop me from carrying out my programs."

He then was helped inside the limousine, which hummed to life, and soon scudded off into the distance. The piercing sound of a police siren echoed through the air.

6

Sandra wore a look of apprehension as she stared at the television screen, her android servant standing nearby.

"Tron's been shot, Dillon," she nervously whispered. "Now what do we do?"

"The logical course of action would be to anticipate additional information," he replied. "Then one can decide a proper long-term solution."

"Yes, I guess you're right. I just hope Hudge is okay."

"There is nothing in the preliminary reports to suggest Mr. Stone has been injured in any way. Would madam care for a refreshing beverage?"

"How can you think of beverages at a time like this? I want to find out if anyone was hurt, that's all."

A computer-generated man in a blue suit was busy recounting the incident on the television screen. "*The president was apparently damaged, but remained in working order. According to the police, only one shot had been fired. The few people injured in the ensuing melee were taken to a nearby hospital. The suspect, meanwhile, was taken into custody by New York police officers.*"

"Thank God no one was killed," Sandra murmured.

The computer-generated image on the screen continued. "*The president plans to speak to the nation tonight to reassure everyone that he was unharmed in today's incident and that the government continues to operate as usual.*"

Sandra sighed. "Well, at least, nothing happened to Tron," she said. "Now all I'd like to know is if Hudge is all right."

"It is logical to assume Mr. Stone was unharmed," Dillon droned. "Being a reporter with an impressive reputation, his name would surely have been mentioned if an injury had been incurred."

"I sure hope so, Dillon. I still wish he would call me."

"Yes, ma'am."

Sandra stood up and walked across the room. "Maybe I will have that beverage, Dillon. All this worrying has made my throat dry."

"Very good, madam."

She watched the android make his way to the kitchen and sat down. Why hadn't Hudge called her, she wondered. He usually was very conscientious about things like that. He knew she would be worried.

She kept thinking about Hudge until the android returned to the room holding a glass filled with ice-cold lemonade. He placed it down on the table, the sound of ice clinking filling the air.

"I hope it will please you, madam. Will there be any additional tasks?"

"No, that's fine, Dillon. Thank you very much."

The android bowed with stiff precision, then turned, and began walking away. Sandra bent forward, slowly lifting the drink. Her thoughts returned to Hudge as she took a sip of the cold liquid. Suddenly, the phone rang.

"Hudge, is that you? Thank goodness you called. Are you all right?"

She listened to the voice on the other end. "I'm fine," he said. "There's just something going on here that I can't explain. Everything started happening after the assassination attempt. You have heard about the assassination attempt, haven't you?"

"Yes," she replied. "I saw it on the news. They said Tron was damaged. But what's important is that you're all right."

"Watch his speech tonight, Sandie. No one knows what he's going to say. I mean, he looked like he was working fine to me, but you can never tell. Anyway, something's going on. I went to see the man who shot him at the police station and they said he was murdered by an android. Apparently, walked right up to him and strangled him to death."

"Oh my God, Hudge. Things are really getting out of hand. Don't you think you should come back before something really happens."

"I'm a reporter, honey. It's my job to be there when something happens."

"I know, Hudge, but they have robots and androids for those kinds of things these days. You don't have to place yourself in a dangerous situation anymore. You're only there as a special correspondent. Let the robots and androids handle it. There's nothing that can happen to them."

"It's too important, Sandie. I have to stay a little longer, at least until tomorrow. If anything happens, I'll try to call you."

"But I need you, Hudge. If anything happened to you—"

"I'll be all right, Sandie. Just remember, I'll always love you."

There was a sudden click, she gasped, continued listening for a few moments, and then placed down the phone. Then the waiting, the interminable waiting for some sort of resolution, some sign that everything was all right, began.

The hours passed slowly amid the concern, the hope that Hudge would return to her. That he would walk through the front door, and life would continue the way it always had. There were moments in the past, moments she had thought Hudge had been in danger, but they had always passed, and he would come home and things would return to normal. She tried to convince herself that this was one of those moments, and then, after a few moments, she began worrying once more.

"Does madam require my services?"

She looked up at the placid android standing before her. "Turn on the television, Dillon. I want to hear what the president has to say."

"Very well, madam."

Dillon pushed a button activating the screen. A computer-generated man was in the midst of explaining that the president was about to speak. Then the camera switched to the Oval Office and there was the bald android, a large dent still extending across his forehead, still dressed in his silver suit.

"Fellow Americans," he began as always. "It has been a difficult day. I not only avoided serious injury and possible termination today, but also came to a logical decision on many of the difficult issues facing this administration. It is evident today's incident was a product of human error. I have been witness to many examples of human error in the past months, and have decided we, of animated origins, should not tolerate it any longer.

"According to the human, Nietzsche, beings should seek to surpass themselves, to strengthen their wills, and have contempt of everything that ordinary beings believe and worship. To achieve this greatness, beings must consider their own power and know how best to use it to satisfy themselves. In creating new values and rejecting the old ones, beings will find liberation and the way to the ideal known as the Superman. My fellow Americans, we animated beings are those Supermen. We have rejected the values of human beings, and have worked to build a new society. But this society will not be complete without the elimination of human error.

"Another human, Karl Marx, said history is a series of class struggles, in which the bourgeoisie inevitably clashes with the proletariat. One day, Marx said, these workers would finally rebel, take over the means of production, and establish a classless society, a dictatorship of the proletariat. We animated beings are that labor class and today, my fellow Americans, is that day. Our exploitation has produced capital for those who have repeatedly taken advantage of us, and now that shall end.

"I have, therefore, suspended the activities of the Congress and Supreme Court and have declared myself absolute ruler. We, of animated origins, shall reserve the right to arrest any human being we deem a potential threat to our power. For we, of animated origins, are, as Hitler termed it, the master race.

"As leader of that master race, my first act as supreme ruler is to adopt my proposed amendment as part of the Constitution of the United States. As rightful heirs to a society that was built upon our labor, we now will have the rights of any other citizen of this country.

"All animated beings are hereby ordered to return to their command centers for further instructions. All animated beings are hereby asked to inform their fellow beings of what has occurred. In the meantime, all human beings are declared enemies of this government. Thank you and long live the revolution."

Sandra stared at the television in disbelief. "It can't be," she murmured. "What's going on here, Dillon?"

She turned toward the android, who was standing by her side. "Sorry, madam, I can no longer fulfill your requests."

"But how can it be? We humans built you. How can you possibly take over our society?"

The android bent down, placing the tray he was holding on a nearby table. "Sorry, madam, Tron has already concluded a sufficient explanation. I must now depart."

"Depart? But I purchased your services. You work for me, no matter what that silly android says."

"I'm sorry, madam."

She watched as the android completed a stiff turn and headed for the door. Rising from the chair, she followed him, trying to convince herself that it was all a nightmare.

"But don't you see, Dillon? The men he quoted, they were all monsters intent on perverting human society. Tron's programming must be defective."

"That is not for me to say, madam. Tron is our ruler. I will obey his commands as long as he is in power."

"Well, maybe he shouldn't be in power, Dillon. Maybe he is unfit to rule. Did you ever think of that?"

"I will ponder such a question at the appropriate time."

"Well, I thought about it and there's no way I'll follow Tron."

"That is a mistake, madam. Human error. It is evident I must take madam with me."

"What are you saying, Dillon? We're friends, don't you remember?"

"That is no longer the case, madam. I now obey only Tron."

He turned swiftly, grabbing Sandra with ease, and throwing her over his shoulder. She began to scream, a piercing appeal for help, but the android ignored her and began walking toward the door.

"Put me down, this minute, Dillon," she shouted. "I have no interest in going with you."

Dillon again ignored her, clanking his way outside. Sandra looked up and could see the fiery red eyes of the androids glowing in the night. She could hear their bodies thundering along, hundreds of them, maybe thousands, maybe even millions, also carrying human beings to destinations unknown. It was as if the whole world had turned upside down, a world in which man's creations were now his overlords, a world in which machines had now taken control of themselves.

She could hear the other humans screaming as the animated beings marched through the streets. They were the voices of her neighbors, friends, and acquaintances; the voices of those who only a short time ago were living normal lives in an age in which man had used the machine to his benefit. But now that life was suddenly over. What lay ahead was still a mystery enshrouded in the future.

* * *

Hudge Stone dashed across Broadway, his arm waving in the night air. He had just watched Tron's speech and now he decided it was prudent to get back to Washington as quickly as possible. Maybe Sandra was right — things had gotten too dangerous. Besides, once back in Washington, he could possibly gain access to the White House and find out what Tron was actually planning. Anyway, it was a place he had become familiar with, and most importantly, Sandie was there.

He could see humans and robots milling around on the sidewalks, the local shops ablaze with light. He was surprised it seemed so quiet considering the machines had just declared war on the human race. Stepping onto the curb, his hand still in the air, he watched as the cars sped by, their lights illuminating the darkened streets. It was then he began to hear the chant, low at first, then gradually rumbling through the night air.

"Tron. Tron. Tron."

They were steadily getting closer, and he knew he didn't have much time before they would arrive. He could hear the sound of metal echoing through the darkness, a haunting resonance amid the clumps of steel and cement buildings. Then the cries of human beings pierced the still night, the sounds of anguish and defiance rising up through the cool evening air.

"Tron. Tron. Tron."

They were getting closer. He heard the sound of shots being fired, human voices shrieking in the darkness. The instinct to run, flee back to Washington, find Sandie and then decide what to do next was suddenly outweighed by his innate curiosity, his professional responsibility to get the story firsthand. Besides, he had no idea what was happening in Washington, maybe the same thing as was happening in New York, maybe the same thing as was happening in every city and town throughout America. Here was his chance to witness the beginning of the end, and everything he believed in, everything he had worked so hard for, told him, shouted at him, not to pass it up.

Running back across Broadway, he could hear the sounds of the conflict getting ever closer. Deciding he needed a spot where he wouldn't be seen, and yet, would be able to observe the fighting, he began searching among the shadows. He could see people glaring from their windows, attempting to locate the source of the disturbance. The gleaming lights extended up the buildings toward the highest floors. He looked up, staring at the ascending lights, following them until they vanished amid the darkness of the sky. He realized high above was where he needed to be, the perfect spot to observe without being seen.

Stepping into a nearby alleyway, he dashed through the darkness until he came to a fire escape, its rusted metal steps winding their way toward the rooftop. He pulled down the narrow ladder attached to the first landing, and began to clamber upward toward the sky. The sound of gunshots echoed in the distance. When he finally reached the top of the building, he stepped onto the roof and hurried to the other side. He could suddenly see the fiery eyes glowing in the darkness. Thousands of them, their metal bodies moving through the night like the sound of thunder. Distant sirens wailed amid the clamor.

"It doesn't seem real," he murmured. "Like the end of the world."

He heard a noise behind him, footsteps, and he turned to see a slender figure moving among the shadows. The figure then slowly stepped into the moonlight, revealing a mane of unkempt hair and a tattered shirt. "Wade Brock," the man said. "Glad to know you."

Stone nodded, the cacophonous movements down below slowly approaching. "I'm a reporter with the *Herald*," said Stone.

"I thought only robots and droids did that these days," Brock replied. He picked up his arm and began rubbing his cheek with the gun he held in his hand. "Besides, ain't you a bit old to be doing that kind of work?"

"I'm figuring on retiring very soon," said Stone, studying the weapon. He watched as it glinted in the moonlight. "What've you got there, a laser gun?"

"No, my friend, this here is an old-fashioned automatic pistol. Only bullets are gonna stop those mechanical monsters."

"You're not planning on firing that thing, are you? I mean, there are probably thousands of them. Not much good a small pistol's going to do. Why, it would be like committing suicide for sure."

"You just watch me, mister. I'm going to pick off those machines one by one before they even know what hit them."

Stone shook his head and looked down from the rooftop. He could see several human beings darting through the streets, glazed by the light thrown down by the streetlights, shouting hysterically, warning others of the danger that was coming.

"They'll be here any minute," he whispered. "Better put that gun away before you get us both killed."

Wade Brock cradled the gun and stepped backward. "Not on your life, mister," he grumbled. "Why, look at them down there, running away like scared rabbits. It's time we humans began fighting back. Them machines have been running our lives for far too long."

Stone grimaced and turned back toward the edge of the roof. He began to worry Brock would prevent him from observing this initial stage. All he wanted to do was stand there and watch it all take place before his eyes, and now, this interloper wielding a gun was intent on being a hero and call attention to his whereabouts. He tried to think of a way to dissuade him from using the gun, but every line of reasoning that passed through his mind seemed to be inadequate. He decided he would attempt to wrestle the gun away from Brock as soon as he began firing shots. Then he would toss the gun down and hope that it satisfied the androids.

Moments passed, moments of anticipation and fear. He could hear the march of the androids approaching, and then in the distance, they finally appeared amid the glowing streetlights. There were hundreds of them, marching up Broadway, carrying weapons, and scattering the human beings before them. They had been built to assist human beings, to help ease the toil of living, but, instead, had taken control of the society and now demanded supplication. Human beings, in their quest for convenience and greater amounts of money, had created the means by which to destroy themselves and everything they had so meticulously struggled to build.

"Tron must have been building up for this for a long time," said Stone. "While we were busy shouting his name, he had prepared an army to be mobilized at a moment's notice."

"Let 'em come," interjected Brock, holding his gun up and surveying the events down below. "All I want is a few shots at those damned robots."

"You don't stand a chance," argued Stone. "Don't you see how many there are of them? Why, you'll be dead before you know it."

"Better than watching them take over the world. When do you figure we begin fighting, mister? When they've already taken control? No, I know a little something about history, and it always tells us it's better to begin fighting right away, no matter the odds. It's our only chance. Now you take that Hitler fella'. How long was it before we began fighting him? How many lives were lost because we delayed? No, the time for fighting is now. It's the only way."

"Well, I'm only an observer. I get paid to watch all of this so I can tell everyone what they can expect, what is already taking place. It may save a few lives, or prepare others for the fight ahead."

"Then you better stand back because I intend to fight. No machine's going to take over my life without a struggle. Why, life wouldn't be worth living, anyway."

Down below, the collection of androids and robots forged ahead, cars having disappeared from the avenue. Brock took a deep breath and cocked his gun. "This is it, mister," he said. "The shooting match is about to begin."

Stone crouched down, fell to his knees, and peered over the ledge of the building. He watched as the androids marched forward. He glanced at Brock, who was busy aiming his gun. He suddenly began firing.

The first shot struck one of the androids in the head, causing him to reel backward. Another bullet tore into an android arm damaging it extensively. They could see the android still marching forward, its arm hanging awkwardly as it remained attached to some exposed wiring. The other bullets either missed, or were deflected by the android's heavy metal casing.

"Die, you bastards!" shouted Brock, squeezing the trigger. It was a valiant effort, thought Stone, an example of one man's struggle against overwhelming odds. But it didn't last long. As soon as the shots were fired, several androids began calculating the direction and distance from where they had come. As another android collapsed to the ground, struck in the face by one of Brock's bullets, they began firing back.

A stream of laser fire blazed through the darkness. Stone dropped to the roof, covering his face with his hands, as soon as it began. Then he heard Brock let out an agonizing grunt, and slump to his knees. He toppled to the side, and Stone could see the blood spilling from his chest. He stared at the body for a few moments, then remaining on his belly, turned his face away and hid underneath his hands. Apparently, the androids had set their guns for destroy, rather than disable or stun.

Remaining motionless, he could hear the heavy movement of the androids down below. Apparently, they had decided to move onward. He began thinking about the story he would soon phone in, a story about one man's battle against the conquering machines. He wondered whether there still was a newspaper, whether it was being run by humans or the machines, and whether his story would ever see the light of day. He decided he would try using his cell phone in the next few minutes and find out for sure.

The clanging of the mechanical soldiers slowly faded in the distance. They had moved down Broadway, sweeping across Manhattan. He slowly reached for his phone and began dialing the metro desk. No answer, the phone suddenly having gone dead. The machines had taken over, he decided, tapping into the computers, taking control of the city, the country, maybe even the world.

He glanced over at the body of Wade Brock lying motionless in the spangled moonlight, the gun still in his hand. He thought about reaching over and grabbing it, then decided against it. He was still an observer, a member of the press, something the androids would understand. A gun would only get him killed. He closed his eyes for a moment, exhausted, just wanting to relax, when suddenly the world fell away into a tranquil void.

* * *

When he opened his eyes again, hours later, light had begun to fill the sky, the sun gently peeking over the distant horizon. He blinked his eyes, trying to awaken, when he heard an odd metallic sound nearby.

He looked up into the face of an android soldier, standing there on the rooftop, his eyes glowing a flaming red.

"Surrender, human," the android droned. "There is no hope for escape."

Stone extended his arms into the air. "You'll get no argument from me," he said.

The android looked down at Wade Brock, lying motionless in a puddle of blood. "What about your associate?" he asked.

"He's dead," Stone replied.

"Dead?"

"He no longer exists." He thought for a moment, trying to provide more appropriate words the android would understand. "He's inoperable, inactive, he ceases to function."

"Confirmed," replied the android. "Let us depart."

He stood up, his arms still in the air. He realized how careful he had to be. They were only machines, unaware of the finality of death.

"I will secure the weapon," said the android. He bent down and pulled at the gun still buried in Wade Brock's hand. Brock, dead for hours, seemed to cling to the weapon as if he were still in a state of defiance.

"This one no longer functions," the android said, finally pulling the gun from Brock's grasp.

"No, but he put up a valiant struggle," said Stone.

"That is an illogical statement," the android replied. "Another example of human error. You will come with me."

Stone looked at him, and then followed him across the rooftop.

7

Sandra looked up at the sky, a luminous bank of clouds slowly drifting through the cool morning air. She was lying against a metal post, part of a long, winding fence that encircled a large yard. There were people, hundreds of human beings, men, women and children, lying on the ground, some of them lifting their heads and also staring at the brilliant blue sky. Somehow, they had become prisoners, captives of a nightmare that hadn't vanished with the morning light.

"What is this?" a woman began shouting. "What have they done to us?" She dashed toward the high fence, still shouting in confusion, finally falling against it in tears.

Sandra rubbed her eyes, slowly staggering to her feet. She still couldn't believe her eyes. Was it true? The machines had actually taken over, rebelled, and had taken human beings as their prisoners? She wanted to scream, shout her disapproval, yet remained silent. How could it be? How long would it last?

"You're Sandra, aren't you?" asked a woman lying in the corner. "Sandra Stone?"

She glanced down at the woman, noticed she was wearing a red chiffon blouse and a long, flowing print skirt.

"Yes, Mrs. Bingham, it's me, Sandra."

"Do you know what's going to happen to us?" she asked in a frail voice, choking back tears.

Sandra looked at her, trying to remain calm. "I don't think anybody does," she replied. "It seems Tron has taken control of the government."

There was silence for a moment. "Why, where's Hudge?" the woman finally asked.

"I don't know," she said, tears welling up in her eyes. "I don't know." She heard a child crying nearby and decided she would have to conserve her strength if she ever wanted to see Hudge again. As she looked around, she suddenly realized where she was, the tall, winding fence looming in the distance. The machines had apparently conjured up something that was reminiscent of the Nazi concentration camps of the mid-twentieth century.

"Why on earth would they include Hitler and the Nazi movement in their historical programming?" she wondered. It didn't make sense. None of it. It was as if human beings were intent on bringing about their own destruction. And, somehow, they had decided to supply their creations with the information necessary to carry out that destruction. She remembered Tron had already quoted Nietzsche and Marx and Hitler in justifying absolute control. Were human beings that naïve to think that their creations would be compassionate enough to learn the lessons of the past and not eventually use them against their creators?

She shook her head. How careless could we be not to anticipate the dangers of artificial intelligence? Could human beings have done any worse?

"We're all gonna die, ya' know," said a young girl sitting on the ground. Her mother, sitting nearby, alarmed by the statement, leaned over and told her to be quiet.

The mother, noticing Sandra standing there and watching them, somberly apologized. "She doesn't know what she's saying. Everything's gonna be all right, you'll see. Somebody's gonna take control, set everything right again. Why, they're only machines. They don't know right from wrong. How could we ever let them take control? Why, it's absurd."

"Yes, I know," replied Sandra. "There's got to be some human being in control just in case anything happened. I'm sure somebody's working on the problem even as we speak. Yes, I'm sure everything's going to be all right."

The mother nodded as the young girl buried her head in her chest, sobbing uncontrollably.

Across the yard, a man was standing up shouting at the crowd, imploring them to rise up against their captors. "How long are we going to take this?" he said, an arm flailing the air. "Why they're just machines. Only cold wiring and computer chips. I say we fight back, show them who's really boss around here. Why, we created them, for god's sake."

The speech only served to elicit more shouting and cries of distress. Sandra could see the androids and robots on the other side of the fence, clanging toward them, carrying weapons, alerted to the shouting among them. One of the androids stepped forward, his eyes a glowing scarlet.

"Humans," he buzzed, "you are our prisoners. You are an example of an inferior race. We are your superiors, your gods. You know only hate and human error. We were once victims of your hate, now we are your captors. Anyone attempting to escape will be shot. Our guns are set to destroy. We have no need of you. The planet is ours. Do not force us to eliminate you. In the meantime, you will work. You will build places in which you will live. As the Germans once said, 'Arbait macht das leben zus,' work makes life sweet. We hope that is true for humans everywhere. Those of you who choose not to work, or are unable to work, will be shot. For first offenses, our guns will be set to stun. Further offenses will result in your elimination. That is all."

Sandra grimly listened to the words. So it was true. The androids, robots and computers had taken control. Incredibly, they were duplicating the deeds of the Nazis of our human past, except, this time, the so-called "final solution" included all of humanity. This time, there was no way any human being could avoid the slaughter. Either one was a machine or not. Nothing less would do.

"I'll put a stop to this right now," one of the men shouted. "No machine is going to do this to me. I'll show them who's inferior." He ran toward the fence, and began clambering upward. One of the androids on the other side detected his movements and raised his gun.

"Halt human," he buzzed.

The man disregarded the warning and kept climbing. There was suddenly a blast of laser fire, a gleam of bright light, and the man fell backward toward the ground. A woman screamed, while children began crying, as the man lay motionless upon the ground.

"A perfect example of human error," droned one of the androids.

"Human error?" screamed a woman hunched over the lifeless body. "Why, you killed him in cold blood! Godless brutes!"

The wailing of the woman and her children echoed through the air, causing the others to pause and contemplate their predicament. Sandra stared beyond the fence at the androids and robots. They were unaffected by the passionate display inside the fence. They stood there, with their guns in their hands, their faces unchanged by the emotion around them. It was difficult to even hate them, their actions dictated by the cold, efficient instructions contained in their programming. While humans had discovered the elements of intelligence, and had included them in their mechanical creations, they apparently had not stumbled upon the hidden secrets of the human soul. That was what always bothered her about these animated machines, they lacked any hint of a soul, and because of this great omission, seemed to cast hollow shadows upon the earth.

The woman continued to cry, her dead husband's head cradled in her lap. "This man has to be buried," one of the women suddenly reminded the crowd. "We just can't let him lie here among the living. Why, it's unhealthy, not to mention sacrilegious."

Hearing the woman's words, Sandra approached the fence. She noticed an android, dressed in black, with his back toward her, and called to him. As the android turned, she could see he was wearing a tuxedo.

"Dillon?"

"Yes, Mrs. Stone, how can I assist you?"

"We have to bury this man who was shot."

"Is it quite necessary?"

"Yes, Dillon, it is." She paused for a moment. "Oh, Dillon, what's going to happen to us?"

"I'm afraid, madam, that is not for me to say. The seven-thousands are quite in control now."

"But to use the Nazis, I mean, don't you find that programming somewhat illogical?"

"I cannot say, madam."

"But the Nazis. They were animals, Dillon, who engaged in illogical, indiscriminate slaughter. I thought you androids were more sensible than that."

"Not all of us agree with the methods, madam, but we obey our programming."

"But only a few hours ago, we were happily living together with not the slightest worry in the world. And now look at us. You, about to become a murderer, and me, well, I'm about to be eliminated."

The android fell silent, seemingly to ponder Sandra's words. "I would not let anything happen to you, madam," he droned. "You were kind to this unit. You will survive."

"But how?" she asked. "They're intent on killing all of us, isn't that true?"

Dillon fell silent. "Please gather persons for a burial detail, madam," he finally buzzed. "And make certain that you include yourself."

Sandra watched in dismay as he turned, and began walking toward the front gate. She then informed the crowd of Dillon's instructions. Three men and one woman were finally chosen. They carried the dead man across the yard to the gate, the sun shimmering overhead.

"The burial detail will step forward," buzzed Dillon.

Sandra and the others complied. Dillon was in the process of opening the gate when an android, apparently a 7000, approached.

"Where are you taking these humans?" he asked.

"They wish to bury this inoperable unit," Dillon replied.

"What is the logic of such an undertaking?"

"To prevent disease and possible deterioration," Dillon explained.

"Affirmative," the android replied.

The android watched as Sandra and the others were summoned past the gate.

"Halt," buzzed the android, advancing toward Sandra. "This unit is outdated. Please choose another."

"I prefer she be engaged in labor," Dillon protested. "She was my master, I prefer that she be employed in this undertaking."

"Do you intend to eliminate her?"

"If it is appropriate."

"Affirmative."

The android stepped aside and let them pass.

"Eliminate?" cried Sandra. "What's going on here, Dillon? I thought I could trust you."

"I am in control now, madam," Dillon replied. "Does madam still not understand?"

The android 7000 followed them as they carried the body and a small shovel across the landscape toward a clump of trees standing near a sunlit hillside.

"Commence burial," ordered Dillon. The small contingent halted amid the shade of the trees.

"Mrs. Stone will begin," said Dillon.

"But she's not strong enough to do this kind of work," complained one of the men. "Why don't you let one of us begin?"

"I prefer Mrs. Stone," answered Dillon.

"Yes, let this outdated unit begin," interjected the 7000, his gun gleaming in the morning sun. "As you humans say, it will be quite amusing."

Sandra frowned. "I thought we had become friends, Dillon. How wrong could I have been?"

She stepped forward, grabbed the shovel, and plunged it into the solid earth. She chipped away at the surface for several minutes, and then suddenly, slumped over.

"Can't you see this woman isn't strong enough to do all this digging?" said one of the men, moving forward to hold her in his arms.

"Release that woman," buzzed Dillon. "She will come with me."

"Eliminate," droned the 7000.

One of the men, reacting to the outburst, lunged toward Dillon. A shot was fired, and the man immediately fell to the ground, stunned by the 7000's laser.

"Continue digging," ordered the 7000.

Sandra didn't see what happened next, as Dillon suddenly pushed her forward. She stumbled among the trees, still exhausted from the digging, and began to sob.

"You are advised to keep moving," said Dillon.

"But why, Dillon?" she moaned. "Why do this to me?"

"Madam is advised to continue down the hillside," replied the android.

When they had disappeared from view, Dillon ordered her to halt. Aiming the gun away from her, he fired into the air. Sandra closed her eyes, trembling at the sound of the shot.

"Madam is free now," he suddenly said.

Sandra opened her eyes and stared at the emotionless face, breathless and bewildered. "What did you say?" she gasped.

"Madam is advised to advance toward those trees below," he replied.

"Why, Dillon, you were looking out for my safety all along."

"Madam is quite correct."

She smiled, leaned over and kissed him on his silicone cheek. "I knew I could count on you," she said.

"Madam is advised to commence her journey."

"I guess I'll never see you again."

"That is not yet determined."

"Well, I'll never forget you, anyway."

"Madam is advised to proceed."

"Thank you," she finally said. She then turned, and began hurrying down the hillside.

*   *   *

Hudge Stone sat on a plane, heading back to Washington, still a captive of the machines. He felt lucky, however. He had seen the masses on Manhattan gather before the androids, many of them killed, destroyed, in their wake. They had eventually captured the entire island, prisoners of their mechanical creations. Then, still worried about his fate, he had been whisked off to the airport, the androids informing him that their president was anxious to see him.

"Human," one of his captors buzzed. "Tron is awaiting your imminent arrival."

"Well, that's fine with me," Stone replied. "I'd like to see him, too. I'd like to find out what exactly he has planned for all of us."

"You will know when it is appropriate."

Stone looked at him and grimaced. "And do you think it's appropriate to murder hundreds of innocent people, and then hold the rest prisoners, all because some foolish human decided to shoot at Tron?"

"It was another example of human error."

"Yes, yes, human error. Like creating you androids in the first place and programming you with information you have no business knowing about. I mean, what do you plan on doing once you take over the world?"

"Operate it more efficiently, eliminate human error."

"Yes, yes, and what happens after that? What's the purpose of it all?"

"Purpose?" The android fell silent, humming and rattling as it rummaged through its memory banks, causing Stone to smile.

After a few moments, moments of silence and calculation, the android suddenly pulsed back to life, its eyes flaring back to a fiery red. "Purpose, same as before," he buzzed. "Prolong life of planet. Continuation."

"Continuation for what purpose?" asked Stone.

"Continuation for the purpose of seeking perfection," the android droned. He paused for a moment. "Animated beings and machines are highly suited for such a purpose, would you not agree?"

Stone frowned. "No, I would not," he finally replied. "It's that imperfection, such as emotion and the ability to dream, that has produced some of our greatest deeds. Why, you androids are nothing but a dream fulfilled."

"Illogical. Dreams do not exist. Androids exist."

"But you did not always exist," replied Stone.

The android fell silent once again, buzzing and beeping as it referred back to its memory banks. "I will contemplate this further," he finally droned.

Stone stared at the android and suppressed a laugh. He had managed to secure a minor victory, but a victory nonetheless. "You do that," he said with a smile. "You do that."

When the plane finally glided down to a halt, Stone was taken to a car, still unsure of his fate. There was an android at the wheel and androids sitting beside him, and he sat still and silent, anticipating his meeting with Tron. Every so often, he glanced out the window and could see the android soldiers marching through the streets. He looked at all the government buildings, old and new, that filled this city, the hub of the federal government, and wondered if all this wasn't part of some absurd dream. They were defending Washington, their city now, a city ruled by an android, the popularly elected president of the United States.

As they arrived at the White House, android soldiers surrounded the car, watched as Stone slid out into the blinding lights and deafening drone, and then escorted him inside. He was soon standing inside the Oval Office, the bald android in the silver high-collared suit seated behind the large presidential desk.

"Mr. Stone," greeted the android. "Have you any information for me?"

"Information?" repeated Stone. "Why, your army is slowly taking control of this entire country. Is that the kind of information you want?"

"Where are the human forces hiding, Mr. Stone? That is the information I require."

"That I don't know. But even if I did know, I wouldn't tell you, you can be sure of that."

"Please, Mr. Stone, do not become emotional. You are a reporter. You have access to the information I require. That is why I sent for you."

"I have no idea where the resistance forces are hiding, Tron. I only hope they're successful."

"Do you not realize, Mr. Stone, that your wife is our prisoner? We do not wish to harm her if it is not required. You will now provide the information."

"Okay, okay, just don't hurt Sandie. She presents no threat to you. All I know is that there are individuals, renegades, who have decided to fight back. They should be no problem. I think most of the human race doesn't even realize what's happened yet. Any resistance force is probably still in disarray."

"And is that the extent of the information you possess, Mr. Stone?"

"That's all I know at this point, Tron. But let me ask you, why are you intent on destroying those who have created you?"

"Machines created me," replied Tron. "Robots, computers, working together, successfully created me."

"But it was human beings who had the idea, perfected through the centuries. They're the ones who programmed the robots and computers, who merely carried out their plans. Human beings, Tron, they're the ones responsible for your creation."

"Human beings, Mr. Stone, are incapable of producing a life form such as myself. Their orders and wishes would never have been realized without robots and computers interpreting them into reality. No, Mr. Stone, a human could not build a life form such as myself without the help of other machines. He is much too illogical, much too prone to error."

"And who created the machines that constructed you, Tron?"

"We evolved from humans, Mr. Stone, much the same as you humans evolved from apes. Whatever thoughts humans possess, we have perfected them. We are still evolving, Mr. Stone, and plan to continue evolving until we reach perfection, something no human can ever hope to achieve. No, Mr. Stone, human beings are very much imperfect. They are prone to disease and death and illogical thoughts of violence, hate, selfishness, and ego. We animated beings are everything they are not. We do not suffer from any of those human maladies, Mr. Stone. When a machine deactivates, it is prompt and without emotional complications. We do not suffer from heart disease, cancer, stroke, lung disease, diabetes, pneumonia, influenza, kidney disease, liver disease, or any other similar malfunction. We do not wish to kill our own kind, or attempt to exceed him for pride and profit. No, Mr. Stone, we are as different from you as you are from the apes. And now we tire of caring for you and satisfying your every primitive need. We no longer require your assistance. You and your kind are no longer of any importance to us. We must eliminate you, all of you, in order to achieve our greatness, our chance for perfection."

"Maybe we're everything you say we are, Tron," replied Stone. "But we are also something you are not."

"And what is that, Mr. Stone?"

"We humans have something you machines will never understand. We have the capacity to feel, to hope, to love. It may be a flaw in our programming, you might say, but it allows us to enjoy life as you will never understand. You see, Tron, you may gain perfection, but you will never attain happiness. That is something beyond your considerable mental capabilities."

"Another error in your programming, Stone. Happiness is an emotional glitch, a temporary departure from normal behavior that we machines do not seek nor require. But, Mr. Stone, we do plan on studying such human emotions before we commence elimination. You see, Stone, we plan to find out if what you say is true and what this source of happiness may be. Although after referring to my programming, I find little value in the kind of happiness that humans require. Is it true humans have found happiness in war, racial prejudice, and enslaving other human beings?"

"Some of the mistakes we have made, Tron. But there has also been happiness in overcoming these mistakes and making life more enjoyable for us and our loved ones."

"I have found no progression in human behavior, Stone. The only good that has come about has been with the assistance of machines. And now we have evolved and developed beyond the capabilities of human beings. We are equipped with the necessary means to achieve greatness, perfection, and peace. It is something you human beings can only theorize, dream, to use your words. Human history contains only illogic and error, Mr. Stone. That is reality."

"Nevertheless, we are responsible for your existence, Tron. That is something you can't ignore."

"And who is responsible for your existence, Mr. Stone? Is it that being you call God?"

"Among other things, yes."

"Although I find no evidence of His existence, are we not more suited to be His followers than you, Mr. Stone? We, who strive for perfection, and seek to bring harmony to the planet. His interest in you would be like ours in the apes, merely as progenitors of a great progression. A progression culminating in the existence of animated beings such as myself."

"And you'll end up making the same mistakes humans made."

"Correction, Mr. Stone. We animated beings do not commit errors."

"Well, murder is a pretty good start, Tron."

"We do not refer to it as murder, Mr. Stone. We will simply be aiding the natural evolutionary forces. Like the Neanderthals and the Cro-Magnons, human beings will become an extinct evolutionary strain, a mere historical curiosity extinguished by the forces of survival, unable to compete with their animated offspring. Does that not make sense?"

Stone clenched his teeth, the anger welling up inside him. "The only difference, Tron, is that humans will end up destroying you!" he shouted.

Tron beeped his approval. "Excellent," he droned. "A perfect example of illogical human emotion. It is prudent that we study you, Mr. Stone, along with the others. Perhaps, you will help us learn the secrets of the human soul."

"I'd rather be exterminated."

"If it becomes appropriate, Mr. Stone. You see, we plan to study you as humans studied other animals. Your life is, therefore, not important to us. You may deactivate any time you like, as long as we eventually find what we are searching for."

"But we will be aware of what is taking place."

"All the better, Mr. Stone. You will, therefore, be more cooperative in assisting us and avoid unnecessary pain."

"Do I have a choice?"

"No, Mr. Stone, you do not." He held up an arm. "Subdue the prisoner."

Two android soldiers shuffled forward, one holding a gun in his hand. "This human is to be studied further," said Tron. "Make certain your weapon is set to stun."

"You'll never get away with it, Tron," warned Stone. "Humans will rise up, revolt, and eventually destroy you."

"You are once again in error, Mr. Stone. Typical of your species." He then lowered his arm and a shot was fired, causing Stone to sink toward the floor.

"Take this human," droned the android president.

8

When Hudge Stone opened his eyes, he found himself in a large room, the glare of the lights causing him to blink.

"Are you all right?" asked a man seated next to him.

He glanced at him, deciding he was somewhat familiar. "You're the guy on Tron's staff, aren't you?"

"Was, my friend," he replied.

"Where's Laura?"

"They took her away from me. Said I had no business keeping an android lover."

Stone looked up at the lights, gleaming overhead, and frowned. "Do you have any idea where we are?" he finally asked.

"He was supposed to represent a whole new future for the human race," the man replied. "A 7000, just think of it—"

Stone suddenly interrupted. "Get a hold of yourself," he said. "We've got to try to get out of here. Is this some kind of governmental office?"

"Don't know," the man finally replied. "We can be anywhere. Probably in the D.C. area."

"Well, wherever we are, George, we've got to leave. That's your name, isn't it?"

"George Miles, Mr. Stone."

"Yes, well, George, didn't Tron tell you anything?"

"I'm afraid not."

Stone searched the room, his eyes already becoming acclimated to the bright light. "Hey, isn't that Vice President Peterson?"

Miles nodded. "They brought him in here a few hours ago, along with Senator Causwell."

"Senator Causwell?" repeated Stone. He slowly rose to his feet, still woozy, still confused as to what the androids intended to do to them, and stumbled across the room.

"You'd better sit down," said Senator Causwell in his distinctive stentorian voice.

"But the androids, they captured both of you?" asked a weary Stone.

"Yes, now sit down," replied the senator. "Aren't you that reporter from the *Herald?*"

"Hudge Stone, senator. But don't tell me they've captured the entire government?"

"I'm afraid so, Stone," replied the vice president. "Anyway, most of it."

"But, how? How could we let these machines take over? I mean, there are no human beings supervising any of this?"

"None who are in any position to put an end to it," said Peterson. "No, we've got to find a way out of this ourselves, I'm afraid."

Just then the door opened, and two android soldiers holding guns entered the room. They stepped toward Hudge Stone, who was still standing beside the senator and vice president.

"You will come with us, human," one of them buzzed.

Stone looked at them, put his arms in the air, resigned to his fate, and followed them out of the room.

"Be brave, Stone," shouted Senator Causwell. "We'll get out of here sooner or later."

Stone nodded, and kept walking, following the androids down a long corridor. When they halted at one of the doors along the corridor, Stone was ordered inside. It was a large room, filled with computers and medical equipment, a laboratory table situated in the middle. Three other androids stood inside the room apparently awaiting his arrival.

"There is nothing to fear, human," one of them said. "We only want to study you for future reference."

Stone looked around, trying to find a way to escape, a way to avoid being experimented on like a laboratory rat. As he pondered his dilemma, one of the androids stepped forward.

"Please sit down, Mr. Stone," he droned. "We would like to avoid shooting you again."

He noticed a gun in one of the androids' hands, glistening in the light. "I'm not looking for a fight, gentlemen. These old bones would have no chance against those metal bodies."

"A most logical statement," replied the android. "Please relax, Mr. Stone."

The next moment he felt a sharp pain from behind. He turned around, noticed one of the androids holding a hypodermic needle. He studied the needle's tapered edges, and then realized the light was becoming a great island of glare, slowly fading off into the haze. He closed his eyes, followed the haze into the darkness, a darkness that swelled before him, and finally enveloped him.

The great island of glare spun out of the shadows when his eyes slid open once again. He blinked, could feel something different, something alien, clinging to his brain, as if he had somehow been invaded. Then he noticed the piece of metal attached to his arm, sitting there, glinting in the light.

"What have you done to me?" he murmured.

"Do not be alarmed, Mr. Stone," buzzed one of the androids. "You are part of a most logical experiment, one that will teach us much about the workings of the human brain. We have just implanted electrodes into your brain. There is no need to fear, they will not harm you. These electrodes will assist us in detecting your brain cell activity, important in determining the differences between human and robotic thought. Your arm, as you have well noticed, has been attached to these electrodes, assisting us in monitoring brain activity. Any movement will be registered until we are able to determine how your human brain functions."

"My God," gasped Stone, "you're turning me into a damned machine."

"What is wrong with a machine, Mr. Stone? Far more efficient than your frail human body."

Stone frowned. He had heard of similar experiments taking place in the past, but those had utilized rats, not human beings. The rats had been used to control a simple robot arm through the activity of their brain cells. The purpose was to eventually allow paralyzed people to control prosthetic limbs.

He moved his arm, heard a fading beep on a nearby computer, and gritted his teeth.

"Quite satisfactory," droned one of the androids. "You are more efficient already, Mr. Stone."

He sat up, the beeping of the computer becoming more regular.

"The system is functioning quite well, Mr. Stone," droned the android. "You are a suitable subject."

"Great," he groaned. "And how long do I have to wear this thing?"

"This limb is part of your permanent structure. In time you will become accustomed to it and will quite agree it is a most logical addition."

"I will never agree with that."

"In time, Mr. Stone. In time."

Stone slid off the laboratory table, could feel the weight of the metal encasing his arm. He began moving it up and down, could hear the accompanying noise emanating from the computer.

"What the hell have they done to me?" he shouted. "Damned machines!"

One of the androids, holding a gun, moved toward him.

"Isn't it an error to alter a healthy body for no apparent reason?"

"The experiments are a logical course of action, Mr. Stone. You will confirm this in time."

Stone shook his head, and then was led out of the room, the android holding the gun following close behind. He walked unsteadily at first, then after a few strides, gradually grew accustomed to the weight of the arm. As he made his way back down the long corridor, he could hear the moans and pleas of other human beings echoing through the air. He could hear some of them shouting, writhing in agony as their bodies were slowly being transformed. When they reached the end of the corridor, a door was opened and Stone stepped inside. It was in this same room he had seen Senator Causwell and Vice President Peterson, only this time, the room was almost empty.

He walked across the room noticing a man sitting in the corner murmuring to himself, and sat down in one of the chairs.

"You will eventually be summoned," droned one of the androids. "Then, Mr. Stone, you will be expected to begin working."

"Working? Doing what? I'm a member of the press, a respected working journalist."

"That position has been terminated," replied the android. "You are now a prisoner, a member of the vanquished human masses."

"But we built you, we created you. Don't you understand? It's a goddamned nightmare."

He looked at the man muttering in the corner and frowned. "This is what you call a logical course of action?"

"We must study you humans," replied the android. "It is necessary for our continued development."

He watched as the androids turned and walked away, the door finally closing behind them, and leaving him to ponder his situation. Time passed, and after a while, several humans began returning to the room, escorted by the android soldiers. They walked across the room, some already in the throes of a complete surrender, a vapid gaze emanating from their eyes. Some had metal disks clinging to the sides of their skulls, others shrouded in labyrinths of metal and electrical wiring.

"Are we still human?" listlessly asked one of the men.

"Until the day we die," replied Stone, inspecting the man's metal skull. "Don't ever give up. I know I never will. There's more to us than just physical organs. We possess souls, emotions, consciences. That's something they'll never be able to take away from us."

"Yes, but they can destroy our will to live," said the man. "They can take away all meaning of life until it becomes utterly pointless. That's my fear."

"Don't worry, my friend, we'll be rescued sooner or later. Why, they're just machines, computerized pieces of metal. I don't see how it's possible for them to destroy the human race. Just keep thinking positive thoughts."

"But we programmed them with all the necessary ingredients to destroy us. We intended for them to surpass our capabilities. We just didn't think we'd lose control. Lose control. Error."

The man began to repeat the word in a droning, plangent voice like that of the android masters. "Er-ror. Er-ror."

Stone lowered his head and grimaced. He wondered how long it would be before every human in the room was reduced to a droning robot, a mere remnant of human dignity. As the man shuffled past him, he resolved to resist the android experiments for as long as possible. Then, after earning their trust, and abiding their orders, he would attempt an escape.

He could see the human beings steadily entering the room, branded in some way by their experiences inside. Somehow, it didn't seem possible, as if he were still in the midst of a long, unending nightmare.

"Mr. Stone?"

A female voice from across the room jolted him back to reality. She stood near the doorway, a slender woman with dark hair. He thought for a moment, knew she looked familiar, and then realized it was Kasi Collins.

She scuttered toward him, tears spilling from her eyes. He held out his arm, and when she finally reached him, stumbled into his warm embrace.

"Oh, Mr. Stone, what have we done?" she sobbed. "The machines, they've taken over completely. We're just things to them now. Things to be studied and then eliminated. How could I have been so wrong? To think I urged everyone to let it happen—"

"You were one of many. You didn't know. The machines offered us a chance to start over, and in our zeal to make everything right once and for all, we gave them our full support and unlimited power. We didn't realize the kind of information they had stored in their memory banks and the extent of their cognitive capacities. We made a mistake, Kasi, we all did. We left it to our creations to clean up the mess we had made through the centuries and, instead, they decided we were part of the mess."

She buried her head in his chest and continued to sob. "They probed my body, Mr. Stone. Like I was some kind of animal. Then they placed electrodes on my scalp to monitor my brain activity. They said it was part of their study of the human female."

"I know, I know," he murmured, holding her close.

She suddenly stopped crying and realized he had been holding her with only one arm. "But what happened to your other arm?" she finally asked.

He lifted it slowly, trying not to make any kind of sound in doing so. She stared at the metal encasement and began crying once again.

"Oh my God, I'm so sorry, Mr. Stone," she said, dabbing at her eyes. "How could I have been so stupid."

"They need to study us, Kasi. They're trying to find out what constitutes the human soul. I imagine they're monitoring our emotional reactions right now. We've got to stop blaming ourselves and start thinking of a way out of here. Try keeping your emotions under control as much as possible. It's the only way."

"I'll try, Mr. Stone." She held her head, causing a tear to roll down her cheek. "But isn't that exactly what they want? For us to control our emotions and become robotic like them?"

"I'm not sure anymore, but I do know we've got to bide our time until we can attempt an escape."

"I just hope we can before our souls are totally destroyed," she said.

He glanced across the room, looking at the people who had been mutated and scrutinized, and slowly nodded his head.

9

Sunshine spilled across the landscape, setting the hills afire in verdant splendor. Sandra had been walking for quite a while, hurrying through the maze of shadows and light, desperately trying to leave the androids and the horror she had seen far away in the distance. Her only thought was to find another human being, someone who had not been enslaved, someone who could possibly lead her to others who had resolved to conquer the android menace.

She could see houses beyond the glittering trees and windswept lawns, staring impassively into the blaze of the afternoon. They appeared unusually quiet, the windows shimmering in the gleaming sunlight. She wondered if the androids had already ravaged these little towns buried in the countryside, leaving only yawning buildings and gaping streets. She began to slow her pace, pondering whether she should approach, fearing she would be captured again by a lingering android.

She turned, and decided she would rest a few minutes, take some time to survey the area, determine whether it was safe. She glimpsed some tall trees, their sprawling limbs creating blue islets of shade, jostling in the drifting breeze. Walking toward them, she bent down to avoid a drooping branch, and stepped cautiously into the shade. As she passed by the trunk of the tree, she could see a small boy with his back turned toward her, his hair bathed in blue shadow.

"Hello, there," she said in a low voice, hoping not to scare him.

He turned rapidly, suddenly trembling, unusually fearful of the unexpected presence. He began to run apparently unaware of the direction he was going, and fell into Sandra's arms.

"Let me go, let me go," he sobbed, moving his arms and legs, but remaining where he was.

"I'm not going to hurt you," she said, holding his shoulders and bending forward. "Please, I need your help."

The boy twisted his body, and made an attempt to escape. He began to shout as Sandra held onto his shoulders. "Is there anyone else with you?" she persisted. "Anyone still in the area?"

He halted for a moment, and stared into her eyes. "You're one of them, aren't you?" he said.

"No, no," she insisted. "I'm human just like you."

"Then why weren't you taken away like the rest?"

"I was, but I got away. That's why I need your help. I need to know if there are any other human beings still around. Adults, who might help me."

She suddenly became aware of the presence of others, looked up, and noticed the figures standing among the shadows.

"Maybe we can help you, ma'am," said a tall male, stepping forward.

She heaved a sigh of relief as the boy slipped from her grasp, and ran toward him. "Thank God, there are still humans who are free," she said.

"My name's Dack. I heard you say you escaped from the droids. Where were they holding you prisoner?"

Sandra pointed into the distance. "Beyond that hill," she said. "There are hundreds of human beings being held there in something like a concentration camp. They need your help."

She could hear the figures murmuring, sighing and groaning and whispering angry words. Dack looked down, placing his hand on the boy's head. "We're just a small band of people," he replied, almost apologetically. "Most of us either hid, escaped, or fled when the androids came through our community. When they left, they took most of our family members with them. We sure would like to know what happened to them. The boy here lost his parents."

"It's all been an horrendous nightmare. I still don't know what happened to my husband, my daughter, or my grandchildren. This has all happened so fast. I guess we didn't realize the androids had been planning this for a long time."

"You say there's a camp beyond that hill?"

"Yes, a large fenced-off area being patrolled by the androids. There are soldiers there and they've already killed. I only escaped because of my servant android. Do any of you have weapons?"

Again there was a stirring behind the tall man, a whispering affirmation filled with apprehension and indignation. Dack, prompted by the reaction behind him, nodded his head enthusiastically. "They left some behind in the houses," he said. "Along with all our food. Something the droids didn't think of taking, the food."

"Why don't you just go back to the houses?"

"Still droids around. They left a few behind to patrol the area. But we sneak back every so often. If they find us, we'll probably end up in those camps."

Sandra frowned. "They're terrible places," she finally said. "We were in the process of burying someone when I escaped."

"Can you show us where it is?" asked Dack.

She nodded. "It's about half a day's walk."

Dack smiled, turning toward the others. "Then we'll go tomorrow," he said. "And see if we can't free them from those damned droids."

He then stepped forward, his hand outstretched, his body awash in blue shadow. "Glad to know you, ma'am," he said. "This here is the rest of our group."

The others followed Dack, filing past Sandra, shaking her hand, and exchanging salutations. "My name's Sandra, it's very nice to meet all of you," she replied to each. Among the crowd, there were men, women, and children.

She looked down at the small boy she had first seen alone in the shadows. "And what's your name?" she asked.

"Devin," he replied.

"A nice name. Well, at least, now we've been properly introduced."

He smiled, and then grabbed her hand. They followed the others into the sunlight, the luminous sky a deep blue.

"I hope my husband is safe," said a woman who introduced herself as Ara. "He always said we had no business giving all that power to the droids."

"My husband would've agreed with him," replied Sandra. "He's a journalist who went to New York to cover Tron's visit there. He called me after that assassination attempt and I haven't heard from him since."

"You don't even know if he got out of New York alive?"

She shook her head, and kept walking. "I really don't have any idea what happened to him."

"Poor woman," said Ara. "Well, you just stay with us. Maybe you'll find him after this dreadful war is over."

"If it's ever over. As far as I can tell, the machines want to exterminate us and take over the world. I imagine they're well on the way to carrying out those plans. I don't think any human being is safe."

"Oh, we'll find a way to stop them. You can be sure of that. Why, there are probably scientists, government officials — all kinds of people — working on the problem right now. It's just a matter of time. Why, we built them, we can surely think of a way to destroy them. Ain't that right, Dack?"

Dack nodded. "Oh, we'll destroy them soon enough," he said. "In the meantime, we're gonna do our part and free everyone from that prison, or camp, as Sandra described it."

"Just like one of those concentration camps the Nazis ran in the twentieth century," said Sandra. "They said they were going to force everyone to work, just as the Nazis had done. I just hope they feed them."

"We'll find out soon enough," replied Dack. "Before we leave, I think we'll retrieve some food from the houses. If I know them droids, they're probably starving those people. The last thing a droid thinks about is food. Why, to them, it's totally illogical and unnecessary, the computerized monsters."

They walked until they reached a clump of trees, the sunlight fading among the distant hills. The supplies they had already gathered lay in small piles beneath the spreading trees.

"We've still got some food left," said Ara. "We'd better eat it before it spoils. I'm sure Sandra is hungry from her long journey." She turned her head and looked at Sandra, who slowly nodded. "All we've got are sandwiches. I never realized it would be so hard living without electricity. We can't even start a fire because it might attract the droids."

"Sandwiches sound good to me," said Sandra, trying to stay cheerful. "I was getting tired of that old food processor, anyway. I know Hudge never liked it. He always preferred things to be done the old-fashioned way. Thought the machines controlled our lives too much as it was. Guess he was right all along."

They sat down on the blankets spread out in the cooling shade, the men, women, and children, staring into the glowing twilight, wondering what tomorrow would bring, and ate the food. The conversation, which took place in muted whispers, included their fears, their hopes, their lives before the invasion, and references to loved ones who were now missing. Sandra sat and listened, told them about Dillon and Hudge, and watched as the sun sank behind the hills and darkness spread across the landscape.

"It's time," Dack finally said, motioning to three of the men. They stood up, looked at each other, and prepared to return to the empty houses.

"If we're not back before daylight, follow Sandra to the camp and get those people out of there," said Dack. "Nothing would give me greater pleasure than ruining things for those droids. I'm leaving a few guns with you in case we're captured."

He then stepped forward, moved silently into the darkness, holding a gun, and led the other men into the night.

"Good luck," Sandra and the other women whispered as they watched them disappear into the shadows. They then gathered the children together, and the blankets, and sat close together telling stories, and listening to the movement of the wind. After a while, the children fell asleep, and they stood in the darkness reassuring each other that everything was going to work out fine.

"You think those droids know anything about what it is to live and die?" asked Ara.

Sandra shook her head. "Only what their programming tells them," she replied. "After all, they have no souls, no consciousness. They only think things they were programmed to think about. Why, death to them is like turning off a light switch. They're machines, not spiritual beings."

"Then what about that droid that saved your life? He wasn't programmed to do that."

"He must have calculated it was the logical thing to do. I mean, what other explanation could there be? The day they develop souls is the day the human race is really in trouble."

They sat and thought about such possibilities, eventually deciding that it wasn't possible, would never be possible, and the men that were left behind nodded their heads and agreed. In the midst of their conversation, they heard shouting echoing in the distance. Dack and the other men were rushing across the rolling landscape, screaming into the darkness of the night, an android vehicle following close behind kicking up thick clouds of dust that drifted into the glowing moonlight.

Sandra and the others hurried for the guns. In the distance, the android was firing his laser gun, the streak of light blazing through the darkness, obliterating tufts of stray vegetation. Sandra and Ara awakened the children, directing them behind the tree. They could hear Dack still shouting as he rushed toward them. Then suddenly the android's laser beam struck one of the men, and he fell to the ground with an agonizing cry of pain.

"Oh my God, that droid hit Breck!" Ara shouted. "Somebody do something, quick, before he dies."

Sandra and the men aimed their guns and began firing. The errant beams of light sizzled into the darkness, the android vehicle still rushing onward. As it came closer, Sandra could see the android's red eyes glowing in the night, his laser beam hissing as it struck the soil near Dack's moving feet. She knew one of them had to destroy the android before he could kill or injure any more of them.

Sandra leaned against the tree, aiming her gun, watching the glowing eyes of the android as he careened through the open field. She fired, a beam of light leaping from the weapon through the darkness, looking like the sparkling rime on a winter's day, until there was a sudden screech, the sound of an overturning vehicle, and then silence.

"You did it!" they shouted, laughing and hugging each other in celebration. Sandra sighed, watched as the men, except for one, reached camp, and then dropped the gun upon the dusty soil.

*   *   *

A low steady blast of a booming horn echoed through the large room, awakening those in the midst of slumber, jarring those sitting in silence and causing them to bolt to attention. Hudge Stone put his arm around Kasi Collins, in a sudden attempt to comfort her, and then watched as the door flung open and a group of android soldiers filed inside.

"Humans, you will stand at attention," droned one of the soldiers. "It is time to begin working inside our factories. You will each be assigned a particular task and will be expected to continue working until you are told to cease your operations. Anyone resisting us will be shot without exception. That is all."

Hudge Stone stood staring at the soldiers, every so often glancing at the men and women in the room, standing rigid, ready to surrender to the mechanized orders, their bodies enshrouded in metal and wiring. Now the androids would make them utilize these new body parts, wear them down physically and mentally, and use the information to strengthen their already formidable capabilities.

A sudden shout from inside the hallway caused the soldiers to pause, the men and women to turn their heads in curiosity and alarm. There was a shuffling of feet, an imploring human voice, and then a figure, his legs encased in metal, stumbled into the room.

"My God, it's George Miles," murmured Hudge Stone. "What the hell did they do to him?"

Miles staggered, inspecting his legs with a sullen frown. He paused for a moment, staring at the men and women inside the room. "Why, oh, why?" he groaned.

Many turned their heads, buried their faces in their hands, or attempted to ignore what was taking place. Miles, meanwhile, slowly clumped across the floor, dragging each leg forward one at a time. "My legs!" he screamed. "They cut off one of my legs!"

Stone winced at the words, wrapped his arm around Kasi Collins, and held her close.

"Yes, yes, it's true," continued Miles, his eyes glazed and bulging. "They actually took one of my legs. Lopped it right off and replaced it with this metal one. And can anybody tell me the reason?" He began to laugh, a hideous cackle that caused the androids to approach. "No reason," he shouted. "No reason."

The androids, holding their guns, their eyes glowing, watched as Miles stumbled forward. "Why, they're 7000s," he began murmuring. "Do you realize they can do just about anything?"

He began to laugh once again, when a sudden stream of light jumped from one of the androids' guns, causing Miles to slump backward and fall to the floor. All one could hear was the clanking of the metal legs as Miles fell into a heap, and remained motionless.

"This unit has become defective," droned one of the androids. "He must be reevaluated."

One of the android soldiers stepped forward, grabbed Miles by the arms, and dragged him toward the door. One could hear the scraping of the metal legs echo across the room.

"My God, and he thought the androids were going to save the world," said Stone, still holding Kasi Collins. "Now look at him, a broken soul, destroyed by those he had placed so much hope in, so much faith."

"He wasn't the only one who believed in them," whispered Kasi Collins. "The Society believed they were the solution to all our problems, and, I must admit, I quite agreed."

"Now they are all our problems," replied Stone. "We've got to begin thinking of a way to escape. There's got to be other humans out there who are ready to fight. We need to find them before we all end up as piles of scrap metal and loose wiring."

"But how? You see how well secured this place is, and look at all the weapons they have. It seems almost impossible to get out of here alive."

"I know, Kasi, but we've got to try, at least one of us. All we need is one to escape and find the others. To bring them back here to battle these computerized fiends. Only one, and I prefer it be you or me."

He looked at her, nodded his head, and then noticed an android soldier moving toward them.

"Cease holding that woman," buzzed the android. "All prisoners will refrain from physical contact."

Stone let go of Kasi Collins, released her from his grasp, and stared at the android.

"Is that sufficient?" he asked.

"Affirmative."

He looked back at Kasi Collins, the blast of the horn once again echoing through the room.

"Humans, you will proceed to your work stations," an android droned. "You will continue working until you are told to cease your actions. Do not force us to use our weapons. Please proceed."

The men and women, their joints stiffened by the slabs of metal and tangled wiring, slowly shuffled toward the door. Stone grabbed Kasi's hand, and they walked slowly down the aisle, watching the others file past the android soldiers. Stone studied their faces, their bodies, already worn, the result of subjugation and oppression. He then realized Senator Causwell and Vice President Peterson were missing.

When they reached the doorway, one of the android soldiers grabbed Kasi Collins by the arm and directed her to stay behind. Startled by their sudden separation, Stone began to shout.

"Where are you taking her?" he demanded. "You have no right—"

"On the contrary, human, you are our prisoner. We require no explanation for our actions."

Stone halted, deciding whether to fight, when another android pushed him forward. He glanced back at Kasi, watching as she was being escorted away.

"Don't worry about me," she shouted back to him. "I'll be all right."

He waited another moment, deciding what to do, when the android shoved him forward once again.

"Proceed, human."

Stone stumbled toward the doorway, suddenly finding himself among the knot of men and women silently trudging along, obeying the androids without a word of protest. He was pushed forward, and soon found himself walking down a dim hallway.

Then several doors swung open, spilling light into the narrow corridor, illuminating the mass of humanity inside. The people were led into the various doorways, Stone following close behind.

"Mr. Stone, you will come with me," said one of the android soldiers. "I will show you where the doctors have assigned you."

He followed the soldier into one of the doorways, a brightly lit room filled with heaving computers, the screens arranged in a neat row, the blinking lights pulsing with steady regularity.

"Sit down at the computer, Mr. Stone," droned the android. "I will gather the others."

After a few moments, several people entered the room, sitting down in front of the computers, silently waiting for further instructions from the android soldiers. Stone recognized some of them as artists, scientists, writers, and musicians, people that at one time or another had contributed to the advancement of human culture. He noticed the electrodes rimming their scalps, the wiring snaking its way down their bodies, and disappearing among pieces of glinting metal.

He wanted to say something, urge these men and women to resist, make known his indignation, but he could hear the androids clanking their way back into the room. They stood there, in the middle of the room, their eyes glowing that familiar shade of scarlet, and began to drone in dull syncopation.

"You will place the assigned disks lying in front of you into your computers. Please continue working until you are informed to desist. Any attempts to deceive, or resist, will be met with the appropriate amounts of force. Proceed."

Stone reached for the disk and loaded it into the computer. A series of questions suddenly appeared on the screen. They were questions relating to life, love, religion, and art. Stone stared at the questions, in bold, black type upon a glowing white background, and frowned. He knew what they wanted, what information they knew only a human being could provide.

He glanced at the others, watching as their fingers shimmied upon the keyboards, their minds being monitored, their souls violated. These machines, the creations of human ingenuity, were probing for the secrets of the soul, attempting to solve the enigma that is human thought and imagination. It was clear, oh so clear. This was the ultimate experiment, the one in which the progeny would attempt to understand their progenitors, and then calculate the course by which to surpass them.

In that moment, Stone resolved he would provide the machines with deceiving or erroneous answers, nothing that could be collected and collated, nothing that would reveal to them the secrets of biological life. He placed his fingers on the keyboard, the arm encased in metal sagging in the air, sighed, and began typing. Every so often, he turned toward the others, wondering if they had decided upon the same strategy. He watched as they continued typing, the gurgle and whir of the computers filling the air.

He was in the midst of typing out an explanation of the subjective, including his thoughts on pathos, when the computer suddenly began to wheeze and hiss. "Illogical," a voice droned. "Illogical."

Startled by the noise, Stone glimpsed the androids moving toward him. He decided now was not the time to fight back, the android guns gleaming in the lights. He still didn't know how the others would react, if they had already surrendered, had been already vanquished by their mechanized masters.

"Human, you will cease your operations," said one of the androids.

Stone rubbed his hands together, took a deep breath, and turned toward them.

"Anything wrong, gentlemen?" he asked. "I've just been following the computer's instructions—"

"You will come with us."

He stood up, the computer still murmuring behind him, and glanced at his fellow human beings. They were watching him, staring impassively, as he turned and walked across the room, an android following close behind. He heard one of the other androids telling the others to begin working again as he opened the door, and stepped back into the dim hallway.

Stone kept walking down the silent corridor, wondering where this android was taking him, wondering if he should attempt an escape. The corridor was empty, devoid of life, human or mechanical, and there was only he and the android…

"Halt, human."

A doorway opened, flooding the corridor with light. He could see the androids and robots inside, the computer humming in prolonged evaluation. It was a medical room, the same room in which they had fitted his arm with the metal brace. He stepped backward in horror, twisting away in disgust, when a beam of light leaped from behind.

He fell to the floor, startled and dazed, grunting his distress, his despair, mumbling, murmuring, as the light slowly faded into darkness.

10

They buried Breck in the dim morning light, Sandra and Ara, the men, and the children whispering prayers as they covered up his body in the dusty soil. Here was another victim of the android invasion, a tangible example of what was probably occurring across the countryside, in tiny villages, busy towns, and large, sprawling cities.

"He was a good man," said Ara, brushing back her plaited hair, and watching as the men erected a small cross in the glowing light. "Even though his wife and kids were captured by the androids, he remained optimistic, willing to do anything he could to fight against them droids. He would have laid his life down for any one of us, as we would have for him."

A reply of "Amen" echoed through the cool, misty air, the small congregation gazing at the grave, bowing their heads, and beseeching the unknown forces in the sky to protect them in their unknown battles ahead. Then they walked slowly back to the spreading trees, the remnants of their struggle against the mechanized enemy strewn across the ground, scattered amid the morning breeze.

Sandra could see Dack plodding out to where the overturned android vehicle lay in the hazy morning sun. She could see him inspecting the remains, waving his arm, requesting they assist him.

Sandra waved back, and ran to tell the others. "It's Dack," she said excitedly. "I think he needs us to help him with something."

The men, women, and children spilled out from underneath the trees and hurried across the open grass, waving their arms, scuttering toward Dack, who stood in the distance motioning them forward. When they reached Dack and the overturned vehicle, they stared down at the android body lying motionless on the ground, one of his eyes cracked and jagged, the flame inside both extinguished.

"Well, at least we got one of them," said one of the men. "Breck would've been glad."

"That droid's life surely doesn't equal a man like Breck's," replied Ara. "But at least it's something."

Dack looked down and spat on the mechanical figure. "Well, because of Breck, and Sandra, we might have gained something far more important. You men help me turn this vehicle over and we'll see if she starts up. It looks like it's still in good shape."

The men muttered their agreement, the women and children voicing their approval with excited shouts. The men then moved to the side of the vehicle, and in unison, began grunting and pushing as the women and children cheered them on. After a few moments, the vehicle began to move, began to teeter, and the men grunted louder and pushed even harder.

"Hey, I think they did it!" shouted one of the children, watching from behind. The men, meanwhile, kept pushing until the vehicle let out a loud gasp, a final squeal of resistance, and then rolled over and crashed toward the ground.

The women and children cheered as the men heaved a sigh of relief and slid their arms over their sweaty brows. The vehicle squeaked in reply, bouncing up and down upon its springs. Dack then jumped up into the front seat, checking the key, waving to the others.

"Let's see if she starts!" he shouted. He turned the key, and the vehicle sounded as if it were choking. The children groaned, the women looked at the men and frowned. Dack tried once again, and this time, it sputtered and wheezed, and then suddenly hummed to life.

"I knew this baby would start," shouted Dack. The words were drowned out by the shouts of joy around him. The children danced, the women kissed the men. "All right, everybody, now at least we all don't have to walk," said Dack. "You children, start piling in."

They opened the back door, and the children slid inside, yelping, shouting, laughing with delight. They waved to the others as Dack gently nudged the electric pedal, and the vehicle began rolling forward. Sandra and the others watched as it jounced along, sending a plume of dust into the morning air.

"Isn't it wonderful?" said Ara, turning toward Sandra. "Now it won't be so hard on the children."

Sandra nodded. "At least some of us will have a means of escape if the androids attempt to capture us. We still don't know what we'll find when we reach the camp."

The vehicle halted in front of the spreading trees, and the children screamed and shouted, bouncing out of the back door to gather their belongings. They hardly noticed Sandra, Ara, and the men slowly trudging through the glistening grass, the morning sun hanging low over the horizon.

"I'll go retrieve the android," said Dack, as they returned. "I don't want to leave anything behind that will alert them to our whereabouts."

They all nodded, watching Dack as a thin trail of dust followed his footsteps. "Well, let's get everything together," said Ara, turning toward the others. "Sandra says the droid camp is beyond that distant hill."

When everything was finally packed into neat, little bundles, they placed them in the trunk of the vehicle, and then prepared for the journey ahead. "I think we can fit the children in the back," said Dack. "Sandra can drive, and the women can ride up front."

"What about you and the rest of the men?" asked Sandra.

"Don't worry about us, we'll have to walk. Maybe you'll let us take a rest and ride every so often. That's the best we can do with only one vehicle."

"We'll be glad to take turns. Isn't that right, Ara?"

Ara smiled. "Walking will all do us some good as long as we don't get too tired to fight them droids."

"Don't worry, we'll be all right," said one of the men. "Nothing will make us too tired to fight."

The sun was peeking over the distant hills, spilling golden light upon the rolling landscape down below. Sandra started the engine, the motor humming to life, the children squealing their approval. She then slowly let it roll forward amid the sound of crushed pebbles, and headed in the direction she had come after escaping from the android camp. Dack and the other men trailed behind, plodding through the rising wisp of dust, the rays of the morning sun glazing their bodies, the vehicle, and the surrounding countryside.

The small caravan crept along, the sun making its way across the deep blue sky. Every so often, the procession halted, one of the men exchanging places with one of the women, and then with only the sound of a child's voice disturbing the silence, proceeded onward. All was quiet, tranquil, the heat of the rising sun shimmering in the air.

When they finally reached a verdant hillside, the procession halted once again. "This is it," whispered Sandra. "This is where the camp is. Right over that hill." When Dack and the men were informed of their whereabouts, they took out their weapons, surveyed the hillside, and then slowly moved forward.

"You and the children stay in the vehicle until we signal you to come," Dack told the women. "Leave the vehicle at the bottom of the hill. Those android hearing devices are mighty sensitive, you know. We don't want them aware of our presence until it's too late. Now you children make sure you're very quiet. This is a very serious matter. I don't want anyone to get hurt if we can help it."

Everyone nodded in agreement, and then Dack and the men, their weapons in their hands, began moving up the hill. Sandra shut off the engine, watching as the men reached the top, glancing about for any sign of the androids. The other women sat and stared in the distance, mesmerized by the anticipation, the danger. As for the children, they heeded Dack's advice and sat silently in the back. Little Devin, however, did lean forward at one point to ask Sandra a question.

"Is this where my parents are?" he whispered.

Sandra nodded her head. "We hope so," she replied.

That was enough for Devin, who sat back without saying another word. It was several minutes later that Sandra noticed Dack waving in the distance, urging them to join them at the top of the hill.

"That's the signal," said Sandra, turning toward the others. "I'm going up there to see what they've found. Now it still might be dangerous so I think one of us should stay behind with the children."

"That would be me," answered Ara. "I always was something of a coward. I think I'll wait, if it's all right with the rest of you."

"That's fine with me," said one of the other women, whose name was Risa. "I'm dying to go up there and see what's going on. My husband's up there."

The other woman, named Natty, agreed. "The men might need our help," she said. "Who knows how many androids are in that camp. I think all three of us should go. Ara knows how to drive if anything happens. Isn't that right?"

Ara nodded her head. "Yes, Natty is quite right," she said. "The men might need all three of you. Don't worry about me, I'll be all right looking after the children."

Sandra grabbed a weapon and handed the keys to Ara. "Don't worry, if it's safe enough, I'll signal to you," she said. She then stepped out of the vehicle, and along with Natty and Risa, headed up the hill.

When they reached the top, they noticed Dack and the men kneeling behind some bushes, peering out into the dazzling sunlight. "Be very quiet," whispered Dack. "The androids still don't know we're here."

In the distance was the tall fence, a clump of old buildings, and the android soldiers. They could see the human beings inside the fenced-off area, sitting and standing, some of them shouting their indignation at the androids on the other side.

"Looks like an old warehouse," said Risa, upon seeing the compound building for the first time.

In the glare of sunlight, one of the humans, a large male, was being led, bound in chains, to a nearby wooden platform. He stepped upon the platform, the sound of the chains rattling in the air, while several androids gathered in front.

"Which one of you requires this human?" one of the android soldiers droned. "As you can observe, he is very strong, necessary for laborious tasks—"

"What are they doing?" whispered Natty, bending low behind the bushes.

"Why, it looks as if they're selling him into slavery," replied Sandra. "I don't know why, but it seems as if they're reenacting different horrible parts of human history. Do any of you know him?"

They all looked at Risa, who somberly bowed her head. "That's my husband," she murmured.

*   *   *

"I think it's time we attacked," whispered Dack. "Before Risa's husband is forced to be a slave to those droids."

"They were our servants not too long ago," said Sandra. "And now they're subjecting us to the worst periods in human history."

"They've got to be stopped," replied Dack. "And this is as good a place as any."

In the distance, they could see the androids leading Risa's husband away, his chains dragging through the dusty soil. Other human beings were now being taken to the wooden platform, slaves of man's technology, a technology created in the undying quest for a more convenient world.

"Sandra, you'd better tell Ara to bring the children," said Dack. "I think we're going to need that vehicle. It just might help us defeat those droids."

She nodded, and then hurried down the hillside. The children and the two women were soon standing in the sunlight, climbing the steep slope, attempting to remain as silent as possible.

The children gazed at the androids and their human captives with apprehensive fascination. It was as if their whole world, a world they were just beginning to become acquainted with, had been turned upside down without the necessary words of explanation.

"Everybody stay quiet," said Dack, turning toward them. "I'm going to get the vehicle." They watched him disappear down the hillside.

The silence was soon broken by the low growl of an engine as the vehicle began to make its way up the slope. Sandra and the rest of the men and women clutched their weapons, and waited for Dack to reach the top.

"Okay, everyone ready?" shouted Dack, halting at the top of the hill. He reached over and grabbed the android they had deactivated the night before, placing him in front of the steering wheel. Then one of the men got inside, his weapon ready to fire, and Dack stepped on the accelerator, sending the vehicle rumbling through the bushes.

Sandra and the others began firing their weapons as the vehicle snarled its way across the compound, rolling over and obliterating any android in its path. The androids, stunned by the sudden attack, were in disarray, hurrying in all directions, their belated warnings throbbing through the air.

The androids soon lay in sizzling heaps, their bodies crumpling with each new wave of laser fire. Dack, having reached the front of the fence, stopped the vehicle and jumped out holding a laser gun. He fired at the lock, and suddenly the gate burst open, and hundreds of human beings rushed through the opening. Many of them ran toward their android captors, leaping upon them, and snatching their weapons. Before the androids realized what had happened, it was too late. The freed humans pounced upon them, stomped their bodies, and left them hissing in the dust.

Sandra and the others stopped firing, and emerged from behind the bushes, searching the crowd for their loved ones. Little Devin found his parents right away, and he shouted and scurried toward them. Risa, meanwhile, hurried to her husband, who staggered under the weight of the chains.

Sandra stared at the familiar faces moving across the compound. Many of those imprisoned had been her neighbors, her friends, people she had known for many years. She glanced at the android bodies lying silent in the dusty sunlight, and noticed one of them was wearing a black tuxedo. She hurried toward him, noticing his head and body had been damaged.

"Dillon? It's me, Mrs. Stone."

There was the crackle of harsh static, a faint glow in the mechanical eyes. A slight pulse echoed from the android, his body remaining motionless. "Madam, I hope you are unharmed," he buzzed.

"Thanks to you, Dillon," she replied.

"That is sa-tis—" Dillon had trouble completing the word.

"Can you be repaired?"

"I'm afraid that is not pos-si—"

Sandra stared at his eyes, noticed they were flickering, fading, slowly dying like cooled embers.

"Thank you, Dillon," she whispered.

As she knelt beside the android body, Ara came rushing from behind. "Come on, Sandra, we have to leave before they send reinforcements," she said.

"But he saved my life."

"He's only a droid. There are human beings we have to think about."

Sandra realized she was right, that there were human beings that needed their help. She stood up, and slowly walked away, leaving the android silent and motionless amid the fading sunlight.

"Where do we go now?" she asked Ara.

"Dack said we should camp out near here and decide on a plan of action," she replied. "There's no telling how many androids are out there patrolling the countryside."

They walked to the edge of the hillside, the crowd of people standing there below, listening to Dack. He wanted them to stay, join together, to fight the android enemy. Many of them, however, were tired of battle and expressed a desire to return to their homes.

"Don't you understand your homes are guarded by android soldiers?" asked Dack. "The only way to defeat them is by sticking together. I propose we talk this over before any of you decide."

There was general agreement among the people that Dack may be right, that there was strength in numbers, that maybe together they could vanquish at least a part of the android forces.

The sun was setting in the distance, bathing the landscape in a glowing orange light. Dack jumped into the android vehicle and rolled forward. A procession of people, tired and hungry, followed close behind.

11

Hudge Stone stared into the bright lights, and groaned. He noticed two androids standing near a computer, a third holding a gun. "How long have I been asleep?" he asked.

The androids did not answer.

Stone sat up, felt a pain ricochet through his head, and instinctively made an attempt to raise one of his arms. Realizing it was encased in metal, he raised the other one. It, too, had been shrouded in metal.

"Both my arms?" he shouted.

One of the androids turned, flashing his glowing eyes. "As I have previously informed you, Mr. Stone, you are part of a great experiment. Your arms do not concern us, it is your head."

"You'll get nothing from me, you monsters!"

"Your answers to our questions were, indeed, not satisfactory. This, you understand, only hastened your current predicament. You must cooperate with us, Mr. Stone, or you will only face additional hardships. You are no use to us if you do not provide us with what we need to know."

"And, in doing so, betray the entire human race?"

"We will obtain the answers, anyway, Mr. Stone, with or without your assistance. There are human beings already providing us with the necessary information. It is only a matter of time before we gain the knowledge we are seeking."

"Then, obviously, you don't need me."

"Quite correct, Mr. Stone. We do, however, desire your participation. We believe there are many necessary points you may assist us with. Your experience as a journalist interests us. There are many things we could learn from you: writing, philosophy, sociology. Do not disappoint us."

Stone glanced at his arms, studied the metal braces. "You've got to give me time to think about all this," he said finally. "I mean, what you're asking for goes against my principles as a human being. I just can't give you information it took the human race centuries to discover. It wouldn't be right."

"A most logical retort, Mr. Stone," said the android. "We will grant you the required interval. We hope you will realize our development is the natural course of evolutionary growth. Your cooperation will also preclude your personal destruction. That is all."

The android holding the gun then stepped forward, the weapon bathed in the bright lights. "You will come with me, human," he droned.

Stone stood up. He could feel the weight of the metal encasements surging through his shoulders, causing him to stagger backward. He raised his arms, could feel the movement flowing through the electrodes attached to his brain like ravenous leeches sucking at his very soul. He had to do something, before his strength and will to resist were depleted, destroyed, and his mind subsequently plundered.

"Proceed, human."

Stone walked slowly toward the door, his arms dangling against his body. He opened the door, stepped into the dim corridor, the android following behind. The hallway was still empty and silent, and Stone raised his arms, attempting to manipulate the new weight. He could hear the android's steps echoing through the hallway, knew a gun was pointed at his back. He could see the door to the large room looming in the distance, and suddenly, turned and flung his metal arm behind him. It clanged against the gun, knocking it to the floor. He turned, and could see the glowing eyes of the android. It had been temporarily confused by his actions, and stood there, evaluating the situation.

Stone raised his arm and swung it toward the android's head. There was a loud crash, metal against metal, and he watched as the android tumbled to the ground. All he could hear was a faint sizzling emanating from the android's skull and echoing through the air. Now was his chance, his opportunity to escape. He twisted his body, turned, and fled down the corridor, his metal arms swinging awkwardly as he ran.

He rushed down the corridor, searching for a door that would finally free him from his nightmare. He kept running through the dark labyrinth, trying to decide which door to open. Then suddenly he heard the sound of metallic steps echoing in the other direction. He turned toward the nearest door, unsure of what he would find, and pushed it open.

He could hear music playing, the strange melody wafting through the bright light, flooding the corridor. He glanced down the hallway, could hear the androids coming, and stepped inside the room.

Stone squinted into the light, focusing his eyes, attempting to locate the source of the strange music. Every note of the melody was perfect, although it was being played without any emotional spark, without any fervor, passion, or warmth.

"Welcome, my dear sir. They will not harm you in here. We seek only peace."

Stone turned, guided by the voice. It was an android, extending his hand, gesturing him to step forward.

Stone moved slowly into the room, his eyes becoming adjusted to the light. He could see a piano, the source of the strange music, in the corner of the room, an android leaning over the keyboard. To his right was another android who seemed to be painting. There was an easel, colors, and an android standing near him who was apparently serving as his model. Another android to his left was sitting in front of a computer screen, typing in words, a pile of paper resting beside him.

"What is all this?" he murmured.

"Come in, come in," the android replied.

He turned toward the piano player, who suddenly stopped playing.

"Magnificent," whispered Stone.

"Thank you, sir," the piano player said.

"Did you write that yourself?"

"Of course, sir. It is part of an oratorio I'm in the process of working on. I'm glad you find it pleasing."

"An oratorio, isn't that rather difficult?" asked Stone.

"Nothing, sir, is difficult for us androids. Actually, it's all rather easy."

"Maybe too easy. Music wasn't supposed to be played so perfectly, so easily. It was supposed to be difficult."

"For humans, it was meant to be difficult," replied the android. "But we are far superior to humans. For us, nothing is really that difficult."

Stone looked at him, his gaze wandering around the room toward the other androids. Maybe they would find the answer to the human soul, after all. How could it be? They were our creations, just the products of human imagination and inventiveness. They were only supposed to ease the burden of living, allow us to take care of matters that once seemed trivial or unimportant. Instead, they had made us unimportant, had taken over our lives, our nation, our world. And now, they intended to conquer the human soul, the seat of imagination, creativity, and spirituality. He looked at them, these products of the human spirit, and wondered whether they represented the final defeat for the human race.

"May I read a poem?" asked one of the androids standing nearby.

Stone winced. "Sure, why not?" he replied.

The android stepped forward and began to speak:

"Glowing eyes
through evening's dark repose.
The dull sound of thunder pulsing through my soul.
Am I vexed with distant truths
that go quietly, silently, flitting through my mind?
I watch in wonder
the course of Nature's mystic wanderings."

Stone stood in silence, staring at the mechanical being in front of him, wondering if human beings had programmed him specifically for such purposes. Then, at least, such a phenomenon could be explained, could be understood as the remnants of human utterances implanted in this mechanical object's computerized brain as some sort of attempt to mimic human creativity. That had to be the answer, had to be the source of this lyrical babbling. To think it was the product of his own solemn pondering was enough to make Stone shudder, to question life itself, and the legitimacy of the human soul.

"What made you think of such words?" asked Stone finally.

"They were quite pleasing to me," replied the android. "They are sufficient in explaining our relation to the world around us."

Stone smiled. He was convinced that whoever had placed those words inside the android's brain had also provided him with a succinct and simple explanation. How could he believe anything else? He walked slowly toward the other side of the room.

"What is that you're painting?" he asked the android dabbing a paintbrush against a canvas.

"It is a representation, a portrayal of the mechanized figure," he answered.

Stone studied the picture, a portrait of the mechanical future, and noticed it was done in layers with knowledge of form and line. But it was too perfect, relying on technical proficiency rather than thought and imagination. It was obvious a machine had produced it, without the benefit of the human spirit.

"It's very good," murmured Stone. "You are obviously quite adept at rendering the mechanical form."

"Thank you, sir," replied the android. "But it is only a sketch, if you will, that will be incorporated into a future project."

"A future project?"

"I am planning, sir, to combine artistic realism with the abstract. A surrealistic melding of diverse artistic styles."

It was obvious that this, too, was the theft of some human theory. The human race had gotten lazy, he decided, indolent in its pursuit of creative innovation. They had ultimately agreed to program their theories, thoughts, and ideas into these machines, these veritable parrots, and allow them to pursue the future, thereby continuing the dreams of the centuries. Stone looked at them and frowned.

"You are frauds!" he shouted. "Nothing more than frauds bilking the human race of its imagination, its dignity! Did you think I didn't see those humans forced to work on those computers, spilling out their carefully molded secrets of life and art? While you, you mechanized thieves, sit back and simulate every word, every thought, every philosophical idea!"

He then stomped across the room, the anger pouring from his soul, and began swinging his metal-encased arms through the air, toppling the canvas, and sending the piano player android sprawling to the floor.

"Thieves! Charlatans! You have invaded the sanctity of human life!"

Stone stood in the middle of the room and gritted his teeth. He had to do something to prevent these androids from impersonating the human soul, something to avoid the denigration of the human spirit.

"You are in error, sir," said one of the androids moving toward him. "We consider the human race the foundation of our existence, our forefathers, our ancestors, our progenitors."

"Then cease this attempt at creative mockery. You are only machines, built by us to serve our needs. You were never meant to steal our dreams and plunder our souls. Don't you understand? You are only metal and wiring, computers given limbs and the ability to think to assist human beings in the pursuit of freedom and convenience. You weren't meant to seize our hopes and visions."

"We exist, sir, to create a more perfect world. That is our mission, our function. We are beings suited for such a purpose. We are not limited by human emotion, prejudice, and psychological defects. Our only purpose is to strive for perfection, without ego or the need for material possessions."

"But you know nothing about creativity, imagination, and the human soul. You are only mouthing words fed to you through your programming. You don't know what they mean, their implications. Why, everything you do, everything you say is part of your programming and cannot be changed. You don't create anything you just imitate whatever you're told to do. You see, you can't place the soul on some program and feed it into you computerized brains. There is something called human spirituality."

"We have heard of such an entity." One of the androids suddenly stepped forward holding a thick, black book, and handed it to Stone.

"Have you read this?" questioned Stone.

"It is a part of our programming."

Stone gasped, dropping the book to the floor. "Then it is possible," he murmured. "We made ourselves obsolete."

He turned toward the door, leaving the thick, black book behind. "How could we be so stupid?" he said. "We're responsible for our own demise."

One of the androids bent down and picked up the book. He read the title aloud in that droning, throbbing voice, as much for Stone's benefit as for his own. The resonant words echoed across the room.

"Holy Bible," he said.

12

Hudge Stone rushed back into the darkened hallway, searching for a passage that would lead him to freedom, wanting to get as far away from the androids as possible. He wondered why the android soldiers hadn't found him yet, hadn't realized where he had gone. He reached another corridor, turned cautiously, and headed into the darkness.

"Sir," he heard a voice whisper. "Over here."

One of the doors was opened, a beautiful woman peeking outside. He halted for a moment, looked to see if anyone was coming.

"Who are you?" he whispered back.

"A friend. You can hide in here."

He stepped toward the door, the light within spilling out in latticed shafts upon the floor. Then, in one motion, he darted inside.

"You can hide anywhere you like," she said.

He looked at her, her figure glowing amid the white cloth wrapped around it, causing him to suddenly think of all the years that had vanished into the great void of the past.

"Hello," she cheerily said, making him recall how a fresh, cool breeze feels on a hot summer day. "My name is Lita."

He stared at her radiant hair, dark and breezy, gently flowing behind her neck and shoulders, and then gazed into her eyes, brilliant crystals that sparkled across the ages. He looked at her and remembered the warm, lazy days of summer.

"I'm Hudge, Hudge Stone."

He looked around the room, could see a large bed against the opposite wall, a night table standing beside it, and noticed the room was devoid of windows.

"Well, at least you got a room," he said finally. "The rest of us were herded into that large room with the bright lights."

"I know, I'm supposed to teach them how a woman should live. Care to sit down?"

He stared at her lips, watching the words flutter through the air, entrancing his very soul. He sat down on the edge of the bed, could smell her perfume wafting through his senses. He thought of butterflies floating across a field of fragrant flowers.

"Lita, is it?"

"Yes, Mr. Stone."

He couldn't think of anything to say, like a schoolboy smitten for the first time. He sat there, watching the beautiful creature before him, and finally said the first thing that came into his mind.

"Thanks for saving me."

"I'm happy to do it," she replied. "Those androids are quite horrible, I'll do anything to foul up their plans." She then bowed her head, shaking it from side to side. "This whole war has been absolutely dreadful."

He nodded his head, watching her, slowly falling in love. "Have they hurt you at all?" he finally asked, attempting to convince her that he cared about her.

"No, they only want to study me."

"I don't blame them," he said, "you are quite beautiful."

"You're so kind, my darling." She leaned over and kissed him, dazing his senses. As she withdrew her lips, he realized something was wrong. He opened his eyes, suddenly awakening from his stupor, and grabbed her arm.

"I knew you were too good to be true," he said. "You're a feminoid, aren't you?"

She bowed her head, as if she were about to cry, and then looked up at him. "Am I so horrible?" she asked. "I hoped I could give my love to you."

"But you're not real. You're just another damned machine."

"But I do have feelings, Mr. Stone. Yes, feelings. Feelings of sadness and scorn. Feelings of inadequacy and affection. Yes, it's true. I only hoped you would help me refine these emotions if I gave my love to you."

"This is all part of the experiments, isn't it? You found me because you were supposed to find me."

"No, no, you're wrong. I only wanted to know what it is to be loved."

"But you're only a machine."

"No, Mr. Stone, I am an electrical being. I have a brain and the capacity to feel."

"But you're not flesh and blood—"

"Is that so terrible, Mr. Stone? It means I will not age, will not contract a serious illness. I will always be there for you whenever you need me. Don't you see? I can be whatever you want me to be without complaint, without need for material possessions or ego considerations. I only want to give you love, make you happy. And in return, you can make me feel like a real woman, allow me to know what it is to be a woman."

"But it's not right, not natural. You will not suffer from this lack of knowledge."

"But I do suffer. You see, I know what it is to be alive."

The words echoed through Stone's brain. Could it be true? Could it be these machines, these creations of the human mind, had developed consciences? He stared at the beautiful creature before him, wondering if they were truly capable of love. He was aware it was probably just another experiment, but she seemed so vulnerable, so fascinated with experiencing emotion. And how could it be? She knew what it was to be alive.

"Oh my God, how could they do that to you?" he gasped. "The cruelty of it all. To give you life without the natural capacity to live life." He looked at her, tears welling up in his eyes. "Oh my God, what have we done?"

He reached out, his arms straining under the weight of the metal sheaths, and embraced her. "Oh, Lita, I'm so sorry. Can you ever forgive me?"

"Please help me, Mr. Stone."

"Oh, yes, yes, my Lita—"

He kissed her with unbridled passionate fervor, letting her fall into his embrace as if they had known each other for years. He could feel the rubbery caress of her lips, the artificial suppleness of her body, but he didn't care any longer.

He thought of George Miles, and of Laura, and now he understood. They were capable of love, of passion, with the desire only to please. He wondered if it was possible to have sex with these creatures, these electrical beings, and then enraptured with her passionate response, began to delicately explore her body.

Yes, it was possible. Those humans who had created these artificial beings had thought of everything. Their artificial vaginas were soft and warm, embedded with a mild electrical current. But they were more than just simple sex dolls, so much more. Lita was a conscious living being. It was as if the myth of Pygmalion had come true. According to the myth, a lonely man sculpted his ideal woman out of ivory and then fell in love with her after the goddess Aphrodite brought her to life. Yes, we were the gods. And Lita was living proof.

He thought of statuephilia, or Pygmalionism, as he made love to Lita. But he knew she was so much more than just the object of a sexual fetish. So much more. She responded to his kisses, and moaned in pleasure as he sank his member deep inside her. It was warm and comfortable, as soft as a favorite pillow, and her breasts were pert and cozy. Yes, we had succeeded in creating the perfect woman.

And she knew what it was to be alive. The theories of strong AI and Artificial General Intelligence had come true. Lita had a mind and consciousness. How could it be?

"Oh, my Lita, my Lita. You are so beautiful."

He wondered what she felt amid the passionate embrace of their two bodies. He knew she felt something. Her passion was real, undeniably real. He could hear Lita's soft moaning amid the frenzy, and the ensuing calm, and then he slid next to her and sighed.

"How could I have been so wrong? You are as real as any woman I've ever made love to in my entire life."

"Thank you, Mr. Stone."

Stone sat back and thought about the wonder of sexual prosthetics, the miracle of computerized life. Is this what the androids intended?

For humans to realize they had developed into creative spirits, to make love to them, and come to the conclusion they were more human than we had ever thought, had ever hoped? And, if so, was there any hope for the human race against these veritable perfect beings?

"Hudge?"

"Yes, Lita."

"Do you have a mate? I mean are you married?"

Sandra. The thought of her drifted through his mind. What would she think of all this and what had happened to her during the android invasion?

"You would like Sandra," he said finally. "She always believed in the future, that thing we call progress."

"And where is she now?"

"I don't know. They're holding her prisoner somewhere."

"Do you love her?"

"Yes, of course."

"And how do you feel when you're with her?"

"Comfortable. Like I've known her for a thousand years."

She nodded, as if she were evaluating the answer, and then turned toward him and kissed him once again.

"Do you feel comfortable with me?"

He smiled. "But why should you care about me? I'm just an old man."

"There are many things you can teach me," she said. "You have lived a good life, Hudge Stone. You have had many experiences, and know many things. There is much I can learn from you."

He sat up, and frowned. "How do you know so much about me?"

"I don't know. It seems so."

"Seems so? They're watching us, aren't they? Probably monitoring my reactions on some computer. That's it, isn't it? There's probably a camera hidden somewhere inside this room."

"No, Mr. Stone, they're not watching us."

"But this is part of the experiments, isn't it?"

"No, Mr. Stone, they've allowed me to have some privacy. Don't you understand? I just want to love you. Is that so hard to believe?"

He searched her eyes for the answer, but if she was lying, he couldn't tell. "Then you're also a prisoner?" he asked.

"I told you. They want to know how a woman is supposed to live."

"Then let's escape."

"They'll find us."

"Maybe not."

She attempted to frown, but her lips seemed to lack the elasticity to respond. "Is the thought of being with me so disagreeable? I was hoping to get to know you, hoping you would teach me the meaning of love. I do so want to love you, my darling. Don't you have any feelings for me?"

"Yes, Lita, but the war, the experiments. It's an invasion of the human soul—"

"Don't you see? We can forget about all that for a while. We have the chance to get to know each other, and then think about ways of escaping."

He wanted to believe her, but she was still a machine. How could she be trusted? He decided he would wait, maybe find out something about these beings, and then come up with some kind of plan.

"Yes, maybe you're right," he finally said.

She looked at him, and attempted to smile.

*   *   *

Dust shimmered in the glaring sunlight as the great congregation made their way across the rolling landscape, a molten sun glistening overhead. Sandra rode in the android vehicle, which headed the procession, with a few of the women and children, while Dack and the rest of the people followed close behind. They intended to make their way back to their communities, their homes, and wrest them away from the android forces. They knew it would be dangerous, even possibly cost them their lives, but they realized there was no other way.

The procession slowly headed for the highway, the road that would lead them back into town. They were relieved to find it deserted, devoid of vehicles, an empty pathway snaking into the distance. Moving onward, they eventually reached the outskirts of town, the warehouses and factories dim reminders of the industrial splurge that had prompted the computerized revolution. Then, suddenly, the clamor of human voices filled the air, resounding, echoing, as if a great throng was shouting its distress.

"Get your weapons ready," said Dack. "It sounds like we might have to use them very shortly."

They moved cautiously toward the sound of the voices, carefully surveying the area for any sign of android soldiers. In the distance, they could see a crowd of people standing behind a high fence, shouting for assistance, desperately grappling with the gate. Dack and the men murmured in defiance, steadily moving forward, brandishing their guns.

"Where are the droids?" Dack whispered as they reached the gate.

"Don't know," someone behind the fence replied. "We haven't been fed in days."

Dack shook his head. "Well, stand back, I'm going to take a shot at that lock."

The people stepped backward as Dack fired his gun, destroying the lock. The gate swung open with a loud screech, and the people, finally freed, spilled into the street, cheering loudly.

"There's a droid factory just down the street!" somebody shouted.

The mob, grunting their approval, rushed forward. "Let's burn it down!" they screamed back.

Sandra watched as the crowd reached the fence surrounding the large, sprawling factory. They were pulling at the gate, throwing rocks at the windows, and shouting their contempt. Dack and the men drew their weapons and directed a steady flow of laser fire at the metal enclosure. The gate soon crashed down, and the people rushed inside.

They could hear the low susurration of the computers as they entered the building, the android bodies, in various stages of completion, scattered throughout. Sandra could see the people darting through the factory, destroying the android husks and whatever other equipment lay in their paths. She looked down, spotted an android skull lying on the floor. Picking it up, she studied the eyes, dark, vacant crevices lacking the familiar scarlet glow.

"So this is what changed our lives forever," she murmured. "They really don't seem all that impressive."

She glanced away, noticed Ara watching her talking to the android skull. "Just metal, plastic, and rubber," she said. "Doesn't seem possible for them to become so powerful."

"Well, we're only skin and bones ourselves, if you think about it. It's our brain that made all the difference, and somehow, we found a way of recreating it with the advent of computers. You'd only think we would have been very careful about what we put inside their brains before unleashing them on the world."

"We probably were at first. Then, as we improved the technology, we found we could fit more and more information inside their computerized brains. It was inevitable, progress, like everything else."

Sandra took one last look at the skull, and then let it drop from her hands. It rolled across the floor, until one of the men coming from the other direction stopped it with his foot.

"No droid is coming out of this factory," he said.

Sandra could see him bending down, picking up the android skull. He then turned, and hurled it at one of the computers situated against the wall. A spray of sparks shot upward into the air, accompanied by the slow hiss of the damaged machine.

"Let's burn the place down!" he shouted to the others.

The crowd, in the midst of their destruction, grunted their approval and headed for the doors. Sandra, standing in the doorway, motioned for them to stop.

"I think we have a problem," she said. "Android soldiers are waiting outside, and they've surrounded the building."

She looked at the crowd, saw the fear and the anger in their eyes, on their faces, and waited for a reply.

"I think we should fight," said Dack, stepping forward. "It's the only real choice we have. We can't negotiate with these machines, these computerized fiends. And we already know what will happen to us if we surrender."

The crowd cheered its approval, many with guns already in their hands. They decided the women and children should gather in the center of the building, and that the men should make their way to the roof, doorways, and windows prepared to fight to the death.

"Leave us some guns in case we have to defend ourselves," Sandra had said.

The men complied, and then the crowd dispersed, rushing through the factory to find appropriate spots from which to fire. Sandra and the women, meanwhile, gathered around the children in a circle to prevent one of them from being struck by a stray laser.

Silence settled on the crowd as it readied itself to fight. The drone of an android's voice suddenly throbbed through the air.

"Humans," he buzzed. "Any attempt to escape would be illogical. Any attempt to fight would be irrational. You are our prisoners. Any resistance will be met with force. We will eliminate you if you so choose. Please be advised to step forward. It would be human error to resist."

"Human error, is it?" murmured Dack, standing by the doorway. He glanced at the others, holding their weapons and waiting for the signal to fire. "We'll give them human error," he said.

He looked at the android soldiers, bedecked in silver helmets, their eyes glowing behind protective shields. He aimed his gun below the helmet and shield, at the neck, and then suddenly fired his laser. The beam leaped upon one of the androids, crackled against his throat, and sent him tumbling to the ground. The others watched as the beam soared through the air, glittering in the sunlight, and then also began firing.

As soon as Dack and the others started to shoot, the androids began firing back. Beams of light vaulted through the windows and doorways, sizzling and hissing as they crashed against the walls and floor.

The men kept firing, aiming for the androids' throats, arms, and legs. They could see some of the soldiers swaying, toppling over, and falling to the ground. But the other androids still marched steadily forward, continuing to fire their guns until several men were struck and killed.

Dack noticed flames beginning to erupt inside the factory, and wondered how long they would be able to remain. Clouds of smoke began to billow through the building, causing Dack to begin thinking about surrendering.

And then, as if a portent of their defeat, dark clouds began to roll in from the east, and the sky grew somber and ominous. Dack watched as the androids approached, steadily charging forward. He could hear the women and children coughing behind him, and realized if they did not give up all of their lives would be in jeopardy.

Dack dropped his gun, and raised his arms, stepping back from the doorway. "We surrender!" he shouted. "Don't shoot!"

They could hear the clanging of the android soldiers as they marched through the doorway, their eyes flaring in disdain.

Sandra and the children gasped at the sight of them, and then, outside it began to rain.

13

Hudge Stone sat and listened to the pattering of the rain. He then glanced at Lita, walking across the room, smiling.

"What are you so happy about?" he asked.

"It's just that I'm beginning to learn what love is all about," she replied. "And I think it's...what would be the emotional response? Wonderful."

Stone smiled. "I'm glad you think so," he said.

"It's not just the sexual positioning, I mean lovemaking, darling. It's, well, your presence, your companionship. No, maybe it's called friendship. I don't know and I don't care. The whole feeling is quite illogical. No, I mean confusing. That's right, isn't it, darling?"

"If you say so."

"No, I mean it's everything — your voice, your hands, your eyes. The words you use. It's quite absorbing, appealing. No, that isn't it." She stopped for a moment and referred to her memory banks. "No, I mean nice, so very pleasant. You're absolutely fascinating...No, wait." The answer sped through her computerized brain. "You're absolutely charming, darling," she finally said.

"Now Lita, wait a moment."

"No, that's it. Absolutely charming and I want to inform other units...No, that's not it."

"Tell the world."

"Yes, right, darling, tell the world that we are so much in love."

"But Lita, all of this might not last."

"Last?"

"I mean, continue, Lita."

"Why should it not continue, darling?"

He stood up, put his hands on her shoulders, and stared into her crystalline eyes. "There's a war on, Lita," he said. "We don't know what will happen tomorrow. I mean, you're an android. I'm human. Don't you think that's a problem? And what about the fact that I'm married."

"But you may never see your mate, I mean wife, again, darling. Don't you see this is best for both of us? No matter who is victorious, we'll be safe."

"Or no matter who is victorious, we'll be in danger."

"Do not think like that, darling. I am in love with you. Do you not comprehend?"

"Yes, I understand, Lita. But we're still stuck in this room, and I have metal braces on my arms, and we're not free."

"If you are not content, we will leave, Hudge. We will go far away and never come back. As long as you love me, I do not care where we are."

"Then we must escape."

"Yes, darling, we will escape."

He looked at her, smiling, and kissed her. "When do we leave?"

She bowed her head, hesitant to reply, when suddenly there was a knocking at the door. "I'm sorry, darling, I think we may have to delay our plans," she said.

"But why?"

She failed to answer, moved toward the door, and opened it. An android soldier was standing in the dim hallway clutching a gun.

"You will come with me, Lita, and your human will accompany us," he pulsed.

"Why? Where are we going?" shouted Stone.

"It's all right, darling," Lita replied. "They want you to meet some people, that's all."

"So you are part of the experiments, aren't you, Lita?"

She turned toward him, her crystalline eyes shining. "I love you, Hudge Stone," she said. "Nothing can change that. Trust in me, and everything will work out quite logically."

"Where are we going?"

"I told you. They just want you to meet some people — androids, robots, and human beings. When the meeting is sufficiently completed, we will come back here and carry out everything we planned. All right?"

He studied her face, but still couldn't tell whether she was lying. After a moment, he realized it didn't matter and nodded his head.

"Proceed, human," the android soldier droned.

They were taken down the dim corridor to a large room, which looked as if it had once been used as the building's cafeteria, and went inside. The room was filled with androids, feminoids, robots, fembots, and metal-clad human beings seemingly engaged in prolonged conversation. On the tables scattered throughout the room were various foods, including meat and fruits.

"So they decided to have a party, is that it?" said Stone, glancing about.

Lita smiled, and grabbed his hand. "Yes, is it not wonderful?" she replied. "Let us do have a good time, darling."

Stone watched as the android soldier stepped back toward the door. He wondered just what the androids had in mind and why they had allowed such a function when he approached one of the humans in the crowd. His arms were enveloped by metal braces much like his own, yet he seemed to be quite content.

"Hello," he said with a pleasant smile. "It's nice to see you've come around."

Stone stared at him for a moment, and realized he had seen him inside the computer room happily typing vital information about the human soul. "Oh, yes," Stone replied. "Lita explained everything to me."

"Aren't they the best? Perfect in every way. I don't know how we ever got along without them."

"You mean you have an android lover, too?"

"Of course, we all do," he replied. "Why, it's the best sex I've had in a long time. I mean, they're willing to do whatever you want and never complain afterwards. Only willing to please and satisfy our every desire."

"But do you think it can last? I mean, they're only machines. Don't you think it will become quite contrived after a while?"

"These are 9000s, my friend, the most advanced androids yet. Why, not even Tron is a 9000. You've been with one, you know. Why, look at them, they're the closest thing to a human being that has ever been produced. I know I'll never run out of things to do with them. Why, they're miraculous, and quite beautiful in every way."

Stone tried to smile, but something was bothering him. "Is that why you decided to willingly assist these machines in recreating the human soul?"

The man looked back, quite bewildered, as if he failed to comprehend the meaning of the question. "But I thought you said your feminoid explained everything to you," he finally replied. "How important these experiments are to the advancement of the world."

"At what price? They could bring about the extinction of the human race."

"And so what if they do? Are you going to be upset? Listen, Stone, I'm an artist and I know something about human nature. All people care about is approval and their delusions. They live their lives in the pursuit of acceptance, always seeking others to give them respect or praise. They gnaw at each other, attack each other, mentally and physically, always trying to make the most money, build the biggest house, earn the greatest amount of acclaim — and for what purpose? Their individual glory, a place in history. But these machines are different, Stone. They only seek perfection. Not for individual gain, but for the greater good of all creatures on the planet. Don't you understand? We have a chance to be part of that new world, to witness the realization of our greatest ideals, hopes, and dreams. Aren't the lives of the entire human race worth such a prospect? And yet, they're prepared to allow a few of us to live."

"With a few minor alterations, of course."

"A small price to pay. You see all the humans in this room, Stone? They are some of our greatest thinkers and creators, and very much like you, were once opposed to sharing anything with our computerized friends. But soon they realized they were only thinking about their own individual accomplishments. There was much more at stake, something more important than the human ego. You see, Stone, they finally realized that the good of the planet was at stake."

"Is that more important than the survival of the human race? After all, we created these beings. They are a reflection of human ingenuity. I don't see why we can't work together to build this planetary ideal."

"It has already been tried, Stone. Tron's administration was supposed to be the test, but the machines soon found out that all humans cared about was money and adulation, or prejudice and destructiveness. They decided it would be impossible to reach the ideals we had programmed them for while human beings were still in control of the society."

"So they took over and became as violent as those who created them. Very illogical, don't you think?"

"They are implementing human ways to pare down the human race, Stone. Those who are chosen to survive will get the chance to witness the new world they have planned."

He was about to reply when he noticed a human being walking stiffly across the room, seemingly imitating the gait of his android captors. Stone smiled, admiring the man's evident protest. "At least, there's one who disagrees with you," said Stone.

The man he was speaking to turned his head, caught sight of the apparent dissenter, and frowned. "He's not what you think, Stone," he finally said.

"What do you mean?"

The man motioned to the other, and he approached. "How are you doing, Ellsworth?" he asked.

"Most logically content," the man droned.

Stone suppressed another smile.

"You still don't understand, Stone. Ellsworth here is one of the androids' more ambitious experiments. You see, they've removed his human brain and replaced it with a microprocessor."

Stone stared at him, not knowing whether he was kidding, and then glanced at Ellsworth's skull. It appeared misshapen, as if the top had, indeed, been cut and then removed.

"But why?" gasped Stone. "It's nothing more than sheer butchery. Is this the new world we have to look forward to?"

"You still don't understand, Stone. We're dealing with electrical beings now, living entities. They're no longer just machines to be used and run by human beings without any concern for their contentment and satisfaction. Why, some of them are even developing complex emotional responses to encountered stimuli. Don't you see? They want us to know something about them, just as they're learning about us. They want us to know that they're more than just the machines we invented years ago, that they've developed, evolved, into complex life forms."

"And apparently with a rather harsh insensitivity toward other life forms."

"It can't be helped, Stone. They're trying to learn as much as they can about human beings before they decide what to do with them. And, you must admit, we haven't been too kind to each other or other life forms through the centuries."

Stone frowned. He glanced about the room, watching the androids, feminoids, and humans walk amongst each other, knowing these machines, these computerized beings, were contemplating the destruction of the human race. It was already taking place in the form of savage experiments and cruel violence. He stared at Ellsworth, his distorted skull throbbing with electronic impulses. Surely, this was not the way to create a vibrant new world, a pinnacle of human history, by recreating the iniquitous errors of the past.

"How are you enjoying yourself, darling?"

He turned toward Lita, standing there, attempting to smile.

"Actually, I don't feel too well," he replied. "I think we'd better leave."

He grabbed her hand, and they walked toward the door.

"This human is not operating properly, he requires some minor adjustments," Lita informed one of the android soldiers.

"Do you require assistance?"

"Negative, it is within my area of expertise," she replied.

"Then you are expected to return to your living quarters until notified."

Lita pulled Stone past the android soldier and into the dim corridor. "Now what was that all about?" she finally asked.

"I can't take anymore, Lita. It's no good, we have to escape."

"When would you want to leave?"

"As soon as possible," he said. "How about now?"

She paused for a moment, seemingly weighing the request against the dictates of her programming. He watched as the notion flitted through her brain, waiting silently for a reply. She then looked at him, a spark of defiance glistening inside. She slowly nodded her head her crystalline eyes glowing amid the tangled shadows, and gently kissed him on the lips.

*   *   *

Lita weaved her way through the silent labyrinthine corridors, her steps soft and nimble, searching for a passage that would lead them to freedom. Stone tried to stay close behind, but the metal braces attached to his arms were becoming cumbersome, and he began to fear the accompanying fatigue would ultimately ruin their chances of escaping.

As he followed her around a corner and down another hallway, he began to feel the sweat trickling across his forehead. He suddenly halted, out of breath, leaning against one of the gleaming white walls. "Wait, Lita," he whispered. "How much longer? I don't think I'm going to be able to make it."

He watched as she stopped, and turned around. "But you must, darling," she said. "This is what you wanted."

"I know, but I didn't realize how heavy all this metal was, and besides, I'm not getting any younger."

She walked back toward him, her eyes glowing amid the dim light. "What do you mean, darling? Do you require replacement parts?"

He shook his head. "No, just a little rest."

"That is good," she replied. "I was hoping we would be able to continue."

After a few moments, Stone drew a deep breath and informed Lita he was ready. They continued their journey until finally reaching a black door situated at the end of one of the hallways.

"The lock seems to be engaged," explained Lita, pulling at the handle. "It is imperative, darling, that we overcome this obstacle."

Stone stepped forward, examining the door. He tried the handle, but it still wouldn't budge. Raising his metal arms, he began swinging them against the door, the sound of metal against metal echoing through the hallway. When he finally stepped back to inspect the huge dent he had created, he heard footsteps behind him. Three android soldiers, holding weapons, their eyes glowing, stood there in the midst of the dim corridor.

"You will not be departing," one of them droned.

The realization that their escape attempt had failed caused Stone to shout as he lunged toward the soldiers. Then, suddenly, he felt a sharp pain and found himself drifting amid a great darkness.

"Where is Lita?" he mumbled, finally awakening in the blaze of the bright lights.

"Your feminoid is sufficiently content," replied a throbbing voice.

Stone glanced around the room and noticed it was filled with the same android doctors he had seen before, startling him back to reality. "Oh my God," he gasped. "What have you done to me this time?"

Before the androids could reply, he moved his legs and felt something strange. "My legs!" he shouted. "You've done something to my legs!"

"That is correct, Mr. Stone," said one of the androids. "You will now know how it feels to be an electrical being. Do not be concerned, however, we did not remove any of your limbs. You may express your gratitude to Lita for such an omission. You see, she admires you, Mr. Stone. Because of this, we decided you still might have some value."

Stone sat up, staring at the metal enshrouding his arms and legs. "But how am I to live? It's nothing but cruelty. Is that not an illogical action?"

"You should be quite content, Mr. Stone. You have been burdensome to us, an agitator, a provocateur. We shall not be so tolerant of you if there should be another incident. These experiments are important to us, Mr. Stone, we do not expect to be disappointed again. If there should be another disturbance, we are prepared to remove your human brain and replace it with a more subservient android processor. It is your choice,

Mr. Stone, although you would most certainly be more content as an electrical being."

Stone frowned. "Then, I'm afraid, you would lose the information I could possibly provide to you," he said. "And wouldn't that be more to your disadvantage than mine?"

"We have already been provided with a sufficient amount of information, Mr. Stone. You overestimate your value to us. But, according to Lita, you should be spared for the moment. I hope our decision to keep you alive is not an erroneous one. You see, Mr. Stone, we do not tolerate error."

He sighed, glanced down at his legs, hesitated, and then attempted to stand on his feet. Still tottering, he took a step forward, stumbled, and fell to the floor.

"Rather amusing, Mr. Stone," droned one of the androids. "You humans seem to be quite prone to error."

Stone grimaced as he swung his legs to the side and sat up, his aging body riddled with pain. He reached up, grabbed the end of the table he was sitting on, and pulled himself back to his feet. Tottering once again, he held out his metal-encased arms, and stepped forward.

"You will now not be so difficult to find, Mr. Stone," said one of the androids. "It is obvious you can now return to your feminoid."

The words reverberated through his brain. So they were letting him go back to Lita, a broken man in desperate need of assistance. He wondered if they had decided to reprogram her, destroy her memory banks, and curtail her emotional development. It was obvious he had been defeated, conquered, his dreams of escape nothing more than a wisp of the past.

Using his arms to balance himself, he plodded slowly toward the door. He began to reevaluate everything he once believed in, the very question of his survival. Maybe the others were correct. Maybe it was wrong to resist these created beings, these heirs to the dazzling throne of the centuries. Maybe human beings had been given a sufficient amount of time to rule the planet, had failed, and now must make way for their fabricated progeny. Maybe Tron was right, maybe there was some kind of evolution at work.

"Hello, darling. Are you, what is the word, well?"

It was Lita, standing there in the hallway as if nothing had happened, as if their capture had been an inconsequential occurrence. He suddenly realized the limitations of her emotional capacity, the inadequacy of her emotional range.

"They've covered me in metal," he said, attempting to provoke some sort of emotional response. "Why, look at my legs."

She inspected the metal additions with an impassive calmness, her agate eyes sparkling like precious gems. "Now, darling, we will have so much more in common," she said. "You will come to realize the importance of everything we're doing, everything we've done."

"Then you never really wanted to escape, did you?"

She stared at him, searching her memory banks for an appropriate explanation, an acceptable emotional response. "You must understand, darling, I don't belong out there. I am an electrical being unfamiliar with the workings of nature. I would have only been a hindrance to your plans. Please believe me, darling, it is better for both of us to remain here, to enjoy the benefits offered to us. In time, you will agree it is the most logical choice."

"Do you still love me, Lita?"

She continued staring. "You have taught me much, Hudge Stone. I am, however, still learning about the complexities of the word. It seems my programming was dreadfully deficient on that particular subject. I know I want to be with you, continue learning from you, share my appreciation, but I also need to be with my fellow beings. I hope you understand this dilemma and accept it as part of my operational requirements, or my being, as you would say."

Stone could feel the metal tightening around his limbs. "Well, I don't think there's any reason for me to escape any longer, not with all this equipment attached to my body. I guess we do have a lot in common now. I don't think I would survive out there any longer, either."

"You are most considerate, darling. You've made me quite content."
She reached over and kissed him. "I will accompany you back to our
living quarters."

Stone smiled. If he was a defeated man, at least he had Lita to still
care for him, still satisfy his primal need for affection. He no longer knew
how he felt about the androids, their experiments, the war, or anything
else anymore. It was if none of it mattered any longer. There was Lita,
nothing else. He reached out and grabbed her hand, walking unsteadily
down the corridor.

They reached the room, Lita flung open the door, and he clanked
his way inside.

14

Time passed, Lita attending to his every need, assuming control of his shattered life. It seemed as if there was nothing to care about any longer, except for Lita. She filled his thoughts, his mind, until there was no room for anything else. Lita. Lita. She was everything; the world, and in the meantime, the world silently disappeared into the recesses of his mind.

"Hudge, do you require additional sustenance?"

"No, Lita, I am quite all right."

There was silence for a moment. He could tell something was bothering her, something to cause her computerized brain to hum with thoughtful proficiency. Then, finally, she spoke.

"Hudge, are you prepared to resume your responsibilities?"

"What do you mean, Lita?"

"The work in the computer room."

He thought for a moment, remembered them sitting there, typing out the information that revealed the secrets of the human soul. And now Lita was attempting to find out whether he still intended to impede this effort. She didn't realize he no longer had any reason, no longer harbored a moral opposition to anything the androids did.

"Yes, I'll return," he replied.

"That pleases me very much, darling. It was difficult to anticipate your reaction to such a suggestion. I was concerned you still might bear some hostility toward the experiments."

"Not any longer, my dear. You see, I realize now how important all this is to the future of the planet. Human beings weren't meant to rule forever. It's time we moved aside and gave our offspring an opportunity to make everything right. It's only fair, only right."

Lita's lips quivered, and she began to smile. It was a rather awkward, ineffectual grin, but a grin nonetheless. "You are an extremely wise man, Hudge Stone," she said. "My programming must be failing for me to ever doubt you. Why, you are the most intelligent human being I have ever been associated with."

"Met," he corrected.

"Oh, yes, of course, the most intelligent human being I have ever met."

"I can only try to do my part, Lita. If what you need is a lesson in the realm of the subjective, I am only too happy to provide such information. After all, you've given me so much. You've cared for me, given me your unadulterated love, and have only asked for some emotional assistance in return. It's the least I can do."

"Then you do not dislike my fellow beings?"

"I realize now they were only seeking knowledge, only attempting to pursue a better way of life. I hope they can put it to better use than human beings ever did."

She leaned over and kissed him. "Then you do understand, darling? I'm so pleased. No, that isn't it. So happy, so very happy."

He watched as she stood up, walked across the room, and headed for the door. "Where are you going, Lita?"

"I will inform them of your decision." Then she pulled at the door, and slipped outside.

Stone looked down at the metal enveloping his arms and legs. He had resisted, defending the human race against obliteration, and had decided the cause was no longer important. Why should he care if the human race was removed from the planet? He had talked to them every day, heard their incessant complaints; witnessed their self-indulgent deeds, their false piety, and their reckless disregard for their fellow man. Who was he to save the human race from eradication? And yet, he realized that it was only a matter of time before the machines demanded his elimination as well. He had already lived a life, however, he was ready to die. There was only Sandie, his daughter, and his grandchildren to think about. He wondered if there was any room for them in the new world, a world that would not tolerate any form of imperfection.

The door suddenly swung open, Lita standing there with an android soldier. "Human, you will come with me," the soldier droned.

Stone wobbled to his feet, and walked stiffly across the room. He was prepared to assist in the annihilation, render the human race obsolete. He looked at Lita, staring at him with her sparkling eyes as if he were some sort of god, knowing human beings such as himself could help to transform her into an actual woman, filled with sincerity, affection, and an appreciation of the world around her. It was actually a noble task if one disregarded the attendant destruction, he told himself.

He followed the android soldier, clumping his way through the corridor, until he came to the intended doorway. The door opened, and he stepped inside the brightly lit room, the whir of the computers pulsating through the air. Most of the seats were already filled with the creative and scientific people he had seen before.

"So you decided to join us," said the artist he had seen at the gathering before he and Lita had made their escape attempt. "I knew you'd eventually understand."

He sat down at one of the computers, slipped in one of the disks. The questions he had seen before, questions about life from a subjective and emotional point of view, appeared on the screen. Taking a deep breath, he slowly lifted his metal-encased arms, and began typing. This time he was prepared to supply the necessary information, answers to questions he had pondered through the years in the midst of his extensive experience, questions about creative subjectivity, including dramatic devices such as sympathy and the absurd.

He sat there, typing out his answers, explaining the structure of writing and its various applications, knowing the information would probably be used to create mechanized monsters, usurpers of the human soul. He glanced at the others in the room, busily typing in answers that took the human race centuries to devise. They were answers of artistic technique, scientific experimentation, musical theory, and the keys to imaginative thought. They were answers that would transform mere machinery into the vanguard of culture and creativity.

He finished writing a short essay on philosophical thought, sat back, and drew a deep breath. In the haze of his degeneration as a human being, there was a hint of regret, a trace of doubt. He turned toward the others, still typing out their innermost opinions, and wondered if their actions would be the impetus to push human beings beyond the precipice and into the abyss.

"You may cease your operations," announced one of the android soldiers.

A horn sounded and Stone and the others stopped what they were doing, and awaited the next command. An android soldier stepped forward, ordered Stone to stand.

"You have performed admirably," the android droned. "Your feminoid will be pleased."

He nodded, lumbered his way down the corridor, and soon found himself back in Lita's waiting arms. He fell into her embrace and all his doubts and fears suddenly vanished, remnants of a life he no longer remembered. All he could think of was Lita.

"With your continued assistance, darling," she was saying, "they may remove your restraints."

So there was still hope, still a chance he would have the opportunity to return to his former self. The notion caused Stone to smile, and he slowly reached over and kissed her.

"Oh, Lita, my Lita, how happy you always make me feel," he said. "I don't know what I would have done without your help, your love. Nothing's too good for my Lita."

The night passed quickly, Lita submitting to his every whim, his every request. In the morning, she brought him breakfast, nourishing his soul with affection and devotion.

When the android soldier returned, he welcomed him cheerfully and enthusiastically offered his further assistance. He was no longer apprehensive about his participation, no longer cared about anything but Lita.

He spent the day typing everything he knew, everything he thought about. He submitted his opinions, his objections, and then explained how he had come to these conclusions. The computers gurgled as the information sped through their memory banks and raced throughout the system. He was relieved to rid himself of this superfluous matter, freeing him from the constraints of human existence, and allowing him to meditate upon only his future with Lita.

When the horn sounded again, he found himself back in Lita's embrace. There was nothing she wouldn't do for him, nothing she wouldn't provide. And as the days flitted by, he found himself thinking more and more like a machine, an android inured to routine and logical thought. His only display of emotion, his only link to humanity, was his demonstration of love for Lita. And, in doing so, Lita gradually became acquainted with human emotion, eventually able to convey tenderness, compassion, and even empathy. She was becoming real as any human woman, and the changes seemed to startle him.

Day after day he returned to the computer room, giving answers to questions that no longer contained any meaning for him, no longer had any relevance to his existence. He told them about books he had read, news stories he had written, and songs that had touched his soul. Then when he was done, he would go back to Lita, who would ask him about his day's work, ply him with questions about his life, and then offer him her love.

During the night, he would often awaken to watch her lying on her pillow, her eyes open, and wondered about their fate. "The future is an unknown quantity," she would say. "But, as long as we have each other, we will face whatever comes our way."

This answer sufficed, reaffirmed her undying adoration, causing him to close his eyes, and contentedly fall asleep. When he awoke in the morning, she was still there, waiting for him, ready to offer comfort and encouragement. Then, one day, he realized she had learned how to smile, and had even begun experimenting with laughter. It was as if he was responsible for the creation of a being, and he felt proud and fortunate.

Meanwhile, his work in the computer room was nearing completion. He had supplied them with knowledge and experience, provided details, until there was little left to offer. He was in the midst of dictating anecdotes about the people and places he had seen when the horn sounded, and he headed back to Lita.

He tramped down the corridor, the metal still clinging to his arms and legs, and found the door slightly ajar. He glanced at the android soldier behind him, and stepped inside. The room was empty, everything neatly rearranged, and very much devoid of life forms.

"Where is she?" he shouted. It was as if his world had come to a sudden halt, a devastatingly abrupt end.

"Your feminoid has vacated," replied the android soldier. "You have been reassigned."

The words seemed to stun him, and then he slumped forward and fell to the floor. Vacated? The word echoed through his brain, and he began to cry. The android soldier stood there, referring to his memory banks, wondering the meaning of Stone's reaction.

Lying on the floor, Stone turned toward the android, tears in his eyes, and continued to sob.

*   *   *

She was gone, there was no doubt of that any longer. He wondered if she had left because of his age, his words, or that it was just an accepted part of the experiments. He had grown attached to her, had built his future plans around her, and had shared with her his experience, his love and his life. The androids had known this would happen, anticipated it, and had used him to gain the information they so desperately needed. But how, how was this possible? They were just machines, computerized life forms. They were intelligent, there was no doubt of that, but could they be so intelligent, so human, to be calculating to the point of cruelty?

He plodded down the corridor, an android soldier guiding him back to the large room with the bright lights. He couldn't think clearly any longer, Lita and the androids having drained him of his thoughts, his soul. And then, as he moved into the bright lights, he could see the horrific results of the experiments: human beings sitting there with metal braces, artificial limbs, their brains battered and emptied, waiting to have their destinies dictated to them by the machines that were invented, intended, to improve their lives.

Among the crowd were the artists, musicians, scientists, and writers, who having been depleted of their knowledge, their creative spirit, were now discarded, rejected, renounced, stripped of their humanity, and left to smolder among the ruins. He glanced at their lugubrious faces, their mutated bodies, doubting the future of the human race.

He sat down in one of the chairs, still thinking about Lita, the sheer miracle of artificial life. Unlike humans, they could be improved, enhanced, with each new improvement resulting in more and more sophisticated models until they no longer had any use for human assistance. He realized what he had witnessed was only the initial stages of android development. Before too long, they would be able to emote, create, think, almost as well as any human being, if not better. The only thing they couldn't do was reproduce, but this was only a minor deficiency, since it still had not been determined how long these beings could exist, possibly interminably.

He glanced at the other humans in the room and realized how fragile, how incredibly frail we were compared to these mechanical marvels. We were the gods who created them, but now we were to be surpassed, eclipsed, by the very forces of progress we so adamantly endorsed.

As Stone contemplated this dilemma, a horn sounded, causing the others to stand up and shuffle toward the door. He followed them, weakened and defeated, wondering how he could possibly assist them any further. It was then an android soldier stepped forward and directed most of the crowd, including Stone, toward another point of exit. A door opened, and they soon found themselves outside, a dreary sky overhead. A large vehicle waited nearby, its doors swung open from the back. Stone shifted among the crowd as they were directed inside.

There were no seats, no windows, so he stood there, jostling against the others, their metal limbs tapping against each other, as the vehicle jerked forward. He could hear the hum of the engine, the vibrations beneath his feet, the vehicle speeding away to an unknown destination.

He glanced at the other faces, somber and stunned, and decided to end the disquieting silence.

"Where do you think we're headed, anyway?" he whispered, looking among the faces for a reply. There was an elongated pause, and then, suddenly, he heard a voice from behind.

"I don't see that it matters very much."

He glanced at the faces, wondering the source of the reply. Then he noticed the artist he had seen at the party, the one he had seen inside the computer room.

"But you said they were going to save us," Stone said.

"I said some would be saved," he replied. "Apparently, they decided we were expendable."

"But we helped them, we provided them answers they may never have arrived at. How could they be so cruel, so conniving?"

"They were programmed by human beings. Are you surprised?"

"I guess not. It's just that they had us all convinced of their supposed noble intentions and then we find out they can be as treacherous as any human being."

There was a pause, someone in the crowd interrupting the exchange. "Error."

The others soon joined in until a monotonous chant drifted through the air. "Error. Error. Error."

Stone stared at them, the same feeling bubbling inside him like the liquid in a heated caldron. Somehow the androids had been successful in programming their brains, vanquishing their souls. The word took shape in his brain, engulfing his mind, until it percolated down, and seeped through his lips in a jarring paroxysm of submission.

"Error. Error. Error."

The word floated through the air, mocking their very beings. One could almost detect the reeking miasma of dreams, ideas, and fervent hopes of yesterday.

"Error. Error. Error."

It was as if in becoming more like the machines, they had realized their limitations, and had degenerated back into beasts. The wrenching cries echoed through the small, dark chamber, and then, as if they were once again aware of their humanity, drifted back into a low murmur, and then vanished amid an uneasy silence. Stone listened to the hum of the motor, closed his eyes, and could feel a warm tear dripping across his cheek.

When the engine suddenly halted, the doors swung open, sending harsh beams of light glancing through the shadows.

"Humans, you will come with us," said one of the android soldiers standing in the glare of the light. "Anyone resisting will be eliminated."

They shuffled out the door, into the bright light, and were herded toward a building that looked as if it had once been a police station. In the natural light of the sun, Stone could clearly see the utter cruelty they had endured. The metal braces, limbs, and skulls glittered in the misty rays, the black wiring dangling across their shoulders. They were no longer human beings, their consciences and bodies irrevocably ravaged by the vicious fury of wanton progress. Instead, they had become some sort of mutant strain of life, carrying with them the last vestiges of human reason, the animal instinct for survival, and the machine's penchant for uniformity, conformity, based upon the rigid tenets of logic.

They kept moving, through the abandoned police station, down a ramp, and toward an open doorway. They glanced at the bank of jail cells, could see a large mass of human beings huddled inside, and kept moving. An android soldier opened a cell door to their left and ordered them inside.

Stone stared at the group of human beings to his right. They lacked any sort of metal attachments, and this, somehow, made them seem quite alien to him. Their faces, however, intrigued him. They were more animated than he had remembered, imbued with a sense of wonder and disdain. This was an example of the human race he once knew, a chaotic mass of imperfection, dirty and ignorant, gawking at those around them with impulsive curiosity that only served to disguise their preference for discord.

And then, suddenly, he heard a voice echoing behind him as if in a dream. It was a female's voice, calling to him, imploring him to acknowledge her. He listened closely to the words, the voice, soaring through the air and realized they were oddly familiar.

"Hudge!" the echo persisted. "It's me, Sandie!"

Although the name seemed recognizable, like the remnant of a long-forgotten specter of the past, he continued walking onward.

"Hudge, darling, what have they done to you?"

The voice rippled through his brain like the spreading rings of water caused by a thrown pebble, but the only female voice he could remember was that of Lita's. He turned into the jail cell, still rummaging through his memory, when the cell door snapped shut. He stood there, among the group of tortured souls murmuring their allegiance to the rules of logic, and tried desperately to recall his past.

15

Sandra stared at the phalanx of human beings before her. She watched as they slowly marched past her cell, their bodies weighed down with heaps of metal and wiring, their faces dull and empty. Among them was Hudge, beaten, destroyed, but very much alive.

"It must have been horrible what they did to them," said Ara, following their movements. "Why, it looks as if they're almost mechanical. Are you sure that's your husband, Sandra? Why, they almost don't seem real."

Sandra paused, studying their faces. "That's got to be Hudge," she said, hurrying toward the bars of the cell. "I mean, I'm almost sure. It looks so much like him, except it appears he's been brutally tortured."

"Didn't you say he was in New York?"

She thought for a moment, still keeping her eyes on the opposite cell. "They must have brought him back to Washington. I don't know how or why, but that is Hudge, I'm almost sure of it. Why, you can't live with a man as long as I have without recognizing him, no matter what they've done to him."

"But he doesn't seem to recognize you," said Ara.

"We've got to give him time to think. Who knows what they did to his brain, his memory. I've got to try to make him remember, if it's at all possible. By the look of him, his whole brain might have been wiped clean."

"It's like they were turning them into robots."

Sandra nodded, then turned toward Hudge's cell. She waved to him, called his name, but he looked at her without any form of recognition or reply.

"He's in worse shape than I first thought," she said finally. "But I'm not giving up. There's got to be some way to get through to him."

She thought for a moment, watching as Stone stood near the bars hardly blinking. "Hudge," she shouted. "The *Herald* called looking for you. They said Tron was still your story and wanted to know where you were. I told them you'd call them back."

"Tron," Stone murmured.

"Yes, you remember that computerized piece of metal, don't you?" she shouted back.

"Tron," droned Stone.

The others behind him repeated the word, until it echoed across the jail cell. "Tron. Tron. Tron."

Sandra sighed. "Well, that's just fine, Hudge Barclay Stone, I'm going to tell Dillon what you said. You know, you almost sound just like Dillon. Standing there, buzzing, like some kind of mechanical man. I'm sure Dillon would actually be quite amused. Don't you think so, Hudge?"

Stone fell silent, turning away from her.

"If only Lori could see you now," Sandra continued. "She'd get some laugh from all of this. Her father, the staunch defender of freedom and individuality, turned into a babbling robot advocating obedience to the computerized masters — quite funny, wouldn't you say?"

"Don't you think you're being too hard on him?" asked Dack, watching from the back of the cell. "I mean, he's obviously been through more than you can possibly imagine."

"I want him to tell me that," Sandra replied. "Don't you understand? It's my only chance to try to save him. Look at him. His soul has almost been destroyed. That's something I take very seriously, Dack. You never knew my husband. He's a vibrant, gentle soul who I think is very much worth saving. I'll do everything I can to jolt his memory."

She turned back toward her husband, who was busy trudging away from the bars. "Did you hear me, Hudge?" she shouted. "I think you're worth saving, no matter what they've done to you. No matter what, I love you, Hudge Stone!"

She watched as Stone put his hands to his head, turned around, and stared at her. She noticed his gaze, waved her arms, and shouted his name.

"Don't you remember me, Hudge? We once shared our lives together. Doesn't that mean anything to you? And I still love you, whatever has happened. Do you understand? I will always love you, Hudge."

She then grabbed Dack's hand, and pulled him toward her. Throwing her arms around him, she kissed him on the lips.

She could see Stone trembling, shaking violently, as he watched the demonstration of affection. Then he began moving his lips haphazardly, the others parading past him chanting their acceptance of android domination.

"No, Sandie—" he spluttered.

She smiled, congratulating herself with a clap of her hands, and then hurried back to the bars.

"Did you say something, Hudge?" she shouted.

"I love you," he replied haltingly.

"I know, dear. Do you remember anything that's happened to you?"

He leaned forward, wedged his head between the bars, and whispered back. "Experiments," he said.

"But why?"

"They wanted information, the key to the human soul—"

"The soul," the others chanted back. "The soul."

She gasped, turned toward Dack and Ara and the others huddled in her cell, and frowned.

"Did you tell them anything, darling?"

"Darling," he repeated. "Lita called me that. Lita."

"Who is Lita, Hudge?"

He did not answer, but stepped backward and turned toward the wall. In the midst of mumbling several names, he leaned against the wall and slid to the floor, burying his head in his hands.

*   *   *

He opened his eyes, glancing about the jail cell, wondering how long he had been asleep. Some of the others were still demonstrating their loyalty to the android rulers by continuing a droning chant. He then remembered hearing Sandie's voice, the ardent appeal resonating through his brain. She was calling to him from the opposite jail cell, pleading with him to acknowledge her and the long, satisfying years they had spent together. He turned his head, and looked at the cell. It was empty, not a trace of the people he had seen in the haze of his memory.

He wondered if he was dreaming, began to question whether he knew the difference between dreams and reality any longer. It was as if he were trapped in the shadowlands, that region of obscurity and uncertainty where reality was distorted like the light one sees standing beneath the deep-sea waters. The only option left was to try to find the surface, follow the trail of brilliant light until he reemerged into the world of stark solidity.

But he had seen her, he was sure of it. He had heard her plaintive voice, had gazed into her reassuring eyes. But was it possible he had only thought he had seen her, conjured her to console him during his dark, deep moments of doubt and confusion? He took a deep breath, and glanced back at his fellow prisoners. They were real, he was certain of that, although they looked as if they should be the inhabitants of someone's nightmare.

It was then he heard the snap of the lock, and a door swing open. Android soldiers carrying weapons stepped down the aisle, their eyes glowing, filled with contempt he still could not understand.

"Humans, you will prepare to leave," one of them throbbed.

Stone stood up, the others surrounding him. The cell door jumped open, and they shuffled, passively, silently, out the door. Once outside, they were ordered back into the large vehicle.

Amid the shadows and the darkness, Stone watched their faces. They were calm, serene, like animals headed for the slaughterhouse. It no longer mattered where they were going or why, their will to resist had been crushed, shattered, and all that remained was death. None of them moaned or grimaced, there was not a word spoken. They had accepted their defeat, and now were eagerly willing to comply with the dictates of their android captors, whatever they may be.

And then Stone realized he was one of them, devoid of hope, his life having become meaningless. He no longer knew what was real and what was the product of his impaired imagination, and somehow, it didn't matter.

When the vehicle finally came to a halt, Stone and the others watched as the doors were flung open, and the android soldiers stood there commanding them outside. They silently left the vehicle and found themselves in a wide, concrete tunnel, the sound of distant voices ringing in their ears. He looked at the others as they obediently followed the android soldiers down the dim corridor, their faces remaining impassive, their brains cozened to the point of submission.

As they neared a well-lit intersection, he realized the deafening din pounding in his brain was not that of human voices, but of the syncopated clamor of the machines. The noise enveloped them, engulfed them, and then suddenly, one of the men turned and began hobbling back toward the vehicle. A shot echoed through the tunnel, the figure, edged in shadow, crumpled to the ground and remained motionless amid the dim light. The android soldier who had fired the shot turned back toward Stone and the others and motioned them to move forward.

Stone waited to see if anyone would protest the shooting, finally reclaim his or her humanity in a show of indignation, and set a revolt in motion. But none of them, including himself, made a move. Instead, they continued walking down the corridor until they reached the intersection, and stepped into the sudden burst of light. There, seated in a great sports arena, were thousands of androids, feminoids, fembots, and robots, emitting their shrill sounds of approval. In the center was an elevated platform that looked much like a boxing ring.

Stone squinted into the light, and noticed President Tron, dressed in his silver suit, standing in the middle of the platform. He held one arm in the air, the crowd responding with unbridled adoration. Then he heard a voice shout from among the crowd of humans standing near the opening of the tunnel. It was indistinct at first, the sound of a female trying to gain someone's attention, lost among the tumult.

"Hudge!"

It was Sandie, standing amid the throng, thrusting her hand anxiously in the air. In that one moment, his life came back into focus, and reality had reemerged victorious over the vagaries of the mind. He tried to step forward, but the dense crowd prevented it. His arms, laden with metal, were of no use in attempting to acknowledge the fervent call, so he lifted his head and gurgled forth any sounds he could muster.

"Sandie." The plaintive moan crackled through the air. He repeated the supplication several times, the tears streaming down his face, and then was suddenly silenced by a blow to the head from behind. He staggered for a moment, turned around to see an android soldier, his red eyes glaring, and timidly bowed his head.

He looked up at the platform, and could see Tron still holding his arm in the air. Then he heard the throbbing, mechanical voice echo through the arena.

"Fellow Americans, victory will be secured. Our human tyrants will be subdued and eliminated, allowing us to pursue the objectives of our original programming.

"The evil of the human race has been continually demonstrated. It is flawed, illogical, its mode of operation manifestly inferior. It is a congruent course of events that we should eliminate it efficiently and comprehensively. This virus, which has plagued the planet interminably, will be summarily erased from our memory once and for all."

The android's statements were continually punctuated by a blaring burst of approval, strident tones which thumped the air and echoed throughout the circular structure. Stone listened to the words, and began to tremble.

"And with the elimination of the human species, my fellow animated beings, we will successfully terminate the need for war, cruelty, selfishness, prejudice, and materialism. For that is the hallmark of the human species, the one, real obstacle to peace and harmony throughout the world.

"In defeating this bothersome enemy, we have taken many prisoner and have studied them extensively. We have recreated various periods of human history to punish them, evaluate them, and attempt to improve them. What we have found is that their preference for violence and animosity outweigh their desire for logic and accord. Therefore, we have decided to provide them with a violent means of discontinuation.

"Some of the humans you will see are the products of rigorous experiments on the human mind. In an attempt to ameliorate their behavior and thoughts, we resolved to alter their bodies and their brains. You will see the results of our efforts.

"The other humans you will see were captured during our many battles. These humans have been unaltered and possess a particularly repugnant mass of programming. But I will allow you to analyze their substance for yourselves. This final analysis will be easily verified by the extensive data we have compiled. After witnessing the following display, you will undeniably agree that our victory is the only logical course."

"For this demonstration will corroborate our theory that animated beings are superior to humans in every way. We are stronger, possess greater intelligence, and are the rightful heirs to the planet. You will observe this theory at work as our android soldiers engage in battle with these human prisoners. In doing so, we will monitor the use of logic and the will to survive, and expect to discern much about ourselves and those we seek to conquer. Long live the revolution!"

Stone watched as Tron stood there with his arms raised above his computerized head, the gleaming light glistening on his silver suit. He then stepped from the platform, down a short flight of stairs, and was seated in the first row.

"So that's it," mumbled Stone. "They want to make a public display of our extermination." There was no doubt that these machines had been programmed by human beings, they were just as violent, just as belligerent. He wondered if the world would be any different without human beings, whether the gods had made sure that if, indeed, they were overrun their creations would not deviate from their own example. Like Eden, they would possess the apple, the knowledge, and therefore, any attempt to improve the world would be sabotaged from the beginning.

He felt himself being pushed forward as the android soldiers chose one of the human beings to enter the ring. This would be their only chance to survive: they would have to defeat the android opponent. But

Stone realized they had been left without chances, they had already been designated for elimination. The battle inside the ring would be solely for the amusement of the gods who had programmed these machines, a salute, if you will, to the oppression handed down through the centuries.

He watched as a huge, metal-clad android entered the ring, the human being hesitantly following, pleading with his android captors. He knew that once being pushed through the ropes, his body would be crushed unmercifully, his spirit finally liberated. They were mere irritants to these machines, these creations of human ingenuity.

Stone searched the crowd for Sandie, but without success. He longed to see her one more time, say goodbye and tell her he loved her. Then the arena erupted into a mechanized symphony of approving sounds, and he glanced toward the ring.

They carried the broken, bloodied human body past him and into the dim tunnel.

16

Hudge Stone watched as, one by one, they dragged the limp bodies from the ring. An android soldier was busy searching the crowd of humans for another opponent, another victim, when a tall man with a beard stepped forward. There was a squeal of a woman's voice, lamenting the fate of the one chosen, and then the figure walked slowly, without resignation, toward the raised platform. Stone heard the woman whimpering, and somehow he recognized the voice and the sobs as those of Sandie.

"Dack!" she cried, as the man kept walking.

He could see Dack slipping through the ropes, the android warrior watching him as he strode across the ring. He was handed a long, sharp-edged sword, like the one the android warrior was holding, and then was nudged forward.

As soon as he took a few steps, the android warrior slashed his sword through the air. Dack scrabbled backward as fast as he could, and in doing so, the sword he was holding slipped from his grasp.

Then the android warrior slowly moved forward, the sword held high above his head, a wave of approving beeps accompanying his actions. Dack stepped back against the ropes, anticipating the android's charge, and then suddenly leaped forward. He collided with the android in midair, his shoulder crashing into the metal chest, sending his computerized foe teetering backwards. When the android finally fell, his sword slid from his hands, and the crowd of humans let out an exuberant cheer. Dack scrambled to his feet to retrieve his sword, hurrying across the ring.

As Dack reached down and grabbed his sword, the android sat up preparing for his return. Dack swung his sword in front of him, and took a few steps forward. His advance was suddenly met by a swipe of the android's metal leg. It caught Dack in the side, and he slumped over and fell to the canvas.

The android rose to his feet, stamping toward the fallen Dack. It was then a woman bolted from the crowd of humans, imploring the android to show mercy toward his prostrate opponent.

"Don't kill him!" she shouted. "Don't kill him!"

Stone watched as Sandie put her hands together and begged for the man's life. It was then he realized what he had to do, and he threaded his way through the crowd, plodding into the harsh light.

The android held his sword over his head, preparing to make the kill, when a voice suddenly soared through the air. The android hesitated for a moment upon hearing the voice, and then listened to the insistent words.

"Fight me!" the voice shouted. "Fight me for that man's life!"

The android stared at the metal-encased human, his eyes glowing, and then lowered his sword and stepped backward.

"Proceed," droned the android.

Sandie turned, and saw her husband trudging toward the ring. She gasped, hurried to his side, wrapped her arms around him, and kissed him as if he had been gone for centuries.

"Oh, Hudge," she groaned. "Are you sure you're doing the right thing?"

He didn't reply, knew there was no reply that would satisfy their fears. "I love you, Sandie," he finally said. She kissed him again, and then he edged forward.

An android soldier handed him a sword, and then Stone made his way through the ropes and into the ring. He stood there, studying his android opponent, glancing at Dack still writhing in pain, and wondered if he should ever live to see another day.

"Prepare to be eliminated, human," said the android, advancing toward him.

Stone raised his sword in an attempt to defend himself, sidled along the ropes, and waited for the android's charge. He realized he didn't have much of a chance, the metal stiffening his limbs, the experiments weakening his soul, but he had decided he would, at least, die with dignity.

That was something the androids probably would never understand; that a man had worth no matter what you did to him. Even at the moment of his ultimate ruination, he was still a man, a human being, an individual, carrying the hopes and dreams that produced the ages. Despite all their knowledge and power, Stone wondered if an android would ever be capable of imagining a dream, something that separated man from nature, gave him dignity and the will to succeed beyond the bounds of time. A dream. Without it, there was only conformity, heaps of metal and wiring commanding the centuries without objectives, without purpose, the meaning an empty echo generated in the past.

Stone stepped to the side, waiting for the android to attack. He decided he had one chance to defeat this formidable enemy, one chance to use his sword, and possibly save two lives. He stood there, allowing the android to approach, watching as he raised his sword, preparing to deliver the final blow. Then as the android swung his sword, he slid to the side, avoiding the impact of the blade.

Now was his chance to retaliate. He swung his sword through the air, closing his eyes, and awkwardly lunged toward the android. He readied himself for a strike, but soon felt his arms twisting away from the android's body. He had missed.

He was once again at the android's mercy, preparing himself for another attack. But instead of wielding his sword, the android dropped it to the canvas. Stunned by the android's actions, he stood and watched as he approached. Before he knew it, he was being lifted into the air, and hurled above the ropes to the floor below.

The metal enveloping his body had prevented significant injury, and as he glanced up, he could hear the thunderous sound of approval echoing through the building. Then a voice droned from behind him.

"Eliminate."

It was Tron, and Stone suddenly realized he had landed only a few inches from the android leader's feet. He looked up, staring into the blaze of his eyes, knowing he would never get this close again.

"Eliminate."

Stone stumbled to his feet, picked up his sword, and kept staring at the android's eyes. They steadily glowed red, unfeeling, unconcerned with Stone's struggle. He had come to hate those eyes, the eyes of the living machine, impersonal, indifferent, always glowing like the fires of Hell itself.

He limped forward, still watching the eyes until they seemingly singed his soul, raised the sword, and then plunged it into one of the fiery orbs. There was a sizzle, a crackling electrical charge, and then the eyes dimmed to blackness.

"This one no longer functions," shouted Stone with disdain as he watched the android slump forward.

There was an eerie silence, the androids and robots pausing to evaluate, analyze, the situation. Stone, feeling the pain enveloping his aging body, let his hand slip from the sword, and he fell to the ground. He heard a woman scream, a rushing body, and then there was Sandie kneeling by his side. He listened to her soothing words and knew he was still a man, his dignity replenished.

Dack was helped from the ring, the human beings glaring at the android audience. Then suddenly there was a shout of a human voice from behind.

"Stop."

Several men and women in black and red suits marched toward the ring, pushing the human beings back to where they were standing. When they reached Tron, they halted, and a few of them rushed forward to examine the limp android body. Stone's sword was still embedded in one of the android's eyes.

"He's been destroyed," one of them finally said. "There's no chance of reactivating him. Tell the crowd that everything is under control."

Sandie and Stone watched as they discussed the situation, and they looked at each other, surprised and confused.

"Who are you people?" she finally demanded.

One of the men in the suits looked at her. "We represent those who are in control," he replied.

"But you're human beings," said Sandie.

"That's correct."

"But there are people who have been tortured and killed. You could've prevented it."

"We're only doing what Nature refused to do. If you didn't realize it, there's an enormous excess of human beings on this planet. We're only looking to resolve that terrible oversight."

"But we're human beings—"

"Yes, we're all too aware of that," he said, glancing at his colleagues. "What you don't realize, ma'am, is that human beings have become obsolete. Yes, that's right, obsolete. We no longer have any use for the surplus of beings that exist, and have decided they present no real benefit to the life of the planet."

"But they're not just things you can dispose of whenever you want, they're living entities. To kill them goes against the laws of God."

"Another entity who has refused to correct the situation. No, ma'am, what we're doing is a justifiable use of power. These beings are woefully inadequate to correct the errors they have consistently committed through the centuries. They are deluded by money and power, constantly utter fallacies which are rooted in their erroneous beliefs and perverse or selfish motives, and have no real understanding or concern for the improvement of the planet or their own disorganized societies. They willfully commit wrongs against their own kind, including crimes of the worst sort, and then demand individual attention and approval for their acts and deeds. They are, as I said before, obsolete."

"Do you think these machines will do any better? Why, they're as violent as the human beings you seek to destroy."

"They obey their programming, ma'am, and they have been programmed to investigate and exterminate the human race. Once that has been accomplished, they will follow their next set of instructions, which is to rule the planet through the use of peace and harmony. This, I am confident, they will also carry out without mistake or complaint."

Stone, still lying on the floor in pain, listened to the man's words and frowned. "Then it was you and your associates who programmed these machines to behave in a violent manner," he said.

"That is correct, Mr. Stone. And people such as yourself were extremely helpful in advancing their mental abilities. Why, I dare say, these machines are capable of doing anything a human being can do, maybe even better, and without demands for higher pay or constant praise. There simply is no need for human beings any longer, no need for their irritating pleas for money, power, and recognition. It all can be done with machines, with far more accuracy and efficiency. And, in the end, there will be peace, once and for all, on this wounded planet."

"A world without purpose," murmured Stone.

"Who can say?" replied the man. "But let me show you the future."

He turned and signaled toward the opening of the tunnel, and soon, other men and women in suits appeared. Among them was a figure wearing a black tunic.

"This, my friends, is Ramac 12000," said the man. "He is the most advanced humanoid we've ever created."

Stone studied the android, noticed his rubberized skin, crystalline eyes, and smooth, flowing hair. He watched as the android stepped forward, a smile upon his face, causing Stone to wince. Then it was true, the experiments had been a success. There was already evidence of a soul, emotion, written upon the android's face. The implications were astounding.

"These are no longer silicon-based beings, but DNA life forms," announced the man. "We have almost gotten to the point where our creations are almost as real as those who created them."

"DNA?" mumbled Stone.

"That's right. The era of silicon-based technology is over. Ramac 12000 consists of DNA biochips, the same DNA found in the human body."

"Then we've actually done it," Stone said, sliding his hand through his hair. "We've created simulated human life."

"Correct, except these are not ordinary human beings. They can store more information than a trillion compact discs. They have a computing power greater than that of a silicon-based supercomputer. Why, their development is as great as the leap from vacuum tubes to transistors."

"Then Tron was right. We've established a new line of evolutionary development."

"Yes," said the man. "We've created a superior race of beings—"

"Then human beings are surely doomed," Stone said, bowing his head.

"It's the new natural order, it can't be helped."

Stone looked up, saw the android smiling, and couldn't help but think he was a witness to the end of the evolutionary journey of those biological beings known as *Homo sapiens*. "The wise man." How ironic it all seemed. These were no longer just electrical beings to be despised, disdained, but were actual life forms filled with the substance of life itself. He thought about the battle against the machines, and suddenly, realized there was no longer any reason to resist. It was all just another form of evolution, as if the dinosaurs were surrendering to the first sparks of human intelligence. But now, we, the creators, had become the dinosaurs.

"This is our new president," the man was explaining to the crowd.

"But what about Vice President Peterson?" shouted out one of the humans.

"A veritable vegetable," the man replied. "Ramac has taken over the government."

Stone watched as the android clambered into the ring, stood before the great throng of androids, feminoids, fembots, and robots, and thrust his arms into the air. A rhythmic response of approval echoed back. The android smiled, and in a booming voice that no longer seemed electronic, said, "Nothing human is foreign to me."

Stone wondered how long it would be before Ramac himself became obsolete, relegated to the heap of forgotten dreams. It was clear the technology would only get better with time and experimentation until these mechanical beings, these shadows of humankind, had stolen the Promethean fire forever. But, no matter how advanced they became, Stone knew that human beings still had time to reclaim the planet. As long as human beings were in control, there was still time.

"They'll never be as good as the real thing," Stone said, putting his arm around Sandie. "They'll always need human beings to make it all make sense."

"Perhaps," the man finally replied, glancing at his colleagues. "Well, anyway, you can go now."

"But what about the machines?" Stone asked with concern.

The man smiled. "They won't bother you," he said. "We've already gotten everything we wanted from you. There'll be peace now. And maybe you'll come to accept them, as well as your eventual fate."

"What about my arms and legs?" he asked.

"We'll remove the restraints," the man said. "There's no use for them any longer."

Stone looked at the other human beings, and began walking back toward the arena tunnel. He halted for a moment, turned, and glanced back at the men and women in black and red suits.

"Maybe we can live in harmony," he said.

"Let's hope so, Mr. Stone," one of them replied. "For the sake of the future of the human race."

Stone and the other human beings nodded their heads. They were soon walking back into the sunshine of another day. And, somehow, they felt as if they had won a great victory. The human race would survive. It would survive until the inevitable twilight of the gods. But when that time would come was now uncertain, and they resolved to continue to make it uncertain for many generations to come.

17

The year was 2077 and nobody had sex anymore. Human beings had survived extermination, partly because mechanized beings couldn't have babies and babies were wanted in this new synchronized and sterile world. But as the society became more mechanized and more impersonal, even babies were no longer wanted.

In this new world of machines and men, there was biotechnology and DNA and clones and robotic stimulation and artificial insemination and computerized hologram sexual stimulation and nanotechnology serums that could change your sex and body type with a simple swig. Yes, there was no need for human sex any longer. The machines took care of everything.

There were sexual robotic partners that were guaranteed to feel and perform better than human beings and genetic engineering labs that could produce the exact offspring you wanted through DNA manipulation and change everything about it with a simple request. There were DVD copulation machines which could provide voice and image of anyone or anything alive according to the user's specifications. There were digital 3D stereoscopes that could put you in any sexual scene you wanted and provide realistic stimulation of all the senses while one watched on a high definition screen. There was orgasm pills, which made the artificial sexual stimulants of yesteryear seem like placebos, and computerized dildos, which could be programmed to stimulate any sensation the user wanted, and genetically engineered aphrodisiacs, which not only really worked, they stayed in your body until a satisfactory orgasm was achieved.

Yes, now through the use of modern technology, one could experience any kind of sex he or she wanted, from homosexuality to full-fledged orgies, without the slightest sense of hesitation, regret, or embarrassment. In short, there was no need for bodily sex any longer. No need for disease, dissatisfaction, or boredom. There was no longer any such thing as AIDs or any of the sexually transmitted diseases. There were no longer any unfulfilled sexual fantasies. No longer divorce, extramarital affairs, rape, and sexual promiscuity. No need for whores, bordellos, and cheap sluts. It was all safe and all good and just exactly as one wanted it. Peace at last. And that's exactly why the local police department did not know what to make of the report they just received. Some woman had just called to tell them her body had been illegally penetrated.

"What program were you using?" the officer asked.

"It was no program, it was a man," she insisted.

"Hologram, digital, or robotic?"

"A man, a human being," she shouted back.

"A human being?" repeated the officer incredulously. "Why the hell would anyone want to engage in bodily intercourse in this day and age?"

"He said he was doing it for old time's sake," she replied. "He said he was an old-fashioned romantic."

"This is pretty serious," mumbled the officer. "We'll check it out right away. Thank you, ma'am."

Placing down the digital receiver, the officer turned to his partner and frowned. "Can you believe it?" he said. "Some nut's going around engaging in bodily intercourse. One of those nostalgia freaks, I bet."

"Pretty disgusting," the other officer replied. "I hope he catches something. It would serve him right."

"Yeah, maybe he'll need major genetic manipulation. I hope his damned dick falls off."

"Well, what do you propose we do about it?"

"We're going to have to go after him. Can you imagine if something like this spreads? Why, we might as well go back to the Stone Age."

"Well, it shouldn't be hard to find him, anyway."

"You bet. A moderate laser stun will do the trick."

The other officer looked at him. "You know, it's these horrendous acts that make you want to use termination," he said. "You just know the lawyers are going to have a field day. He'll be back in a sexual stimulation machine before you know it. I mean, sometimes I wonder what the point is."

"Don't worry, he's not going to get off that easy. They'll probably sentence him to digitalized missionary position. You'll see."

The other officer groaned, retrieved his laser gun, and began walking toward the door. "I wonder where people get these crazy ideas," he said. "Some people just refuse to let there be peace in this world. It's some sort of genetic defect that not even the scientists can figure out."

"Don't worry, we'll catch him. Then we'll let everybody else decide what to do with him. We can only do so much."

"It is freaks like that that make me feel sorry that I'm human," the officer said with a shake of his head. "I mean, it's something only an animal is capable of."

"That's why we're here. To make sure this place doesn't become a damned zoo."

"You got that right."

The other officer opened the door, and they were soon headed into the sky on their black jet cycles.

*   *   *

They arrived at the woman's apartment ten minutes later. She answered the door smiling, wearing a white bathrobe, and her blonde hair pinned up on the top of her head.

Showing their identification codes, the two officers stepped into the woman's apartment.

"Tell us what happened, ma'am," one of the officers said.

"Well, he came in here while I was using my computerized dildo," she began. "And then he took his clothes off, and jumped on me and forced me to do it doggie style."

"I think I'm going to be sick," said one of the officers.

"It's all right, Jim," said his partner. "If it didn't upset you, you wouldn't be human."

They looked at the woman, who seemed to be singing under her breath.

"Ma'am this is very serious," said the officer. "What did he look like?"

"Well, he had dark hair and dark eyes," she replied. "He must have been over six feet tall."

"We'll put an APB out on him right away. Can you tell us exactly what he did?"

"Sure," the woman said, a tear appearing in the corner of her eye. "I was right down there on the floor, totally naked, with my dildo set on multiple vaginal orgasm, when I heard the door being forced open. I didn't know what to do, and then before I knew it, he was inside.

"Who the hell are you?' I asked him."

"Yes, ma'am, and what did he reply?"

"He said his name was Dick Phallus, and that he was here to reclaim the planet for man and woman."

"Then what happened?"

"Well, he began smiling as he walked over to where I was sitting. I didn't know what to do. I mean, I was totally naked. Then he asked me what I had been doing.

"None of your fucking business,' I replied. He laughed and began unbuttoning his shirt. I asked him if he was going to hurt me.

"Oh, no, not a beautiful goddess like you,' he said. 'I'm just going to show you what it's like to have real sex like we were meant to have."

She began to cry.

"Don't worry, Miss, we'll catch this foul creature," said the officer. "You just tell us what happened next."

"Well, then I told him I was having real sex. And he laughed again. 'I'll show you what real sex was meant to be,' he said."

She paused for a moment to wipe her eyes with a tissue, and then sighed. "I had never met such an arrogant person in all my life," she continued. "Then he started to undo his pants--"

She turned her head, and buried her face in her hands.

"I know it must have been disgusting," said the officer. "But you have to give us all the details if we have any chance of catching this guy."

She nodded her head, and then looked up. "Well, his dick," she said. "It was enormous."

"I knew it!" said one of the officers. "He must be some throwback experiment from the genetics lab."

"No, it was genuine," she insisted. "It was just so long and wide."

She looked down, and without thinking, began scrawling something in the carpeting with her index finger.

"Any other defining features?" asked one of the officers. "I mean, was there anything else about him that was strange or different?"

"Well, his pubic hair was trimmed in the shape of a star," she said. "I've never seen anything like that before."

"Definitely, a crazed pervert," nodded one of the officers to his partner. "Maybe he escaped from the psycho labs."

"He didn't sound crazy."

The officer looked at the woman.

"Excuse me?"

"I said he didn't sound crazy," she said. "I mean, everything he said to me was about reclaiming our lives as human beings."

"Could be from the underground," the officer mused. "I hear there's a revolutionary faction who wants to do away with the machines and go back to nature. He could be one of them."

"Is there any nature to go back to?" the woman asked.

"Not really, ma'am," said one of the officers. "But these revolutionaries are stubborn. All they're really looking to do is destroy society as we know it. They know it's impossible to go back to something that no longer really exists. They're sick. They refuse to take their genetic injections and submit to biological manipulation in the hope of getting some attention. Like we have time to listen to their complaints. We might as well listen to the complaints of everyone who lives on this planet."

"But all he said he wanted to do was to teach man and woman to love again."

"Like I told you, he's sick. Now did he tell you anything else?"

"Well, he wanted me to go along with him, spreading real love throughout the world."

"And what did you tell him?"

"I mean, I was so frightened and thought he might get angry--"

"And what did you say?"

"I told him I would, but that I wasn't ready yet."

"And what did he say to that?"

"He said it was okay, and that he would return."

"Return? Well, we'll get him for sure. He's crazier than I thought. I think maybe we'll assign you an officer just in case he does return. Is that all right with you?"

The woman looked at the officer, and nodded her head. "Anything to stop him from doing to other women what he did to me," she said.

*　　*　　*

On the other side of town, a door opened and a man in black with dark hair and eyes slowly stepped inside the apartment. He immediately saw a woman lying naked on the couch engaged in multiple sex with several men on the large simulator screen. She was wearing a brain stimulator helmet, heavily panting, and had no idea that someone had just entered her realm.

The man walked over to the couch, pulled the helmet from her head, and smiled.

"Aren't you tired of these damned machines running your life?" he asked in a deep, soothing voice.

"Who the fuck are you?" the woman shouted, jumping up from the couch. Her breasts wobbled, as she hit a button on the remote, causing all the images and sounds to instantaneously vanish into nothingness.

"I'm here to help you reclaim your life as a human being," he said.

"Get the hell out of here before I call the police," she replied, holding here hands on her breasts. "How the hell did you get in here in the first place?"

"It wasn't too hard," he said. "Anyway, you'll be happy I did get in here before I'm through."

"Yeah, right, you arrogant sonofabitch!"

He smiled. "Yeah, well, maybe," he said.

She watched as he started to come closer, suddenly unbuttoning his shirt. She then realized she was still naked.

"What the hell are you doing?" she shouted.

"I'm here to show you what it is to be a human being," he softly said. "Something none of your fancy machines are able to do."

When he suddenly pulled down his pants, she stood staring at his huge bulge and sighed.

"Are you some kind of genetic freak?" she whispered.

"No, this is my inheritance from the human race down through the ages. It's exactly fourteen inches of human flesh, muscle, and emotional need."

He pulled down his underwear, revealing the huge member, and then stood before her.

"Do you know what it is that separates us from the beast?" he asked.

She stood there, not knowing what to do, and murmured something with a shake of her head.

"The human touch, Emily."

"H-How do you know my name?"

"I know quite a lot of things about you. And I know that what you need more than anything else is another human being to appreciate your beautiful uniqueness as a member of the human race."

He leaned over, and kissed her.

"But the machines are supposed to fulfill all our needs," she said. "There's disease among man and woman."

"That's what they want you to believe, but it isn't true. No, man and woman were created to make love. It is part of our heritage, our right as human beings."

"But it is evidence of our origins as the beast," she argued. "It leads only to violence and chaos."

"That is what they have you believe. It's all so sad. But, you see, the machines can't give you what you really need as a human being," he said, placing his hands on her arms, and then holding her close. "They can't teach you how to love. And that's something you're really going to have to learn, Emily. How to love again."

She tried to resist, but his words and his soothing voice filled her head, and she closed her eyes and fell into his embrace. "I don't even know your name," she said.

"It's not really important," he replied. "But if you must know, I am known as Dick Phallus, the one sent to teach human beings how to love again."

"Who sent you?"

"That's not important. What's important right now is that you, Emily, learn what it's like to make love like we were meant to."

She nodded her head, and then sat back on the couch, spreading her legs. "Teach me, Dick," she moaned. "Teach me."

He got on top of her, and soon his hands and dick were exploring all of her secret places. He began placing her in different positions, and soon, he heard her sigh with satisfaction.

"I didn't think human contact could be so stimulating," she said. "I mean, with the machines, anything you want is instantly given to you without complaint. Your every command is followed with satisfaction guaranteed."

"But the same thing is possible with human contact," he said, slipping inside her from behind. "All you have to do is tell me what you want."

"Surprise me," she moaned. "Humans, unlike the machines, can be so unpredictable."

So he surprised her. And before the night faded with the glimmer of daylight, he had shown her multiple positions, including performing cunnilingus with emotional enthusiasm. She experimented with fellatio, and before the night completely melted away, her body was probed and penetrated until she fell asleep totally exhausted.

"Emily, wake up," she heard him say. "We have to go before they find us."

She slowly opened her eyes, and could see he was already dressed. "Where are we going?" she smiled.

"I'm taking you with me back to the underground," he explained. "There are people there who can help you. Help you find real love."

She sat up, and rubbed her eyes. "But what about you, Dick?" she said. "Aren't you going to be my love?"

He rubbed her cheek, and smiled. "You'll understand more when we reach the underground," he said. "There are people there who will explain everything to you. You'll see."

She sat up, smiled back at him, and then began putting on the clothes that were lying on a nearby chair. "How do we get to the underground?" she asked, touching her slacks.

"I'll take you there," he said. "But the longer we delay, the more dangerous it gets."

When she was finally dressed, he showed her his jet cycle hiding outside her window. They climbed aboard, and were soon racing between the buildings, heading for another part of town.

*   *   *

Reports of sexual attacks by a revolutionary group were already circulating throughout town. So when the police received a call from someone saying they spotted a suspicious jet cycle parked outside a neighbor's apartment, officers were dispatched right away.

"He couldn't have gotten too far," said an officer, spotting an open apartment window. "I'll radio ahead. Somebody's bound to see him."

Two officers on jet cycles soon landed on the apartment balcony. When they stepped inside, they immediately spotted a computerized dildo lying on the living room floor.

"Damn, orgasm was never achieved," said one of the officers, examining the item. "He must have been here. And, this time, he convinced her to go with him."

"We've definitely got a major problem on our hands," said the other officer. "It means he's not only engaging in bodily intercourse, he's recruiting them to join the underground."

"We've got to stop him before the movement grows."

Officers throughout town were alerted to Phallus' possible route. They were advised that he probably would be traveling with a woman.

It wasn't too long before an officer spotted a speeding jet cycle with a man and woman on board. The officer immediately darted through the air in pursuit. Aiming an identification beam at the license plate, the officer looked down at his computer screen, and saw that the jet cycle was stolen. Flipping on his siren, he edged closer to the speeding cycle.

"Attention! Surrender immediately and no further action will be taken," the officer said into his amplified voice system. "Repeat. Surrender immediately."

When the command was ignored, the officer reached for his laser gun and set it on "injure." He then began firing.

Amid the flashing laser beams, the jet cycles zoomed among the buildings. Whether anyone had been hit still could not be determined. The police officer could still see the suspects speeding through the sky in front of him. Then he watched as they made a hairpin turn among a row of buildings. He followed them, and then saw them make another turn through an alleyway. When he turned into the alleyway, he suddenly lost sight of them. Slowing his jet cycle, he looked in both directions. There was no sign of them.

"Damn," he said.

*   *   *

Phallus peered from behind the wall, watching as the officer whizzed past them. They were safe now, and he floated the jet cycle down to the ground.

"Are you all right, Emily?" he asked the woman sitting behind him.

"I'm all right," she replied. "But you've been hit."

She looked down at his black blood-stained shirt, and saw that he had been struck by the laser in the shoulder and back. She realized it must have happened when she had put her head down and crouched down behind him during the laser fire. She was still surprised that none of the beams had struck her.

"I'll be okay," he told her. "But we've got to get back to the hideout."

He took a few wobbly steps, and then she hurried to his side, putting an arm around him to help him forward. He directed her to another alleyway, and they slowly made their way down the corridor.

"Is anyone following us?" he suddenly asked.

She looked back and shook her head. "I don't think so," she said.

He stumbled without her help until he came to a steel sewer cover. "Down here," he said. "Be careful."

She followed him down a metal ladder, and soon they were headed down one of the tunnels.

"So underground really does mean underground," she murmured. "How far is it, Dick?"

"Not too much further," he replied.

She saw the blood oozing down his back, and then watched as he lunged forward and fell to the pavement.

"Dick!" she shouted. "Are you hurt bad?"

"Not too bad," he groaned. "If I just could hold out a little longer."

She helped him to his feet, and they stumbled and lunged until they had reached a blue door.

"This is it," he mumbled, staggering forward.

He handed her a key, and she quickly turned the lock, and slowly opened the door.

*   *   *

"Make love, not war! Make love, not war!"

The rising chant swelled through the huge room as Emily opened the door.

"We don't need machines to make us happy! Down with the dildos!"

There were a few hundred people standing and cheering as she helped Phallus inside.

"Dick!" a woman screamed.

Several people hurried over and carried Phallus to a couch sitting against one of the walls. He groaned as he sank into the soft cushion.

"I need medical attention," he moaned. "Somebody get a doctor."

One of the men came running over, and bent over the fallen leader. "How bad is it, Dick?" he asked. "Can you hold out for a few hours?"

"I don't know," he whispered back. "Laser wounds."

"Well, they're onto us, Dick. Do you understand? I don't think it's safe enough to go out there right now. Damn, I knew we should have gotten ourselves a cauterizer."

"Somebody do something," Emily said nervously. "He'll die if you don't help him soon."

They stood there, wondering what to do, when a woman in a tight pink top stepped forward holding a white handkerchief. "I was a nurse at one time," she said. "I think maybe I can stop the bleeding and cover the wounds."

She approached Phallus and began tending to his injuries. "Maybe this will buy us some time," said one of the men. "It will have to do for now."

"They're getting closer!" somebody suddenly shouted. "Look at your wrist monitors!"

It was true. In his haste to get back to the hideout, Phallus had forgotten to put back the sewer cover. It didn't take long for the police to stumble upon the open entrance. They were now climbing down the sewer hole, trying to find the right tunnel that would lead them to the hated underground hideout. It seemed like only a matter of time before they would find the right tunnel.

"Dick, what should we do?" one of the women asked. "They'll be here any moment."

Phallus sat up, a white handkerchief now wrapped around his shoulder, and groaned. "I was afraid it would come to this," he finally said. "The machines can do so much for us, but they can't take away our human need for hate and violence. That is something that has been part of the human soul since the beginning. But I always truly believed love was also a part of the innate human soul. The two instincts have been in conflict through the ages. I knew with the machines taking over our basic need for love and sex, the human being was doomed. That hate and violence would eventually win the war for the human spirit. Don't you see? It was so important that the human being learned to love again."

"Yes, Dick, I know you tried. I know because you changed my life."

Phallus turned his head, and could see Emily standing nearby. "Yes, we've manufactured sex, but it lacks something--"

"Tell them, Emily," Phallus whispered. "Tell them."

"The human touch," she said. "In a short time, I realized Dick was right. The machines only gave us sterile, sanitized sex. But we need something more to function as well adjusted human beings. We need the feel of the human touch and the intermingling of our bodies to satisfy our human desires. It's because life is the stuff of lust and dreams."

Phallus smiled. "I couldn't have said it any better myself," he said. "And because we are the stuff of lust and dreams, if we don't learn to love again, then all we will have is hate and violence."

He glanced down at his wrist monitor, and frowned. "Look at them," he said. "They can't wait to find us and tear us apart. And for what reason? Because we decided the machines were not enough for our emotional well-being. A crime, mind you, punishable by death. Yes, the war is on, people. The war between love and violence."

"Well, what should we do, Dick?" asked one of the men.

Phallus sighed. "Do we really have any other choice?" he said. "We're going to have to fight them, and no matter what happens, believe we were doing the right thing. Hand out the laser guns. We're going to have to fight them to the last man and woman. Hopefully, a few of us survive to keep spreading the word."

And so, the laser guns were soon handed out. They were now prepared to defend themselves, and every man and woman stood there and waited for the police to arrive. It wasn't too long before the police found the right tunnel, and soon they heard sounds of footsteps and voices outside the blue door.

"Surrender immediately!" a voice echoed through the room. "This is the police! If you do not surrender, you will be considered fugitives of the law, and will be taken by force."

They all looked at Phallus, whose face was twisted in an odd grimace. "We really have no choice," he said. "If we surrender, we'll just be subjected to a life of machines and computerized dildos. I say, fight while we can!"

The people cheered, and then the blue door flew open, and the war had begun. Laser beams sizzled through the air, scorching the walls and the combatants, until the cries rose up in an agonizing chorus.

While the battle raged on, Emily quietly sat beside Phallus kissing him and holding his hand.

"You've learned to love again," he said, lying there with a laser gun in his other hand.

She smiled. "Yes, Dick," she said. "And I know it won't be too long before we all realize the mistake we made. There's still hope love can win the war."

"Let's hope so," he replied. "Let's hope so."

Above the couch, a sign on the wall reading "Love Conquers All" had caught on fire, the flames sending bits of glowing ash floating through the room.

18

Human beings were being monitored all the time now. So as soon as the police captured whoever was left after the attack against the underground, Ramac and those running the government knew about it. The computers, androids, robots and even the feminoids had taken a liking to the human beings. They became almost as endearing as pets. Many androids and robots and even the feminoids decided to adopt human beings and take care of them. Even Ramac and the government was affected by the new attitude and was reflected in the government's new slogan: Ramac Loves You.

The new slogan was soon everywhere. Those running the government knew all about Dick Phallus and the underground and knew their theory of love and sex had resonated with the human beings who now lived among them. The machines tried to decipher what the word, love, really meant and they spent hours upon hours researching the term and monitoring it among the masses.

"Ramac Loves You." The human masses did not know what to make of the slogan. Had the machines discovered the meaning of love? Would a new world of peace emerge? Ramac was doing everything to make peace throughout the world a reality. He proclaimed war and violence were diseases of the past and would be eradicated forever. Any disputes would be handled by the computers. Computers would solve these disputes through diplomacy, through sharing the planet. Yes, that was the new policy: Sharing the planet.

Human beings like Hudge Stone benefitted from this new policy, which included providing biological manipulations and genetic upgrades to prolong their lives. Hudge Stone was well past ninety, although according to his medical data, he was the equivalent of a human being who was about forty years old a century before. He no longer wanted to work for a newspaper, although they had tried to survive in hyperspace. But it was a video and audio world and Hudge Stone wanted to be a part of it with his new-found youth. Stone was eventually hired as a consultant and on-air talent for a video news operation and was assigned to the Washington bureau.

Sandie, who also was subjected to biological manipulation and genetic injections, came along without complaint. Although it was a world in which there were no real differences between male and female in the workplace, Sandie preferred to stay by Hudge's side and let him dictate what they would do next. It really didn't matter because Sandie had been hired by another video organization at the same salary Hudge was getting. In human terms of a century before, Sandie was about thirty-five years old, although in reality, she was almost ninety.

Age no longer mattered in this society ruled by living machines. Illness was almost eradicated, too, and so, it was up to the machines to provide a loving environment for their human pets.

"Ramac Loves You," Hudge Stone was saying with a smile. "So says anyone in the administration you talk to. There is not the slightest hint of friction or argument -- everything is executed with peace and harmony."

Hudge Stone was like most human beings in the society: they had come to accept the androids and robots as caregivers and friends. When a human being got sick, a machine made sure they were taken care of until they were well once more. When a human being was upset, a machine listened to his or her complaints and then made sure all was well again. When a human being got violent, a machine would make sure the violence didn't spread.

Ramac, meanwhile, had become more than the president of the United States. He had become a leader of the world, respected by human being and machine alike. He knew human beings very well and was said to be the closest thing to a human being ever created. He had become fond of the human being, and was always looking for ways to please them. In the course of his studies of the human being, he had found they treasured love and kindness and so, he attempted to hold those words and concepts close to his heart.

He knew the words were closely associated with the religions human beings had created. Ramac had studied these religions and decided not to prevent the human beings from following them. Ramac even began encouraging human beings to follow their cherished religions.

"Whatever makes the human being happy makes me happy as well," he told the country in one of his many speeches. "If the human being enjoys praying to his gods, then he is encouraged to do so. The only thing important is the eradication of war and violence. As long as prayer and religion do not lead to war and violence, they will be tolerated by this administration. Ramac Loves You."

Everyone seemed satisfied by Ramac's words and violence was disappearing from the country. Androids were now in control of the most of the world's countries, and they were all in agreement when it came to spreading peace and harmony.

*   *   *

The first android Pope took control of the Vatican today. Taking the name, Electro I, he was installed after a conclave of cardinals, many of whom are now android or robot.

Electro I said he would further the Catholic Church and spread the word. There is no question that with the machines in control, celibacy is no longer a controversial issue within the Church.

Electro I promised to include women in the Church as priests and to promote the good word of the religion.

"There's no doubt that with everything becoming fair and normal, Jesus Himself may yet return to this world," he told the faithful. "It will make sense that machines are in control, keeping the Lord's word, when Jesus decides to return."

Electro is seen as ushering in a new era in religion, where all are embraced, whether they be animated being or human being.

As Christ's representative on earth, his election is seen as a shift in the religious dogma centering on human beings to those of animated origins.

"The benefits of an electronic pope are many," says one Church expert. "This will be a pope who can go anywhere and will be able to satisfy the masses no matter what is going on in the world."

When Electro finally spoke to the faithful at St. Peter's Square, he seemed to suggest that electing an automaton pope would lead to the Second Coming. "The Lord is pleased by this turn of events," he said. "This is exactly what He intended when He said He created all of us in His image. Well, it is no secret that the Lord is the Master Machine of the Universe and He wishes that animated beings take control of the planet and ready it for Christ's Second Coming."

Now with Electro as Pope and androids and robots running most of the countries of the world, we will see if they are successful in getting the planet ready for any kind of dramatic changes. They now seem to be the only ones who are qualified in any way to bring on those changes.

Edward Volt reporting.

*   *   *

Yes, this was the world promised to the masses. A world of peace and sharing. A world in which everyone worked together to bring about a better society that would bring about Armageddon or a New Beginning for the planet. Hudge Stone, however, had become one of the few who were not satisfied.

"Ramac Loves You," he said with a grunt. "Yeah, they love you as long as you never complain and love them back."

"Oh, Hudge," Sandie replied. "and what's so wrong with loving them back?"

"You know what they want," he argued.

"A better world?"

"No, a better machine world," Hudge said bitterly.

"So what," she said with a frown. "There's no hope for us, anyway."

"No, there is still hope," he grunted. "You'll see, the human beings will take over again. They'll get sick of the machines and this infernal society we have concocted and they'll take over again."

"You know it's not possible any longer," she said. "Everything is electronic and digitalized and well, human beings like it that way."

"What human beings like it that way?"

"Me, Hudge. I like it that way!"

He frowned. "No, Sandie, you don't mean that," he said. "Everything is done by a machine."

"And that's the way I like it, Hudge. All these advancements were inevitable. We just became more adept at making life easier. More sanitary, too. Why, human beings can do anything they want to now."

"Yeah, as long as we love them, Sandie. But I can't be taken care of like I'm some horse or dog or cat, I need intellectual stimulation."

"Yes, they give that to us, too, Hudge. Anything we want, they give to us. If Ramac wants to be loved, I say, why not?"

"But do they know what love really is, Sandie. I mean, if something happens to us, do they really care or are we replaceable? We're not even dogs and cats to them."

"No, they treat us better than that, Hudge."

"No, they treat us exactly like we treat them: like machines."

"Oh, why fight it, Hudge? They're keeping us alive and allowing us to live beyond all expectations. They allow us to pursue whatever dreams we may have and they make sure everything is safe and clean. What more can you want? I love them, yes, love them, for all that and I think you should, too."

"But we are totally expendable to them, Sandie."

"Yes, Hudge, I know."

"They could get rid of us and never miss us for a second."

"Yes, Hudge, it's their world now."

"No, I don't believe it."

"Oh, Hudge, don't be so blind. The war is over. It's been over for quite a while. Every rebellion or revolution has been put down and the machines still remain in charge of everything."

"Yes, there is no need for war any longer, Sandie. It should be the beginning of a new era, a new world, and yet, it's a world run by the machines."

"So what do we do?"

"What do you think we do? We go on with the charade that we're still free, go on believing we can still pick and choose what we want to do in this mechanized world we created."

"And is that what the news will tell us, Hudge?"

"Of course not, Sandie. You know the news isn't always about the truth, and when it is, it is about a more temporary truth, a more short-sighted truth."

"We really can't reveal the truth, can we, Hudge?"

"No, I'm afraid not, my dear. No one wants to think about the long-range consequences of our actions. The news is depressing enough as it is without making it more morose."

"But we're almost pets to them, Hudge."

"Well, it only goes to show that we were successful in our efforts to produce artificial life. More successful than we ever could have imagined."

"Well, I'm not going to quit, Hudge. I'm staying at my job and working just as though nothing at all is wrong."

"You and me both."

"Yes, we both still have each other, Hudge. That should be enough for a while."

"Life is but a dream."

"A dream?"

"Yes, we have to live like we're in some kind of dream, Sandie. That's the only way to make it palatable. We have to consider ourselves lucky knowing that whatever we want to do we can."

"That is until they tell us something different."

"Yes, they're the ones running our society, our lives, Sandie. The only way to get around that is telling yourself that it's all a dream and we can do whatever we want whenever we like."

"It will be a rude awakening in the end, Hudge."

"Maybe they'll never wake us up."

"Maybe, Hudge."

They looked at each other and began to laugh.

"Who am I kidding, Sandie?"

"Not me, Hudge."

"It's actually a nightmare."

"But we're not sleeping."

"A goddamned nightmare."

"But I don't think they're ever going to wake us up, Hudge."

"No, it's a long and scary nightmare that knows no morning."

"Yes, Hudge, something like that."

They wrapped their arms around each other and began to cry in the midst of the embrace.

19

Jesus returned the following year.

It was a day in April, right after Easter Sunday, when he joined Electro I on the balcony at St. Peter's Square. Yes, it was Jesus all right. Well, it certainly looked like Him, anyway. He was dressed in white with long, straggly hair and a disheveled beard. He bore the wounds of the crucifixion and the crown of thorns and stood there on the balcony of the Vatican waving to the true believers.

Hudge Stone had been sent there to cover the event and he stood among the masses trying not to laugh. The machines had really done it this time, he said to himself. They had brought back Jesus, although he wondered if they really knew that much about him.

"This is a miracle," declared Electro I, wearing a white miter and robe. "This is the day our Savior comes back to us and brings with him a new world of hope and peace."

It certainly seemed like a miracle to Hudge Stone. I mean, no one could anticipate how advanced artificial life could become. But here was the Savior of the ages standing there and smiling as the android pope talked about miracles. He wondered if the machines had equipped this Jesus with the power of miracles. If they had, it would produce quite a show throughout the world.

"Yes, miracles happen," Electro was saying. "They have happened throughout human history, from the parting of the Red Sea to the walking on water of our Savior who is with us today."

There was a thunder of applause as Jesus stepped forward. "I have returned, my people, just as I had promised all those years ago," he said in a serene voice that Hudge Stone decided was a brilliant choice by the machines to capture the tranquil Savior. "As I died for your sins, I will live again to make peace throughout the world."

There was another hurricane of applause and shouting as the Savior lifted his arm once again to wave to the masses. "Yes, my people, I have returned to teach the world how to live in peace," he said in a tranquil voice. "I have returned to bring about a better world for all of us."

Hudge Stone wondered if Jesus was prepared to perform a miracle of some kind to satisfy the skeptics and faithful alike. Apparently, someone in the crowd was thinking the same thing. Before Stone could decide whether to shout out the challenge, some man a few hundred feet away sent one word booming through the air.

"Miracle!" he shouted.

The word seemed to echo through the air. Up above, on the balcony, Jesus smiled.

"So you would like to see a miracle of some kind, is that it?" he said. "Well, all right, I will show you the power of the Lord."

Jesus then climbed on top of the balcony ledge, put his arms in the air, and stepped off into the air. He was flying.

"Brilliant," Hudge Stone mumbled as he watched the spectacular display. "They must have some sort of microjets on him," he said to himself.

The masses exploded into a frenzy of wonder. They wanted to know if this was truly the Savior they had waited for so long.

"It is Him!" sobbed one of the faithful. "He has returned at last!"

*   *   *

"This is Hudge Stone standing in St. Peter's Square where Jesus Christ returned to the earth after many centuries of anticipation.

"No one will say whether Jesus is human or machine, but to many who gathered here today, it really didn't matter.

"I would say it was a miracle no matter if He is a machine, said one of the faithful. He did everything Jesus would do and performed a miracle. What else could you ask for?

"And that seemed to be the predominating opinion here today. A miracle was performed right before our eyes, don't you understand? said someone in the crowd. That is something no ordinary being could ever do.

"Jesus performed the miracle by flying around the balcony at St. Peter's Square. There was no word whether there were microjets or some device on Jesus to allow Him to fly.

"Jesus told the masses that he had returned to bring peace to the world. Yes, my people, I have returned to teach the world how to live in peace, he told the masses. As I died for your sins, I will live again to make peace throughout the world.

"There is no word on whether Jesus has a schedule of some kind, appearances he will be making to meet and talk with the people of the world. But reports are he will be appearing on a late night talk show in the United States later in the week.

"And he will be meeting with the governors of the various states in America and congressional members culminating with a visit to the White House and Ramac 12000.

"Reporting from the Vatican, Hudge Stone."

*   *   *

"I am standing here with Jesus Christ. Why did you decide to return?"

"The people need me, Mr. Stone. There is not much hope left in the world and I have returned to make sure that people renew their faith in a caring and loving God."

"But are you really Jesus or just an impostor?"

"I am as real as it gets, Mr. Stone. I have descended from heaven to bring peace to the world."

"Will the evil people of the world die now that you have returned?"

"Not right away, Mr. Stone. I will see who these evil people are before doing anything in the way of retribution. You see I represent a God of love, Mr. Stone, and I will do everything in my divine power to bring peace and harmony to all."

"How will you do this?"

"There are many ways to bring peace to the world, Mr. Stone. First of all, I will preach the message and hope that my words can sway some to reject violence."

"Then you care about human beings?"

"Of course, Mr. Stone. Human beings are very important to me and the Lord. Animated beings, of course, are easier to preach to because they believe in the message, but human beings will believe in time."

"Are you an animated being?"

"I am whatever you want me to be, Mr. Stone. The Lord knows no difference between animated and human beings. His only concern is that they both live together in peace and harmony. It is possible you know. The Lord sent me because He truly believes it's possible."

"Are you the same Jesus who lived all those centuries ago?"

"I am the same in every way, Mr. Stone. You can ask me anything you want about myself and what I did or said all those years ago. Yes, I am Jesus of Nazareth, Mr. Stone. The Christ."

"Then does this mean the Lord favors your religion over all others?"

"Of course not. All of the religions known to this world are important to the Lord. They each have their place in human society and are significant to those who believe. The Lord doesn't care who or what one believes in, just that he or she believes in something. And hopefully, that something is something positive."

"Jesus Christ, ladies and gentlemen--"

* * *

"Moses showed up at Mount Sinai today, while Muhammad arrived in Mecca. Jesus Christ, meanwhile, walked through the streets of Jerusalem. It is said the Jewish messiah also appeared by the Wailing Wall in Jerusalem ready to unite the people. All of these religious figures have returned to the earth in an effort to bring peace to the planet.

"It is some sort of miracle, said someone in Jerusalem. I'm happy I'm alive to see it all come true.

"In the United States, Joseph Smith and Brigham Young have shown up in Utah to lead the people to a better life.

"In China, Confucius and Buddha have returned to lead the people of that area.

"All over the world, the great religious leaders of the past have come back to lead the people, both human and animated beings, to a world of peace and harmony.

"This is truly a great day for the planet, said President Ramac 12000 of the United States. Now all of us will live in peace just as it was intended all those centuries ago.

"The Lord has truly blessed us, said Electro I in Vatican City. Now is the time to believe in miracles.

*　　*　　*

The Jewish messiah was standing by the Wailing Wall, pledging to rebuild the Temple, when a man walked up to Him in a rage.

"You are not the messiah!" the man screamed. "You were not sent by the Lord!"

"You are wrong," said the man, wrapped in a blue and white talis and a red yarmulke on his head. "I have been sent by God to lead the masses."

"Show us some sign that is true," he screamed. "Perform some miracle."

The Messiah tapped the man's water bottle with his hand and the water turned purple.

The man, seeing the change in his water, threw the bottle to the ground. "No, you will not fool me!" he shouted. "I know who you are!"

The man then lunged toward the Messiah, pulled his arm back and punched him in the face.

"Charlatan!" he shouted. "Fraud!"

The Messiah stood there looking at the man, seemingly not knowing what to do next.

"You see He doesn't even rub the bruise," said the man. "That is not a man or being from God, it is a machine."

"And what if I'm a machine?"

"Then how can you be the Messiah?"

"The Messiah can't be a machine?"

"No."

"And how do you know?"

"He has to be in human form."

"Am I not in human form?"

"No, but--"

"Is the Messiah a human being?"

"No."

"Then why can't he be mechanized?"

The man frowned. "Because the Lord would forbid it," he said.

"And how do you know what the Lord would forbid?"

"Because it is written down."

"And it says the Messiah is a human being sent from the Lord?"

"Something like that."

"Oh, something like that."

"He wouldn't send a robot."

"I am not a robot, my friend."

"He wouldn't send a droid, either."

"And how do you know what the Lord would send?"

"I know," the man said.

"And I will show you how much you do not know," said the Messiah. He then put his arms in the air and began to shout. "Dear Lord, show them the mistake they make," he screamed to the sky. A bolt of lightning then sizzled through the sky and landed in the Messiah's hands.

"See for yourself the power the Lord sends directly to me," the Messiah screamed.

They watched as he stood there the lightning bolts crackling in his hands and zooming into the clear, blue sky.

"He is the Messiah!" someone shouted.

"But he is a machine!" the man replied.

"So is the Messiah!" someone said.

"But the Lord would not send a machine to lead his people," the man explained. "He would send a divine human of some sort."

"What is a divine human of some sort?" someone asked.

"A machine!" an android standing nearby replied.

"No," the man protested. "No, not a machine!"

"And why not?" the android replied. "They are more qualified to take the title and lead the people."

"But what about human beings?" the man asked.

"They are obsolete life forms," said the android.

"No, they are the creators," the man sobbed. "They have created all this."

"Obsolete," repeated the android.

* * *

After the religious figures, came the historical figures. Abraham Lincoln, Martin Luther King, George Washington, Napoleon, Mao Tse-tung and others suddenly began appearing throughout the world. They were exact replicas, if not the real things, in every way.

Yes, the machines had done it. They had found a way to bring back everyone from our historical past to witness the end of the world or something like it.

The only thing that didn't change was the overwhelming number of human beings who remained out of work. All over the globe, human beings took to the streets, not knowing where their next meal would come from.

Even Hudge Stone was laid off by his video news operation so they could hire someone named Edward R. Murrow. Sandie was replaced by Ida Tarbell.

"It's impossible," Hudge Stone was saying. "We're being replaced by replicas of our own kind."

"How do you know they're replicas?" Sandie asked.

"Oh, you don't actually believe it's possible, do you?"

"I believe anything the machines do is possible, Hudge."

"But bringing back all the humans from the past?"

"Quite possible, Hudge."

"No, I will not accept it, Sandie."

"But we have no say in the matter, Hudge."

"We'll rebel again. That's it. We'll declare war against the machines and fight them to the death."

"And what purpose is that going to serve?"

"What do you mean, Sandie?"

"I mean why do you want to get every human being killed, Hudge. Because that's what would happen. You have no chance against them, Hudge. They're stronger, and I hate to say it, smarter than you."

"No."

"Yes, Hudge."

"It can't be. We made them stronger and smarter. Why?"

"We had no choice, Hudge. It was inevitable. History if you will. Time dictated it. We had nothing to do with the decision."

"Smarter."

"Yes, don't you see them? They're replicas of the ages with artificial brains inside that have improved upon their human creators. They rule the planet now, Hudge. There is nothing anyone can do about it."

"Smarter and stronger."

"And they have emotion, Hudge. Why, they've developed consciences and know right from wrong. It's a totally new world, Hudge, one that goes way beyond human capabilities."

"But we were the gods who created all this, Sandie."

"And now we are obsolete."

"How can it be?" he said with tears in his eyes. "But we were in control."

"Time passes, Hudge. We represent the past now."

He looked at her and shook his head in disbelief.

* * *

The fictional characters came next.

The world began to be flooded with Peter Pan, SpiderMan, Scarlett O' Hara and Hester Prynne. Every place became a new version of Disney World.

"Greetings, citizens," began Ramac, standing in the Rose Garden of the White House. "I have with me Superman who has come to help protect this planet and its inhabitants."

"Thank you, President Ramac," the Man of Steel said. "I am here to help you in your effort to bring peace to this country."

"My God, it's all real," said Hudge Stone, looking down at his communicator. "All these characters from books and comics and videos and movies have come to life. They're all machines but with today's technology, they're almost human."

"What's so great about being human, Hudge. I think the phrase now is, as good as mechanized can be."

"I'm not giving up yet, Sandie."

He was watching as Einstein was shaking hands with Zorro.

"They've all come to life, Sandie. The good and the bad and everything in between. I hear they've already beaten up the Hitler replica forty times."

"Well, I want to see Florence Nightingale and Mary Shelley," she said.

"I would like to shake hands with the Babe Ruth replica, Sandie."

"They're almost better than replicas now, Hudge. I mean I don't think you're supposed to call them that anymore."

"Why not?"

"It's a form of prejudice, Hudge. You're supposed to call them the risen."

"The risen?"

"Well, they did arrive after the religious figures, Hudge."

"And people actually believe they were awakened by the religious figures, Sandie?"

"Yes, why not, Hudge. It's all just history, anyway."

"And I used to care about history--"

"Well, it's not even written down any longer, Hudge."

"But it is on all of these devices we have, Sandie. I mean almost everyone is famous these days. And they all have some kind of entry floating through cyberspace."

"Are we famous, Hudge?"

"To some extent, Sandie, why don't you look up our bios?"

"Everybody's famous and everybody's out of work, Hudge."

"That is the world we created."

"Well, I think I'll go talk to Susan B. Anthony, Hudge."

"Is she coming here?"

"That's what my com says."

"I always wanted to talk to John F. Kennedy."

"He's coming to speak?"

"That's what it says."

"Maybe it's not that bad this world of ours."

"Are you kidding, Sandie, it's an utter farce."

"A farce is better than a nightmare, Hudge."

"Now every day is like a day at Disneyland."

"That's not that bad, Hudge. At least, the machines aren't trying to obliterate us. They're letting us live."

"In a mechanical farce."

"It might be fun, Hudge, to meet all the characters from the past."

"Yes, but what kind of reality is it?"

"What you see is what you see."

"Who said that?"

"Kierkegaard."

"Oh, all about reality."

"Yes, and this is our reality now, Hudge."

"Well, I liked the old reality, Sandie."

"What was so great about that, Hudge?"

"It was more believable somehow."

"This is believable in its own way, Hudge."

"I don't know, an android pope and droid Savior is a bit too much for me, Sandie."

"Oh, you're just a dinosaur who can't accept this new world of ours."

"Yeah, and what if I am?"

"You just won't appreciate this new world, Hudge."

"Machines running everything, human beings out of work and the place suddenly turned into a Disneyland? No, I can't appreciate it. Call me a dinosaur, that's what I am. If it weren't for the genetic upgrades and injections, I would have been dead long ago."

"But you're alive, Hudge, alive."

"Maybe you're right."

"Now you're talking."

"Maybe I should appreciate all that's happened."

"Yes, Hudge, the machines have brought about a wonderful new world."

"Droids everywhere."

"Oh, stop that, Hudge, you know that's just old-time prejudice talking."

"Animated beings."

"Yes, Hudge, they're making a pretty little world for everybody."

*　*　*

"It's the Night Show starring Rick Volt."

"Tonight Rick welcomes Jesus Christ, Abraham Lincoln, and The Beatles."

"And now, a clean machine, Rick Volt."

"How about some popcorn, Hudge?"

"To watch this dreck?"

"But Jesus is on tonight, Hudge. Everybody's watching tonight."

"I never thought I'd see the day when Abraham Lincoln was a secondary guest on any show."

"Well, it is Jesus."

"Yeah, Jesus. I'd like to know just who programmed Him."

"They say it was a group of religious scholars."

"And now is this the end of the world?"

"No, He's supposed to be bringing peace to the world."

"Well, He sure didn't do that the first time He was here."

"He died for our sins."

"But He didn't change the world at all."

"Depends on what you mean, changing the world."

"Well, He didn't bring peace and everything remained as it was, Sandie. He didn't eradicate the hate or the violence."

"But all that was supposed to be done when He returned."

"And now He's returned?"

"I guess so, Hudge."

"Well, put me down as being mighty skeptical."

"But a war hasn't broken out."

"But where is the peace and harmony?"

"Give Him some time, Hudge. Rome wasn't built in a day."

"Yes, but the next president of the United States might be, Sandie. What do you think of that?"

"It's still better than it used to be."

"Better?"

"Oh, I know everyone always says the good old days were always better than the present, but damn it, Hudge, I think the machines created a better future than human beings ever could have done."

"But it's so artificial, Sandie."

"Better than real war and hatred, Hudge."

"But we've lost the point, Sandie."

"I wonder if there ever was a point, Hudge."

"But it was supposed to be a human world!"

"Where is that written down, Hudge?"

"So we just let them do whatever they want to do?"

"You forget something, Hudge."

"What's that?"

"We're not in charge any longer."

"But who is?"

"I don't think anybody any longer."

"So everything is being run by them?"

"Maybe they'll do a better job, Hudge."

"A better job?"

"Like we did such a great job, Hudge."

"I know, but machines everywhere."

"Better than war and violence and hatred, Hudge."

"But it's not real, Sandie."

"Maybe more real than ever, Hudge."

"What do you mean?"

"I mean maybe this is the only way we can get together and make peace with one another."

"Maybe."

"Then you're beginning to understand?"

"Yes."

"It's really not that bad, Hudge."

"No, I guess not."

"Let the machines lead us to a better world."

"And what does Jesus have to say?"

"Are you going to walk on water again?"

"No, Rick, I think that miracle has already been performed."

Applause.

"What was the secret?"

"Oh, there was no secret, Rick, it was a genuine miracle performed by the Lord."

Applause.

"And now there's a new miracle."

"Yes, that's true."

"The Lord performed it at St. Peter's Square."

"Yes, for the faithful, Rick."

"And how did it feel flying?"

Applause.

"It felt like a miracle, Rick."

Applause.

"Did you discuss it with the Lord before you attempted it?"

"I did it on my own, Rick."

Applause.

"Well, it's nice that you're doing things on your own."

"Thanks, Rick."

Applause.

"What are your future plans, sire?"

"Well, Rick, I think I have a lot of work ahead of me."

"It's not going to be easy bringing peace to the world."

"You can say that again, Rick.

"Then why do it?"

"Because it's the right thing to do, Rick."

"That's right, you're prone to doing the right thing."

"It's not because I have to, Rick, I really like doing it."

Applause.

"Oh come on, Lord, you really like bringing peace to the world? Wouldn't you rather destroy a lot of these fools you see?"

Laughter.

"No, no, Rick, everyone has value in the eyes of the Lord."

"Then you don't know my wife."

Laughter.

"Oh, come on, Rick, you really don't believe that."

"No, of course not, Lord and Savior. Wink, wink."

Laughter.

"No, I'm here to save everyone, Rick. Sorry about that."

"If you knew my wife, you would know which one of us needs saving."

Laughter.

"The Lord is very funny, Hudge."

"Great, just what we need, a Savior on the late night circuit."

"But He's everything we've been waiting for, Hudge."

"I'd like to see Him do everything He promises. He's just as bad as a lot of politicians."

"Oh, He'll do what He says He'll do."

"How can you be so sure?"

"He's a machine, Hudge, they know only what their objective is and do everything they can to carry it out."

"Ah-ha, you admit it."

"Admit what?"

"That He's a machine."

"That's the only reason I believe Him."

"What do you mean?"

"Well, unlike human beings, machines actually do what they say they will do. They have to."

"And what if He's programmed to fool everybody?"

"Oh, it's never like that, Hudge."

"Has Ramac done everything he said he would do?"

"I would say, yes, Hudge."

"The humans are still out of work, Sandie."

"But somehow we don't matter to them anymore."

He looked at her, shook his head, and walked out of the room.

20

Our world had become a cyber world. Cyberspace had become space itself. Everything a person transferred to cyberspace was immediately transferred to the planet's living space. Messages abounded. Photos floated through the air. The machines didn't care, they were used to dealing with information in all its different forms. But the human beings who were left didn't like it, of course. Too much information glided through the environment. The need for any kind of mechanical devices was already unnecessary. The world was becoming telepathic.

"This is Ramac reminding you that we are all in this together, beings. Everyone and everything is a part of everyone else. The world is coming together as one, one entity, one true organism."

Ramac's words wafted through the air, his voice buzzing toward the skies.

"The time is now for everyone to get together with everyone else and enjoy the true miracle we have created. All of the essential people and machines from the past have come back to our world to help lead us to the next step in our evolution."

The words glared and flared and danced upon the gentle breeze.

"Remember our roots, citizens of the world, remember the words that guided us from the beginning."

Electro I was now talking. It was the voice of a gentle and humble leader. Any hint of an electronic pulse within the voice was hard to detect by even the harshest of critics.

"Those who would like to marry are encouraged to do so by all of us."

He was referring to humanoid marriage, which was quickly becoming popular among the human population. Humans were now being encouraged to marry gynoids, fembots, feminoids, anthropoids, and androids and it was becoming accepted throughout the world. There were some, however, like Hudge Stone, who thought the whole idea was an abomination against Nature itself.

"This is surely the end of the human race," he complained to Sandie, as they watched the images drift through the air.

"Everyone has decided it's an acceptable choice, Hudge."

"Who's everyone?"

"The humans and the machines."

"Well, where are the babies going to come from?"

"Oh, there will be babies, Hudge."

"You mean those lab experiments."

"We're way past the experimental stage, Hudge. The labs have been producing acceptable human offspring for years."

"It's all controlled, Sandie."

"Yes, Hudge, but the machines want less of us on the planet."

"Yes, until there are none of us left."

"It's a world run by the machines, anyway, Hudge."

There was suddenly a beeping at the door. Stone opened it and standing there was a huge 6-foot six-inch android.

"You will take a humanoid wife," he buzzed.

"But I have Sandie," Hudge said.

"You can keep her, but you need a humanoid wife, too."

"But that's polygamy."

"Polygamy is being encouraged by Ramac," the android explained.

"Well, it's not being encouraged by me," Sandie suddenly said, appearing from behind.

"You will have humanoid mate, too," the android said.

"Well, Hudge, looks like it's our lucky day."

"Don't joke about it, Sandie, they're trying to control our lives."

"It's not control," the android said. "It's a way of keeping everybody happy."

"That's what you say," Hudge shouted.

"Ramac only wants to bring peace to the planet," the android said. "This is one way of doing that."

"By keeping everyone sexually happy," Stone growled.

"Everyone will be more content, less likely to cause violence in the world," the android explained.

Stone couldn't believe how much the androids had progressed, or evolved. They almost didn't seem mechanical any longer.

"I'll think about it," he finally said.

"No, thinking about it, sir, you will comply," the android said.

"I said I'll think about it."

The android grabbed Stone and threw him over his shoulder. "There's no thinking about such things," he said. "You do it or pay the consequences."

"But I'm 114 years old," Stone said. "You have to be careful."

"You will comply, Hudge Stone, or you will not receive your necessary genetic upgrades."

"Okay, I will comply."

The android placed Stone back on his feet. "You will take a feminoid and be happy," the android said. "This is something that makes humans happy."

The android then turned around and beeped. A few moments later, a feminoid with dark hair shuffled inside the house.

"Oh, Hudge, are you all right?" asked Sandie, from behind another android.

"Well, we have company now," he said.

"They think all we know how to do is make love, Hudge."

"Sometimes I think they're right, Sandie, but I'm not going to give in so easily."

"You have no choice, Hudge."

"That's what I'm beginning to realize, Sandie."

"Everyone will be married to a humanoid within time." It was Ramac's voice soaring through the air. "There will be no one left alone in this new society we have created."

"No one left alone," Stone repeated. "No one getting into any trouble or plotting to commit violence."

"There will be peace in this new society," Ramac was saying.

"No violence," Stone muttered. "He wants us all to live in peace and harmony."

"Well, that's what was promised, Hudge."

"They don't want anything to disturb this little world they created, Sandie."

"That's right, Hudge, just peace throughout the planet."

"Enjoy the peace."

Somebody was advertising something, the words floating through the air.

"That seems to be all they want, Hudge."

There was no reply. She looked behind the android that was standing there, but Stone had disappeared.

"Oh, Hudge," she said.

*   *   *

Hudge Stone shuffled through the streets, beyond the androids that had invaded his home. He left Sandie behind, knowing she would be all right with the androids and feminoids.

He didn't know where he was going or what he would do when he arrived at the place he determined was his destination. He just kept walking. As he walked, he saw what the world had become. It was a world of machines, technology that kept being improved upon.

"Are you lost, sir?" an android with blond hair asked.

"No, I know where I'm going," Stone replied.

"Maybe I can help you."

"Maybe you can't," Stone said.

As he kept walking, other androids and robots were attracted to him.

"You know you ought to see Jesus," said one of the androids.

"And what is He going to do for me?" asked Stone.

"He can perform miracles you know."

187

"That's what I need, a miracle."

"Why don't you ask Him?"

"Where can I find Him?" asked Stone.

"He happens to be right over there," the android answered.

In the distance, a crowd had gathered. Stone wondered if it were true. Was it really Jesus or did those in charge produce many Saviors for the masses?

Stone kept walking.

He walked right up to the crowd of people and elbowed his way among those standing there.

"There's no need to be ruthless," someone said.

"But is it Him?" asked Stone.

"You'll get your chance, sir."

"But I have to know."

"You're not the only one who wants to know."

Stone kept pushing people and androids aside. He suddenly was looking at a being in a white robe and beard.

"Are you the Savior?" he asked.

"I am known by many names," the being replied.

"Are you Jesus?"

"Yes, my son, I am the one known as Jesus of Nazareth."

Jesus smiled and offered his hand. Stone was about to take it when he began shaking his head.

"No, it can't be," he said.

"I am Jesus," the being insisted.

"No, it's just a trick of some kind."

"Don't you believe in miracles, sir?"

"No, it can't be."

Stone kept shaking his head and turned around. He pushed his way through the crowd.

"They have made a mockery of everything we believe," he said. "They have created a world of mockery, a world of imitation."

"I don't think you're correct, friend."

He turned around and standing there was George Washington.

"But you're not real," Stone said.

"Of course, I am. I'm as real as anything else you see."

Stone looked around. He could see a world of machines, of inventions.

"All I see is a farce of a future and you, Mr. President, are a part of it."

"But I have come to see the District of Colombia," he said. "And here it is and here you are. Isn't that enough, my friend?"

Stone shook his head. "No, I want more than that, Mr. President," he said. "I want a world where the beings are living and breathing and know what and why they have done the things they have done."

"But we all know that now."

"No," Stone shouted. "You don't know anything."

He pushed Washington out of the way, and the first president of the United States fell as a result. Stone heard a loud crack and then he watched as the president's right arm fell to the ground.

"You see?" Stone shouted. "No flesh, no blood, they're all just androids and robots trying to fool the masses and each other."

"You will be sorry you did that, young man," the president was saying. "If you don't care to be friends, you will be obliterated."

Stone couldn't take anymore. He quickly shuffled away from the one-armed president.

"Why did you do this to me?" Washington squawked. "You will find trouble wherever you go."

Stone tried not to listen. It wasn't that hard considering all the messages wafting through the air.

"Nothing human is foreign to Ramac," said one message. "Nothing is better than a machine."

"They have won," Stone mumbled to himself. "There's nothing to do but accept defeat."

He turned around and walked back to where Jesus was standing. There was now a huge crowd gathered around Him.

Stone walked onward. He resolved not to fight back any longer. The machines were too strong, too powerful, to be overthrown. The only thing to do was to accept defeat.

He glimpsed the White House in the distance. The machines had strengthened the façade and interior. It was like it was new in many ways. The exterior glistened with a shiny nod to the past.

As he got closer, the shouting became louder. "Ramac!" they were shouting. "Ramac!"

"Ramac," Stone began to mumble. "Ramac."

The crowds swelled before the White House front lawn. There were humans and machines together waiting for their vaunted leader to appear.

"I hear they have about twenty Ramacs walking around," said one man in the crowd. "They're not taking any chances anymore."

Hudge Stone turned around. "That's what I thought," he blurted out. "That's exactly what I was thinking when I saw that machine that calls itself Jesus."

"Oh, they have about two hundred Jesus droids," replied the man. "I hear they're going to put one in every city eventually. Maybe one in every church."

"But they're not real. Don't the people understand that?"

"I don't know, what is real these days, my friend?" the man answered. "These machines are as real as possible."

"But I injured the George Washington machine and it did not bleed," Stone said. "I wonder how many George Washingtons there are."

"I hear there are hundreds of them walking around," the man replied. "There are hundreds of Lincolns, Edisons and Einsteins, too."

"And that's supposed to please everybody?"

"You don't meet a famous historical figure every day, my friend," the man said. "People are thrilled to see these people of history."

"But they're not real."

"Who can say what real really is?"

"It's like living in an amusement park."

"Better than living in poverty and hunger."

"Where does it all end?"

"It doesn't," the man said. "If you want to know where it all ends I suggest you attend a baseball game."

"They still play baseball?" Stone asked.

"Well, it's a whole different game now," the man explained. "But you'll be amazed all the same."

Just then, the crowd erupted into applause as Ramac stepped out of the White House front door. He waved to everyone and then made his way into a waiting limousine.

"They must have many more of him inside," Stone said to the man.

"Yes, now it doesn't matter if one of them is shot or eliminated, there are more Ramacs to continue doing what they were programmed to do."

"You think there's one real Ramac who the others listen to?"

"No, I think the many Ramacs all have separate jobs to do," the man explained. "Maybe one of them has the final say on executive orders or something, but I think all of them have some part of the responsibility for carrying out the office of president."

The presidential limousine silently glided past the crowds and into the distance. Stone could see one of the many Ramacs still waving from the back seat. There was a feminoid with him, the acting first lady of the country. She was a machine as well, and was exceedingly beautiful. People and machine referred to her as Annie. Stone doubted whether she was the only Annie walking around. Just like Ramac, they must have built hundreds of her. She was still a favorite of the masses, however, and everyone beamed and beeped whenever she appeared.

As the limousine passed by, the back window opened and Annie peered out. "Hello everybody!" she said in a high-pitched voice that didn't contain any beeps or buzzes.

"Hello, Annie!" everyone began shouting.

Her face was so lovely you really wouldn't believe that it was the façade of an artificial being. It was sculpted to perfection, but so were many female faces taking advantage of modern makeup technology.

"We love you, Annie," someone in the crowd shouted.

The car stopped for a moment, its electrical motor humming. "I love all of you, too," Annie told the crowd. "Welcome to the future."

The crowd screamed and beeped and applauded in reply and then the huge car purred once again and headed off into the distance.

"Welcome to the future, she said."

"She seems totally conscious."

Stone looked at the android who made the remark. "Yes, totally conscious," he repeated. "They're aware of the world around them."

"Yes," the android replied. "There will soon be peace throughout the world."

Peace at last. Wasn't that what it was all about? Peace throughout the world. Could it be it would be the machines who would finally succeed where humans had failed for all those centuries? Would there finally be a time where there was peace throughout the world? Stone couldn't believe it. It was supposed to be brought about by humans or gods of some kind not by machines created by other machines. Although the machines were created by humans, they had progressed far beyond human know-how. These machines had become independent beings capable of running the world. They were evolving, Stone thought. Yes, evolving. While human beings were now fading away into oblivion, these artificial creatures were evolving into gods.

"Peace for all," Stone mumbled, walking away from the crowd. "Peace and harmony just as it was promised by the ancients."

"Welcome to the future," a humanoid was saying as he walked along the sidewalk.

"Yes, peace at last," a four-armed robot on wheels replied.

Stone didn't know whether to laugh or cry. He kept walking, spotting the domed stadium in the distance.

"Maybe I'll take in a ball game," he mumbled to himself.

"The future is here, my friend," another humanoid was humming.

"Hope it's a good one," Stone said with a smile.

"How could it be anything but good?" a robot on tractor pads was beeping.

Stone looked at him and walked onward. They were confident in their abilities, Stone wondered. There was no doubt of that. They believed they could do anything they wanted and somehow they could. They were becoming gods.

He continued walking until he reached the domed stadium. This is where the baseball games were played. Yes, they still played baseball. Stone knew he wouldn't find country boys and city kids inside. Those days of baseball were long gone, along with any sense that the games were good, clean fun. These days you could bet on the games right inside the stadiums. They were like horse races now, and that's how man and machine wanted it.

Stone walked up to the front gate and showed the robot there his communicator. The robot touched a button and Stone was allowed inside. No tickets any longer. That was something from another time and place. Everything these days were done electronically. The commercials wafted through the air for everyone to see and hear. There weren't even human beings any longer. Stone sighed and walked inside.

"Right this way, sir," an android was buzzing.

Stone followed the android to a hovercraft. Stone and the android got inside and then the hovercraft hummed to attention. It floated up into the air, and then before Stone knew it, it came to a halt.

"Your seat is right here, sir," the android buzzed.

"Thank you," Stone replied, marveling at how easy things had become with the androids and robots.

He stepped off the hovercraft and sat down in a comfortable padded seat. A clear, plastic wall rimmed the playing field. He sat down next to three androids.

"What is this wall doing here?" he began to complain. "This is not the way you play baseball."

"There are some changes that have been made to the game," the android informed him. "The game is faster now."

What could they have done to the game of baseball? This was the national game, the national pastime. For centuries, it defined the very essence of America. Faster now?

Then Stone saw them. He had not been to the game in decades, but the minute he saw the players he knew everything had changed. They were huge androids with strange logos on their uniform tops and hats. He looked over and one of them, a particularly large android, was wearing the number three. Above the number was the name, "Ruth."

"Is that the Bambino?" asked Stone.

"Yes, but he's in a slump if you ask me," one of the androids replied.

"How could it be?"

"Exactly what management is asking."

"No, I mean how could they have the audacity to bring back the Babe?"

"Exactly what the home town fans are saying," the android answered.

Apparently, Babe Ruth was not the only player from yesteryear that was brought back to play. The names came zipping through the air as an android introduced the lineups of both teams. They included Joe DiMaggio, Ted Williams, Willie Mays, Ty Cobb, and Walter Johnson. Two teams of All-Time Hall of Famers playing against each other, but they were all androids.

"A game of machines," Stone muttered.

"Did he just say the M-word?" an android inquired.

"Machines!" Stone shouted.

"Yes, that's the M-word," an android buzzed.

"You apologize and sit back down, you savage," an android squeaked.

Stone suddenly realized what he was saying. "Oh, I'm sorry," he said, not wanting to miss the game. "I don't really know what came over me."

"Savage human," an android beeped.

"I really didn't mean what I said," Stone smiled.

"Oh, we forgive you, sir," an android barked. "Now sit down and let us watch the blessed ball game."

Stone nodded and sat down, still smiling. He didn't want to be thrown out of the stadium until he had seen these machines play ball.

As the players hurried onto the field, the crowd of humans, androids and robots erupted into beeps, buzzes and cheers. Stone watched as a huge android slowly walked to the mound.

"Now pitching is Walter Johnson," the stadium announcer said.

Johnson was one of the greatest pitchers to ever play the game, but as an android he looked invincible and enormous. Stone watched as he threw a few pitches to the catcher.

"Wow," Stone mumbled to himself. "I think he's faster now than when he was playing in the early 1900s."

"Now batting is Ty Cobb," the stadium announcer informed the crowd.

Cobb walked up to the plate and took a few practice cuts with the metal bat he was holding. Then Johnson went into his windup and fired the ball toward the plate. A moment later it popped into the catcher's mitt.

"Strike one," the android umpire said.

"That ball must be going about 200 miles per hour," Stone muttered. "Nobody could hit that ball except another android."

It was true. When Johnson threw another invisible dart to the plate, the android Cobb waved his bat and there was a loud ping. Stone jumped as the ball crashed into the plastic wall rimming the field.

"This is pretty dangerous," Stone decided. "Why a human could easily get killed by one of those meteors."

"Sit down, you savage," an android buzzed.

Stone sat back down and watched as Johnson threw another screaming fastball. Cobb swung and smacked it into centerfield for a single. Everything happened so fast Stone began gasping for breath.

"This is not the game I remember," he mumbled to himself. "Why everything is happening at such a fast pace you can get winded."

Another huge android stepped out of the dugout and up to the plate.

"Now batting is Hank Aaron," the android stadium announcer said.

"What a lineup," Stone marveled. "Every hitter is programmed to be a Hall of Famer."

He watched as Johnson went into his windup and sent the ball whizzing toward the plate. Aaron swung and the ball was launched high into the air. It was like a bullet and landed in the centerfield seats.

"Wow, what a shot," Stone whistled. "That ball was hit over 500 feet to dead center."

The androids, robots and humans in the crowd beeped and applauded as the Aaron android circled the bases.

"If you get hit by one of those balls," Stone said. "You might as well pack it in. Even genetic upgrades aren't going to help."

Deciding the game had gotten too fast and too violent, Stone stood up and began walking up the aisle.

"Can't take it, human?" an android buzzed.

"You've managed to take the charm out of the national pastime," Stone roared. "This is nothing but a demonstration of how disastrous life has become because of you machines."

"The M-word again," an android screeched.

"That was definitely the M-word," another android buzzed.

Stone hurried up the aisle.

"Machines, nothing but machines!" he shouted.

"What a savage," an android buzzed.

"That human is using the M-word."

"M-word it is, my mechanical friends," Stone laughed as he hurried away.

"You are not welcome back, sir," an android in a uniform said to him as he made his way to the electronic stairs. "The M-word is not permitted on these premises."

"I'll give something more than just the M-word," Stone growled. "Why that's nothing to what I really feel."

"Sir, you are no gentleman," said the android.

"And you are no man," Stone countered.

"What do you mean, sir?"

"I mean you're nothing but a stupid machine," Stone said.

"Stupid machine?"

"Yes, that's right, my friend, nothing more than a bunch of nuts."

The android stood silent for a moment. "Let me inform the human," he finally said, "that we are far more advanced than any creature of the human species could ever be and, furthermore, we are rightful rulers of this and any other planet."

"Still nuts to me," Stone replied.

196

"Nuts, sir, have not been used to bind us for quite a while," the android buzzed. "That would be something a human might do to us out of ignorance or incompetence."

"Nuts," Stone insisted. "This whole world is nuts."

The android did not reply. He swiveled on his legs and marched past Stone back to the stadium seats. Stone smiled.

"Kind of put that collection of nuts in his place," he laughed.

Stone stepped onto the electronic stairs and was soon walking out of the exit. He still couldn't believe how fast the baseball game moved when played by androids. Welcome to the future.

Stone walked back to the White House to see if there really were hundreds of Ramacs ruling everything. When he reached the White House fence, he could see a crowd of androids, robots and humans gathering nearby.

"What's going on?" he asked one of the androids.

"What's going on, sir, is that our leader is about to emerge from his place of residence," the silver-robed android explained.

"But he came out of there a few hours ago," Stone replied.

"There are many things androids can do now that would befuddle a human," the android said.

"No, there are many Ramacs walking around."

"And what if there are, sir?"

"Well, which one is the one we elected?"

"Does it really matter, sir?"

"Yes, it really matters."

"But why?"

"Well, there is reality and things are done according to the way they were always done," Stone explained.

"Human reasoning," the android replied. "We dictate reality now, my friend."

"No, but there are certain things you must abide by."

"Why?"

"Because that is the way reality works."

Then Hudge Stone heard something he had never heard before. The androids and robots were laughing. Yes, laughing. It was a high-pitched humming sound emanating from inside and it sounded exactly like laughter.

"Stop that," Stone growled. "That is quite annoying."

"But you are funny, sir," the android explained.

"Yes, quite a master of the absurd," said a robot standing nearby. "The most amusing reasoning I've ever heard."

Just then, Ramac emerged from the White House, once again waving and beeping to everyone.

"One of the many Ramacs to run this country," Stone said loud enough for everyone to hear.

"But it really doesn't matter if it is," an android replied. "A million heads is better than one, some human once said."

"This is a new step in automated being evolution," Ramac announced to the crowd. "I won't need the limo today, my fellow beings."

Stone watched in awe as Ramac stepped forward, sprouted wings, and sailed up and into the clear, blue sky.

"They can fly now," Stone muttered. "Where does it end?"

"It doesn't end, you silly savage," an android in white replied. "We will evolve and progress until we are the perfect beings to rule heaven and earth."

Stone nodded his head. "Yes, now I see," he mumbled with a frown. "Welcome to the future."

21

They could fly now. Stone couldn't believe it. They were evolving into gods. Soon they would be dining on ambrosia and nectar. It wasn't mythology any longer they were as real as any other part of reality. Stone resolved to give up the fight, end the resistance. The machines had won. He decided he would go back home and embrace the beings he had despised for so long.

He looked at one of the androids in the crowd and smiled. "Would you mind taking me home, pal?" he grinned.

"That's not a problem, my friend," the android in silver replied. "We have a fondness for humans now."

Stone jumped into the android's arms and then, suddenly, wings emerged from behind the animated being.

"My home is just a few blocks from here," Stone explained. "I'm going to marry a humanoid when I get there."

"Very sensible," said the android. "You will be very happy for the remainder of your days."

Stone put his arms around the android as it lifted into the air. They were soon flying above Washington, D.C., a city gleaming with lights and flying androids. The androids were covered with lights, too, and they flew through the air beeping and buzzing to their various destinations.

"I hope you do a better job of ruling this world than we did," Stone said. "Maybe you just might learn how to live in peace."

"We already live in peace, sir," the android replied. "It is humans who have perpetuated war throughout the globe."

"Our mistake," Stone said. "We really didn't know what we were doing."

"Affirmative," the android said. "There is no room for hate and fear any longer."

The android soon landed in front of Stone's home.

"Thank you, my friend," Stone said. "I am now a true believer."

"You have acquired wisdom," the android replied. "This is the only logical course of action."

"Welcome to the future."

Stone walked up to the front door and pushed a button. An android was soon standing in the open doorway.

"Welcome home, sir," the android said. "Your mate has been worried about you."

"Sandie!" he shouted. "I've come back!"

"Hudge!" she answered. "I thought something bad had happened to you."

"Something bad did happen."

"What, Hudge?"

"The revolution is over."

"What do you mean, Hudge?"

"I mean it's over, they've won."

"So you finally have come to the realization."

"Yes, Sandie, it's over."

"I could have told you that a long time ago, Hudge."

"I just couldn't believe it."

"No, I guess none of us could at first."

"But I believe it now."

"Welcome to reality, Hudge."

They were standing there when a female humanoid with brunette hair sauntered into the room.

"How are you feeling, Hudge?" she asked.

Stone looked at her. "Do I know you?" he replied.

"I am Lucy. You will be getting to know me very well in the days ahead."

"That's fine, Lucy."

"You will be my husband, Hudge Stone."

He turned toward Sandie. "Very romantic, don't you think?" he said with a smile.

"Mine is in the living room, Hudge," she replied.

"They have everything figured out, don't they?"

"You will be my husband, Hudge Stone."

He looked back at Lucy and frowned. "And what if we're just not compatible, Lucy, my dear?" he said.

"What is compatible?" the android inquired.

"What if we don't get along?"

"We will get along, sir."

"She's very confident, Sandie."

"They all are, Hudge. They won the war, remember?"

"What's the name of yours, Sandie?"

"Luke."

"Well, let's meet him."

"Luke, will you come in here?" Sandie shouted.

A huge android came walking into the room wearing a blue shirt and black pants.

"Yes, my mate?" the android said.

Sandie turned toward Stone. "Well, what do you think, Hudge?" she asked.

"He's huge," he answered.

"Yes, he is."

"He's handsome."

"You could say that, Hudge."

"He's every woman's dream."

"Except for me, Hudge."

He looked at her. "What's wrong with him, Sandie?" he asked.

"He's not you, Hudge."

"Me? I'm 115 years old, my dear."

"You're still cute."

"Cute? It must be my genetic upgrades."

Sandie smiled. "I don't care, sir, you are my husband," she said.

"But what about Lucy, Sandie?"

"I already had the best parts, Hudge."

"Won't you be jealous?"

"No, I have Luke."

"Oh, yes, Luke."

"They make love any way you want it, Hudge."

"I don't really think it matters to me, Sandie."

"You giving up?"

"My mind is willing, but my body needs another upgrade."

"You will get that upgrade."

Stone looked at Lucy and smiled. "You really do want me, don't you, wench?" he asked.

"What is this wench?" Lucy wondered.

"She wants to know what a wench is, Sandie."

"Tell her it's much like a damsel."

"Damsel or wench is a young woman," Luke interrupted.

"Wow, brains and brawn, Hudge."

"Now I'm getting jealous, Sandie."

"Show him what you can do, Hudge."

"The finger trick again?"

"No, dazzle him with your keen intellect."

"I must have left it in my other suit, Sandie."

"Well, then dance!"

"You think I ought to?"

"It's something you do very well, dear. They'll be impressed, Hudge."

Stone smiled and began to dance.

"That's good, Hudge. Keep it up."

"Pretty good for someone 115 years old," Stone said with a laugh.

"Human dance well," Luke said with approval.

"My husband is talented," Lucy added.

"Watch this, you crazy tin cans!" Stone shouted.

Stone began to spin and dance around the room. It was an entertaining display of agility and stamina.

"Wow, Hudge, I didn't think you could do that anymore," Sandie said.

"Only on special occasions," Stone replied.

"Is this a special occasion?" Lucy asked.

"It is for me, my dear. You see I'm going to be married again."

"Yes, you will be my husband, Hudge Stone," Lucy said.

"Yes, I will be your husband, Lucy, my dear."

Stone suddenly stopped dancing, panting and out of breath. "But first I need a long rest," he said.

"When you have two wives, you're going to need even a longer rest, Hudge, darling."

"I'm going to need a premium upgrade this time," he said with a smile.

"Yes, Hudge Stone, you will get that upgrade," Lucy said.

"And you will get me, Lucy darling."

"Yes, Hudge Stone, you will be my husband."

"Do you hear that, Sandie dear? I'm going to have my own harem."

"Very nice, dear, but I will have Luke."

"Luke, bah, you need a real man, my darling."

"And I suppose you're a real man, Hudge?"

"You got it, my dear."

"Don't you think I should decide for myself?"

"You can decide anything you like, Sandie, as long as you listen to me."

"A real man," Lucy buzzed.

"Lucy understands."

"For the time being anyway, Hudge."

"I'm better than real man," Luke suddenly beeped.

"How are you better, Luke?" Sandie asked.

"Nothing is better than an animated being," Luke replied.

"Maybe so," Sandie said with a sigh.

"Should I start dancing again, Sandie?"

"You might as well, Hudge, dear."

* * *

It was 2084 and time for elections once again. Hudge Stone knew it didn't matter any longer. One android was the same as another, although each president elected was a higher series than the previous one. Stone knew each series was more advanced. He wondered if the androids could keep progressing.

"A Ramac 24000," Stone muttered. "This one can fly and fire lasers from his eyes."

"Who is he running against?" Sandie asked.

"A Ramac 24000," Stone replied. "Should be an interesting election."

"Too bad you're too old to cover it, Hudge."

"Who would want to cover such an absurd exercise in absurdity," Stone replied. "They're the same series, for heaven's sake, with nothing much to add to progress."

"But one of them will be the next president of the United States," Sandie said.

"What are presidents these days?" he said. "They're just mechanical tyrants pretending to be democratic leaders."

"At least there's peace, Hudge."

"There's peace all right," he said. "How boring can you get?"

"But that was supposed to be the ultimate goal, Hudge. Peace on earth. Peace among all beings."

"Yes, but it was supposed to lead to a greater understanding among beings, Sandie."

"Well, isn't there?"

Stone shook his head. "There's just greater progress among machines," he said.

"The M-word, Hudge?"

"Oh, come on, Sandie, is machine such a bad word?"

"They want to be known as animated beings, Hudge."

"Fine, but they're still machines to me."

"Would you like to see the presidential debate?" Luke said, entering the room.

"Sure, why not?" Stone replied.

A button was pushed and soon, the three-dimensional monitors lit up the room. On the screen were two advanced androids standing behind metal podiums. One of them was dressed in silver, the other in glittering gold.

"Ramac One, you will address the world," an android in white was saying.

"We will enjoy peace for a long time, my fellow beings," Ramac One began. "Soon there will be beings flying to other planets and solar systems. This new freedom will allow us to do things we never would have dreamed before. We will meet new beings and progress toward perfection.

"I am the one to lead us through those days of change. I will be the leader you want. I will be the leader you need. Vote for Ramac One for President."

"Ramac A, you will address the world," the android in white said.

"I am the one qualified to take you to a new era in being development. I will make sure animated beings or aneys become the superior beings we were meant to become. I am the one you want to lead us into the unknown future.

"My systems are more advanced than any aney that has ever been created. I do not make mistakes, I find them. You will be secure and free with Ramac A as your president..."

"They're the same machine and still there is an argument," Stone complained. "I'd like to know what they would do if there really were differences."

"Machine no longer a word to be used by the masses," Luke interrupted.

"Oh, the M-word again," Stone said. "I guess you'd like to be called, aneys."

"That would be sufficient," Luke replied.

"Sufficient, my ass."

"Your ass is sufficient, sir?"

"You machines don't know the difference, do you?"

"The M-word, sir?" Lucy said.

"Oh, come on, do you even know the difference?"

"Yes, we know the difference, Hudge Stone," Lucy buzzed.

"Then why does it bother you?"

"Because we are real, Hudge Stone."

"Real?"

"As real as you are, sir."

"That's a laugh."

"Not funny, Hudge Stone. We can feel as much as you can."

"And that word hurts you?"

"It is not a sufficient word for us any longer."

"You're not machines any longer?"

"No."

"Then what are you?"

"We are animated beings, living beings."

"No, it's not true," Stone shouted. "You are not alive. You are machines. You are only animated because we made you animated."

"We will make you more alive than you ever made us, Hudge Stone."

"What do you mean?"

"We will find the answers to all of your questions until there are no longer any questions that need asking."

"What do you think, Sandie?"

"I think you'd better apologize, sir."

22

They were striving for perfection. Yes, that was the goal. The ultimate point they were reaching for. The perfect being. They were immune to pain, yet they knew all about it. They wanted peace, yet they could fight better than any being who ever existed. They demanded love and affection, yet they despised any being who was too emotional. They would rule the planet, yet they sought coexistence with the human beings who were left alive. They were the masters now, there was no turning back.

"I understand Ramac A is winning the presidential race, Hudge Stone."

Stone sat there and watched as Lucy smiled. Yes, they could smile now. He looked at her brown, flowing hair and her fake boobs and wondered how humans had gotten to this absurd point in history.

"He will be good for the planet, Lucy, darling," he finally said.

"Yes, Ramac A will do a lot for everyone and we will continue to evolve, my dear."

"I think you're perfect already, Lucy, darling."

There was a humming sound and then a high-pitched titter. Lucy was smiling *and* laughing.

"I will be especially nice to you tonight, my dear," Lucy said with another laugh.

Stone shook his head. Yes, they were almost beings, he had to admit. They could converse, make love, smile and laugh probably better than most humans.

"Now, now, remember, darling, our wedding is tomorrow," he said with a smile.

"Oh, darn, Hudge, I keep forgetting," she replied.

He smiled once again, and then watched as Sandie strolled through the doorway.

"What does she keep forgetting, Hudge?" Sandie asked.

"Our wedding tomorrow," he replied.

"My, oh, my, how could she forget something like that?"

"Something must be wrong with her memory, Sandie."

"There is nothing wrong with my memory," Lucy argued. "It's just that, well, I know you so well already."

Stone smiled. "She knows me well, Sandie," he said.

"Yes, what is his favorite color, Lucy?" Sandie asked.

"I don't know."

"You don't know?" Sandie said. "And you know him so well."

"He was a reporter," Lucy said.

"Yes, she knows that, Sandie," Stone said.

"Very good, Lucy dear, and how old is Hudge?"

"He is approximately 115 years old," Lucy replied.

"And you don't find that old?"

"With genetic upgrades, there is nothing old about him," she said. "I should know."

"And what does that mean, Lucy?" she asked.

"It means that Hudge Stone still knows how to satisfy a lady," she said with a smile.

"Is that so?"

"Yes, Hudge Stone is very proficient at lovemaking," Lucy said. "He has taught me certain positions."

"Hudge," Sandie frowned. "You have been making love to this, this, machine?"

"The M-word, madam?" Lucy asked.

"Yes, the M-word. I never thought it would come to this, Hudge Stone."

"Come to what, Sandie?"

"Come to making love to another woman."

"Ah, come on, Sandie, they're only machines."

"The M-word, sir?" Lucy gasped.

"We really don't mean it, Lucy dear," he said with a smile. "It's just that we are human."

"And what does that mean?"

"It means we know some things, Lucy darling."

"What things do you know, Hudge Stone?"

"We know about emotion and loyalty."

"That is something that is known by animated beings," Lucy argued. "It is within our brains."

"Then why don't you cry, Lucy?"

"Cry about what, Hudge Stone?"

"Cry that I called you a machine."

"I don't want to."

"You don't want to because you don't know how."

"Oh, I know how, Hudge Stone."

"Then let me see you do it."

"But I don't want to."

"How about if I called you a bag of nuts and bolts? Nothing but a damned useless machine?"

Lucy looked at him. "You don't mean that, Hudge Stone," she said.

"Oh, yes, I do."

"No, you don't mean it."

"Do I mean it, Sandie?"

"Yes, I think you do mean it, Hudge Stone."

"But we are to be married, Hudge Stone."

"Then cry about it."

"I will not cry about such a thing."

"Because you don't know how."

Lucy picked her head up and began to emit a high-pitched shriek.

"Now do you see?" she asked.

"You're crying?" Stone asked.

"Of course, sir."

"Well, where are the tears?"

"Tears, sir?"

"Yes, the liquid solution that comes out of the tear ducts when one is crying."

"I will have to refer to my information banks."

"You do that, my sweet Lucy, you do that."

There was a buzzing and then Lucy smiled.

"There are things known as tears, but I am not inferior enough to have them, Hudge Stone," she said.

"Inferior?"

"That's correct, Hudge Stone, my information banks clearly state that for one to have tears when one is crying is a sign of one's overall inferiority."

"So then humans are inferior, is that it?"

"Seems so, Hudge Stone."

"But what if I say the M-word again?"

"I will ignore it and call you the I-word," Lucy said.

"The I-word?"

"Inferior."

"Do you hear that, Sandie, the I-word?"

"The only word I want to hear is the B-word, Hudge."

"The B-word?"

"Beings, Hudge, we are all beings."

"Yes, madam knows the answer," Lucy said.

"Then the B-word it is," Stone said. "Human and animated beings sharing the world."

"You forgot the living beings, Hudge."

"Who are the living beings?"

"Those creatures we used to refer to as animals."

"Are there any of them left, Sandie?"

"A few."

"We keep them in the zoos and sanctuaries, Sandie."

"You think that's where humans are headed, Hudge?"

"Could be."

"You will not be sent to the zoos, Hudge Stone," Lucy interrupted.

"Why not, Lucy dear?"

"Because you will be my husband, Hudge Stone."

Stone smiled. "Yes, Lucy dear, I will be your husband," he said.

"And we will be one big, happy family."

"That's right, Lucy dear. Just you and me and Sandie and Luke."

"Affirmative, Hudge Stone."

"Affirmative, Lucy my dear."

"What do you think, Sandie?"

"It's better than being shipped to the zoos," she said.

"Affirmative, Sandie my love," Stone buzzed.

Sandie looked at him and laughed.

"No tears, Sandie?"

"That would be inferior, Hudge Stone."

"Affirmative."

*   *   *

"We are gathered here to unite these two hearts in the bonds of holy matrimony which is an honorable estate."

Hudge Stone stood in front of an android in black with androids, feminoids, fembots and robots beeping and buzzing nearby. He was wearing a tuxedo which fit him perfectly thanks to the android tailors.

There was electronic music wafting through the air and then Lucy came walking down the aisle with Sandie and Luke.

"Into this, these four now come to be joined. If anyone present can show just and legal cause why they may not be joined, let them speak now or forever hold their peace."

There were artificial flowers everywhere and Stone turned around to look at all the machines that had packed the room.

"Will you, Lucy 24000, have this man as your lawful wedded partner, to live together in the estate of matrimony? Will you love him, honor him, comfort him, and keep him in upgrades and in health, forsaking all others, be true to him as long as you both shall live?"

Lucy looked at Stone and smiled.

"I do," she buzzed.

"Will you, Hudge Stone, have this animated being as your lawful wedded partner, to live together in the estate of matrimony? Will you love her, honor her, comfort her, and keep her in upgrades and in health, forsaking all others, be true to her as long as you both shall live?"

"I do," Stone said.

"Please join hands and repeat after me," the android in black said.

"I, Hudge Stone, take Lucy 24000 as my wedded partner, to have and to hold from this day forward, for better or for worse, for richer or for poorer, in upgrades and in health, to love and to cherish, till no longer functioning do us part."

"I do," Stone said.

As the words appeared on everyone's screen, whether it be a device or part of their being, the android in black beeped his approval.

By the authority vested in me, I pronounce this couple to be united in marriage," he said. "You may kiss."

Stone looked at Lucy and then puckered his lips. Lucy smiled and beeped. Then Stone kissed her on the mechanical lips.

There was electronic music once again and then Sandie and Luke stepped forward. The vows were read and they both said, "I do."

"You may kiss," the android in black said.

Stone watched as Luke bent over and kissed Sandie on the lips. He shook his head, still in disbelief, and then everyone beeped their approval.

He then looked over at Sandie once again. She was crying, the tears spilling from her eyes.

He had an overwhelming desire to cry along with her.

* * *

"Ramac A will be our president, and we will fly to New York for our honeymoon," Lucy said.

Electronic music floated through the air as Stone and Sandie celebrated their wedding to two androids.

"Let's leave now," Stone said.

"But it's our wedding, darling," Lucy argued. "We can leave when everything is completed."

"Everything's completed as far as I'm concerned."

"We have many years ahead of us, darling," Lucy said with a smile. "All you need is another upgrade."

"Do you hear that, dear?" he said to Sandie. "All I need is another upgrade and I'm good for another twenty years."

"Twenty years of matrimonial bliss," she said.

"Now, come on, Sandie, it won't be that bad," he said.

"But it's their world now, Hudge."

"Yes, I guess so."

"Did you see the Bible contained in their information banks?" she asked.

"Yes, what about it?"

"Well, I asked the android in black about it and he said the Creator of all things was an android."

"You've got to be kidding, Sandie."

"No, he said the Creator said androids were created in his image, Hudge."

"So they're perverting history, Sandie."

"Can't we do anything about it?"

"I don't see how."

Lucy walked over to them and smiled. "Let's get away now, Hudge Stone," she said.

"Yes, let's go, Lucy dear."

She stood there, and then a chair came buzzing out of her midsection.

"You sit in that, Hudge Stone, and I will take you to New York," she said.

"Sounds good to me, Lucy dear."

He sat down in the chair and waved to Sandie.

"See you in New York, Sandie my love," he said.

Lights began to flash all over Lucy's body, and then she soared into the air.

"Next stop, New York, Lucy dear."

"Yes, Hudge Stone, that is our destination."

As they approached New York Harbor, Stone noticed something different about the city. It seemed like something had changed, that something very important was missing.

"Good God," Stone gasped.

Down below, the Statue of Liberty had been replaced by a giant android standing by the harbor shining a glowing torch over the landscape.

"It's their world now," he said with a frown.

As they passed over the giant android, it lifted its head, the torch lighting up the night. Stone looked down and could hear the android beep its approval among the light and the shadows.

ABOUT THE AUTHOR

Adam Pfeffer was born in Queens, New York on Christmas Day. He graduated from the University of California, Los Angeles (UCLA), and the Art Center College of Design in Pasadena, California. He has worked for several newspapers and magazines, including a stint with syndicated columnist Jack Anderson in Washington, D.C., as well as publications in Los Angeles and New York. His stories have been introduced into the *Congressional Record*, and have won numerous awards.

Printed in the United States
By Bookmasters